Many boats sink and never reach the Sargasso,
but no dream ever entirely disappears
—Nathaniel West, *The Day of the Locust*

AUDREY THOMAS

Coming Down from Wa

VIKING

VIKING
Published by the Penguin Group
Penguin Books Canada Ltd, 10 Alcorn Avenue, Toronto, Ontario, Canada
M4V 3B2
Penguin Books Ltd, 27 Wrights Lane, London W8 5TZ, England
Viking Penguin, a division of Penguin Books USA Inc., 375 Hudson Street,
New York, New York 10014, U.S.A.
Penguin Books Australia Ltd, Ringwood, Victoria, Australia
Penguin Books (NZ) Ltd, 182–190 Wairau Road, Auckland 10, New Zealand

Penguin Books Ltd, Registered Offices: Harmondsworth, Middlesex, England

First published 1995
1 3 5 7 9 10 8 6 4 2

Publisher's note: This book is a work of fiction. Names, characters, places and incidents either are the product of the author's imagination or are used fictitiously, and any resemblance to actual persons living or dead, events, or locales is entirely coincidental.

Printed and bound in Canada on acid free paper ♾

Canadian Cataloguing in Publication Data

Thomas, Audrey, 1935-
Coming down from Wa

ISBN 0-670-86366-1

I. Title.

PS8539.H65C6 1995 C813'.54 C95-930195-X
PR9199.3.T56C6 1995

For all those—dear family and dear friends—who keep me going. You know very well who you are—such a long list!

Acknowledgments

I would like to thank the Canada Council for a grant that enabled me to return to West Africa in 1991, the B.C. Cultural Services Fund for help towards the first two drafts, the Dickey Centre at Dartmouth College, the Hawthornden Trust and its castle of beauty and peace.

There are also many individuals I would like to thank: Marlyn Horsdahl, Barbara Moore, Richard Harrison, Mardele and Fred Harland and the many ex-volunteers I interviewed or corresponded with during my searches and researches; Gordon Ewart for his help with lost wax; Shilyh Warren and Trevor Dodman of Dartmouth; Monty de Cartier; Bob Sherrin; Bill Schermbrucker (as always); my editor Meg Masters and, once again, my cheerful typist Carole Robertson.

Although the place names in this novel are real, all of the characters, with the exception of "Johnny" (who has graciously allowed me to put words in his mouth and make him part of the action) and the woman who formed the model for Mary Ibrahim, are fictitious. The same holds true for all the events, past or present, except for Nelson Mandela's historic visit to Ghana in the autumn of 1991.

The bus had gone on for perhaps five miles before he realized that the two-hundred-cedi note he'd handed down to the orange-seller had really been the one-hundred-dollar Canadian bill he'd been keeping for emergencies. Two hundred cedis, and she had given him change, one hundred fifty cedis change. He stared in disbelief. He had paid ninety-nine dollars plus a few cents, for six oranges.

"Stop the bus," he yelled. "Please, you've got to stop the bus!"

William was in the window seat on the right-hand side, fifth row back. Next to him was an enormously fat woman who had been buying things out the window all the way along, or getting others to do it because she couldn't reach. At the minute the curved stalk of a large hand of plantain rested across William's left knee like the narrow muzzle of a dog. Other produce left little room for his legs, which were long. In the jump seat next to the fat woman a man was sleeping with his head and arms against the back of the jump seat in front of him. The bus was full. William couldn't move; all he could do was yell.

"Please stop the bus, please!"

"Somebody want to vomit," said a voice from the back.

"Somebody wants to free himself," said another.

Without turning round, the driver called something in a language—one of the many languages—William didn't understand. His voice was angry and dismissive. The driver's mate spoke some English, a little bit, "small-small," so William poked the woman in front and motioned her to poke the man in front of her and made signs that he was to poke the mate, who was also asleep. The mate came to with a start and said something in the vernacular; he too was cross. It was a long way down from Wa and they had already been travelling for hours.

The people in the first three rows began to chatter. William caught the word "'Bronie" and the driver's mate stood up from his seat and looked back sourly. He was a small man, very dark, with two tribal scars on his right cheek and a shirt that had been white when they started out. Now it was covered in streaks of red dust. Everything was covered in red dust, every thing and every one. The women wore scarves and headdresses but the men were beginning to look as though they all suffered from kwashiorkor, *the disease that turned the hair rust-red and the skin blotchy.*

"Yes?" he said. "What is the problem?"

"Back there," William said, "at the market. I gave the orange-seller a large sum of money, Canadian money—a very *large sum—instead of a two-hundred-cedi note. They look alike. We have to go back."*

The man stared at him.

"Do you understand?" William said loudly, desperate. "It was a very large sum of money. I need it. We have to go back. It was"—he did a rapid calculation—"it was like giving someone over thirty-four thousand cedis for six oranges!"

The man stared at him for another few seconds and then

began explaining to the driver, in a loud voice, what had happened. The passengers who could hear clicked their tongues against the roof of their mouths. Tsk, tsk. A few laughed. They began to discuss the matter amongst themselves, passing the information back to those who hadn't heard. The driver shouted out a few sentences but he didn't slow down.

"We can't go back," said the driver's mate. "Because of the flat tire we are already late. It is impossible that we go back."

"Please," William cried, "I'll explain to his boss. I'll pay the extra gas. I need that money."

Once again, a rapid exchange of words. Once again the passengers on the bus discussed the matter. Voices grew louder. Obviously some were for but many more were against.

"He can't go back," the mate said. "He is not allowed."

"He is not allowed to take on more passengers than he has seats for, is he?" William shouted. "He's not allowed to do that and yet he does it, you do it. I could report you for that you know."

The mate didn't bother to translate.

"He can't go back," he said.

"Then stop the bus immediately, let me off!" He stood up and banged his head.

"You want to get off?"

"I have to. I have to go back and get the money. It's a lot of money. I can't just let it go. STOP THE BUS!!"

The mate said something to the driver and as soon as they rounded the next curve the driver brought the bus slowly to a stop.

Before William could get out all the people on the right-hand side had also to get out. The two old Muslims who had been *sleeping in the stairwell were woken up and told to step down. The jump seats had to be folded away so the aisle could be more or less cleared. More or less, because the aisle was also crammed with sacks of yams and bags of oranges, sleeping mats, some tins of oil. If you could get away with shoving stuff inside then you didn't have to pay the baggage fee. The driver's mate, who also took tickets and assessed baggage fees, had had shouting matches with two women at the back; each had shoved on enormous sacks that must have weighed a hundred pounds or more. William had seen one of the relatives stagger under the weight as he lifted a sack up off his head and through a back window.*

William stood by the bus door.

"I need my pack," he said.

"You want me to open the luggage container?"

"I know exactly where it is. Please."

He gave the man a hundred cedis and the man shrugged. Why not? Everyone in the front section of the bus had piled off as they usually did, whenever the bus stopped for any reason at all. A man held a small child up to pee. Several people disappeared into the bushes. The driver remained behind his wheel, shouting and cursing. He honked the horn angrily, three times. If they wouldn't come he would leave without them.

*As William walked away, his pack on his back, the mid-afternoon sun beating down on his neck, several people called after him but he didn't turn around. He knew he was being stupid and sulky; he knew they were discussing him right now, as the bus moved on towards Accra; foolish 'Bronie, silly white boy. Even if he found his money it could cost him plenty—*plenty—*to get a taxi to Kumasi where he could pick up another bus to the capital. He must be a rich boy. Or maybe no.*

Maybe he was rich back home but not rich here, one of the hundreds of 'Bronie students who came for a couple of years, sent by their governments. The women had dresses made of the market cloth and liked to dance at festivals; the men wore shirts of the same cloth and had hairy legs. They stayed a while and then they left. They were not important; they were all one face. They were a source of great amusement. They saw the decal Chantal had sewn on William's pack.

"Canada," they said. "Oh. Fine. Fine country."

The young ones wanted his name and address so they could write to him, be his friend. "I want to go to Canada."

The village was farther back than he had thought. By the time he reached it, he was hot and cross and tro-tros crowded the highway, everyone honking. A man walked by holding a goat by its hind legs, pushing it along like a wheelbarrow. Women with headloads were everywhere; women selling oranges were everywhere.

"ANKA! ANKA!" they called in their flat nasal voices. He looked for his orange-seller. How far along had they been? It was only as the bus was ready to pull away that he thought about buying a half-dozen oranges for later on. She had been very pretty, his orange-seller; that's why he wasn't paying enough attention to what he was doing. That and the fact that the bus was about to leave. He had been watching his own long freckled arm reach down to take the oranges from her and then reach down to hand her what he thought was a two-hundred-cedi note. Watching his long freckled arm reach out and down again, watching her young breasts under the faded green jersey, how they rose as her arm rose to meet his, and then once again as she handed up his change. He had seen her breasts rise, and

her brilliant smile and had been thinking about his father, all those years ago, as well as the contrast between her life and his. That's what he had been thinking about as the bus pulled away. It was something else, some intuition, that made him unzip his money pouch and feel for the hundred-dollar bill. Had he not been, suddenly, thinking about his father all those years ago; had he not been tired and confused and burdened now with knowledge he wished he didn't have...

He couldn't find the girl. He asked everywhere. He found a schoolboy who spoke English and he went round with the boy, describing the orange-seller—young, maybe seventeen or eighteen, in a green jersey and a cloth with...what on it? William closed his eyes—in a green cloth with the black spiderweb design, yes, that was it, Anansi.

No one had seen her; no one knew anything about her.

"They're lying," William told the boy. "Somehow she's realized that bill was a lot of money and she's hiding. Tell them I'll offer a reward."

They went back up and down the street of stalls, of people selling yams and charcoal and chickens and goats; they asked the women selling fried chicken, selling kenkey and kelewele. They offered the reward. Nobody knew her; nobody had seen her. The band of little children that William had thought so charming earlier in the day, the little troupe that had followed him, as children always did, laughing and pointing, 'Bronie, 'Bronie, 'Bronie, now infuriated him. They probably knew where she was as well. There would be a big feast tonight—a sheep slaughtered, palm wine drunk, everybody laughing at the stupid 'Bronie who had given the girl all that money for a few oranges.

He wanted to stop and get something to drink but he was damned if he'd put one more cent, one more pesewa, *into this village's coffers.*

A taxi-driver honked and leaned out his window.

"Chief! Where is it you want to go?"

William waved him away. "Later," he said, "maybe later."

He and the schoolboy went up and down three times. They told a policeman who also went up and down. The girl had vanished. She was probably from another village, the boy said, coming for market day. Yes, said the policeman, that was probably what happened.

William gave up. He left his name and the address of the High Commission *in* Accra. *He said to the schoolboy to write out a notice and pin it in a public place. Five hundred cedis reward. No questions asked. He would leave five hundred cedis with—with whom? Could he trust the boy, the policeman? He would leave five hundred cedis with the* High Commission.

The market was crowded, overflowing with buyers and sellers, but the area of the market was not large. All of this palaver had taken less than half an hour. William was tired and hot and discouraged. Had he not just written to Chantal *that these people were the most honest people he had ever seen? Ha. Double Ha.*

The children followed him as he headed back towards the main road south.

'Bronie / How are you?

I'm fine / thank you.

They pointed and laughed, pointed and laughed. The sun beat hard on the back of his neck. Suddenly he bent down and his pack nearly toppled him. But he found what he was looking for, some stones. He began shouting and throwing stones.

"Do you know what would happen to kids in my country if they behaved like you? If they pointed at a foreigner and laughed and made up stupid rhymes about him?" (He threw another stone and another.) "They'd have their bottoms smacked, that's what would happen." (Another stone, another.) "They'd have their mouths washed out with soap!" (Stones. He needed to find more stones.) "Their parents might be hauled up in court as racists." (stones) "Yet I'm supposed to think you're cute." (stones, stones)

"I'm supposed to give you candy and pesewas *and Bic pens and not mind being laughed at by you little brats."*

The children danced out of range of the stones. Eventually, tired of the game, they turned back to the village and William went on alone. Taxis honked, offering him rides, tro-tros went by. "God's time is best," "Except God," "Psalm 100."

He shouldn't be out in the sun any longer, hatless, thirsty. But he couldn't take a ride, not yet. For to his horror and shame he was crying, bawling like a child of six or seven, the tears making white tracks in the red dust covering his face. He had thrown stones at little children. He had cursed them. How could he? He was no better than... Over money! All worked up over money! And his mistake, not hers.

William, walking down the highway sobbing. What was to become of him now?

1991

When William Kwame MacKenzie was six years old his MacKenzie grandparents sent him a box of sixty-four Crayola crayons with a built-in sharpener. William did not know his MacKenzie grandparents because they lived in Montreal and he lived in Victoria, British Columbia, but he liked the sort of presents they sent: a Mickey Mouse bell for his tricycle, pop-up books, rubber stamps and an ink pad, a kaleidoscope.

William was born in Montreal, lived with his grandparents for two months, but had never been back.

"Did they like me?" William asked his mother.

"Of course they liked you—you were their grandson."

"Can we go and visit them? Can we take the train and go all the way across Canada and visit them?"

"Someday," said his mother, "someday." Her own parents were dead.

Only when he was in high school did it occur to William that it could have worked the other way—his grandparents could have come to visit him. But by then it was just one more piece of a puzzle he thought he would never solve: the puzzle of his parents' taking separate vacations every year, his mother usually to visit one of the children in her Child World program, his father to hike the

West Coast Trail or go kayaking by himself (later, with William) up along the Sechelt Peninsula; the puzzle of his parents' polite but distant attitude to one another; the puzzle of their lack of involvement in any cause where they would have to belong to a group; the lies. The lies had started early. His mother on the telephone: "Oh, we would have loved to put you up but we're going away on holiday tomorrow, yes, and some old friends will be staying here I'm afraid—looking after the dog and keeping an eye on things."

William went next door and told his friend Jonah he wouldn't be able to go to the beach tomorrow after all—he was going on a holiday in the morning. No, he didn't know where; he thought it was supposed to be a surprise.

The next morning, when his mother called him down to breakfast he didn't hear her—he was too busy trying to decide whether to take his box of crayons or leave them behind, whether to take his squirt gun or leave it behind. His bathing suit and teddy were already packed.

"William," said his mother from the doorway, "what are you doing? Are you running away from home? I called you twice for breakfast. If you're running away it's better to eat breakfast first, I think."

"I'm packing."

"I can see that. Why are you packing?"

He turned and looked at her smiling.

"It's okay," he said, "I know about the surprise."

"What surprise? What ideas have you got in that funny little head this time?"

"You're a liar," he said at breakfast. "You're a liar and

now I'm a liar. I told Jonah we were going away for a holiday."

She tried to explain to him about "white lies," which weren't really lies at all, just polite ways of getting out of awkward situations. So nobody's feelings would be hurt. They weren't lies, real lies; they didn't count. That phone call—people they had known years ago, dreadful people, but she hadn't wanted to hurt their feelings. You'll understand when you're older. William unpacked his case.

(Over the years, again and again, his mother's voice, his father's voice, "What a pity but we..." "Oh, if you'd only called a little earlier," or worst of all, "William—our son—chicken pox...measles...mumps." White lies. But why?)

They were polite to the neighbours, and one or the other always went to the Home and School meeting or the Christmas concerts. He was introduced early to the public library, the rec centre, even the symphony and the theatre. He knew they loved him and worried about him when he was ill, encouraged him when he learned to ride a two-wheeler, took him skating.

His father was a lab technician; his mother was a speech therapist. Money wasn't the problem, but what was? It occurred to him from time to time that his parents were afraid. They were like people who were on the run from something, who had changed their identity maybe and were afraid of being recognized. This was silly, he knew—weren't there the MacKenzie grandparents in Montreal, his father's position at the hospital, his mother's work?

William should have been born in West Africa, but at the beginning of the eighth month of his mother's pregnancy there were complications and his mother came home to have the baby—or came to Montreal, so that she could stay with the MacKenzies. As soon as the baby could have his shots she took him back to Africa, where she and her husband were teaching. In that country a boy born on Saturday is given the name Kwame, and so William became William Kwame MacKenzie and the girls at the school called him Kwame, never William. Or so he was told. Three months after he arrived he was taken away again because the climate didn't suit him. Or so he was told. Or so he was told by his parents.

"What didn't suit?"

"It was too hot for you; you got terrible rashes, spectacular fevers; we thought you were more important than staying on."

They were sad to leave; those years had been the best years of their lives.

In 1987 William found on the kitchen table one day an invitation to his parents to attend the twentieth reunion of their group. It was a professional day at his high school and he was home early. The letter had already been opened—he wasn't snooping—and so he brought the subject up at dinnertime. Were they going?

His mother and father looked at one another, or rather, his mother stared at his father so long that he was forced to look up from his plate.

"Sandy," she said. "Do you want to go to the reunion?" And then, "I wonder how they got our address." (The phone calls, the white lies, had stopped long ago.)

The look in his father's eyes scared the shit out of William. Contempt plus anger plus something else—pleading?

"Oh I don't think so," his father said to the dinner plate. "I'm not big on that sort of thing."

"What sort of thing?" his mother said. "Exactly what sort of thing are you not big on?"

"Oh, a bunch of people who had something in common twenty years ago, getting drunk together and talking about the good old days."

"I'm surprised they invited us," his mother said.

"Why?" William asked, forgetting to leave well enough alone, forgetting for a minute the excuses, the ripped-up Christmas cards in the wastebasket, the evasive answers to a small boy's questions. "Why wouldn't they invite you?"

His mother rallied quickly. "We haven't really kept in touch, that's all. I thought they might have gotten the hint by now that we aren't really interested in keeping up connections.

"Anyway," she said, "I'll be in Greece at that time. Heleni invited me to come and see her babies and I've already said I will. Your father can go if he wants. It's in Ottawa I believe, just a hop, skip and jump away from Montreal." Grandmother MacKenzie was ailing—instead of hiking or canoeing his father was going to Montreal. William had a job delivering pizza; there was no way he could go to Montreal even if invited by his father. Which he hadn't been, hadn't expected to be. But William was going to McGill in the autumn; he would meet his grandparents soon enough. The thought filled him with a kind of joy that had nothing to do with all the wonderful presents over the years. They were *family*; he had been born from their house on Clarke Avenue. His grandparents had seen him before his father, even. And he felt they understood him, even from three thousand miles away. (The blue pencils with his name on them in gold; the roller skates; the book bag with books already in it—books on myths and legends, on art, on adventure. Lots of picture books, always.) They understood him but they never said "Come and visit." Something had been agreed upon, between his house and theirs. In the letters he sensed, as he grew older, a secret message, like something written in invisible ink—"Hang on, we understand, we'll be together soon."

"We'll see," his father said. "We'll see how I'm fixed for time."

"Your father," said William's mother, "is a very busy man."

Later he thought that it was there, in that moment, that he knew his parents hated one another, that what he felt flash from one end of the dining table and back again was pure hate. He got up and left the table. An arc of hatred, electric, devastating. In his room that night, studying for a history exam, he waited for angry voices. Nothing.

There were round brown pots and woven baskets and a wool rug with designs in red and black. William's puppy chewed a hole through the middle of that one night so his mother cut away the unchewed part and hung it on the wall as a tapestry. Wooden masks, five of them, lined the upstairs corridor. One had legs coming out of the side of its head. One had a bird pecking at its brains.

On Hallowe'en William got to wear a mask. His favourite was a white wolf mask, trimmed with false fur, his mother had brought back from the toy market in Mexico City. He tried wearing it one night when he woke up and needed to pee. He adjusted the elastic behind his head and set off down the hall.

But the first mask spoke to him:

"Foolish boy! Do you think we are afraid of that thing? Do not come around here at night, I am warning you."

He fled back to his room.

("William, what are we going to do about this? Any suggestions?")

There was a small nightlight in the hall and the masks cast dreadful shadows on the midnight walls. There was a period when William endured the shame of a wet bed rather than run the gauntlet of those dark and eyeless faces.

One day, underneath one of the masks, there was a small heap of pale, yellowish dust. Some bug had got in— or out. "We should burn it," his mother said, but even a grown-up hadn't dared. It went someplace to get the bugs removed and was soon back on the wall.

"What are we going to do with you, William?" his mother said, but not unkindly, as she stripped his bed. He wasn't allowed to drink anything after 5 p.m. "Are you worried about something? Is something wrong at school?"

She was always kind to him, his mother, let him keep his new shoes under his pillow, let him have the naughty puppy, helped his small fingers write a Christmas message to his grandparents in Montreal.

MERRY XMAZ WILL.

He always added kisses and hugs, XXXX OOO. He understood about hugs being circles but why were kisses crosses?

"You ask hard questions," his mother said. "I don't really know."

His parents never touched but they were polite to one another, considerate. His favourite beer chilling in the fridge, flowers for her birthday. William couldn't wait to leave but in the end he vacillated, spent two years at the University of Victoria before heading off to McGill. He wanted to save enough money, working summers, working weekends, to pay his own way. He didn't want to be *beholden*.

Did they have their hopes pinned on him? He didn't think so. His mother once, when he came in late and she was still washing up after a dinner party: "I just want you to be happy." But he would never be completely happy because he had the painter's eye without the painter's hand. He would have to settle for art history, like someone who loves good food but can't, in cooking, progress much further than omelettes. Does everyone carry around a dream like this, he wondered. Even the successes? Perhaps Picasso wished he could sing the blues.

She was always kind to him and yet, later on, one of the images of his mother—an image that came frequently to mind—was that of a smiling woman with her arms wide open and a small child, a small boy, running across a playground straight into those open arms. Only just as he got there, just as he was about to launch himself, she put her arms down and stepped to one side.

"Yours does not sound like what I would call an *emotional* family," Chantal said. "Rather cold."

He rose to their defence. "Reserved is all," he said.

"Cold." She implied but did not say, *comme tous vous Anglais*.

"My grandfather isn't cold," William said. He took her to the house on Clarke Avenue where she charmed his grandfather and he charmed her. At the end of the evening, Grandfather played the piano and they all sang hymns.

"No," said Chantal, "your grandfather is not cold. But he is lonely—you must visit him more often."

When he moved to Montreal he was offered a room in Grandfather's house, but even as he offered it, his grandfather wrote, "I will not be offended if you turn this down. You should be among people your own age, fellow students and such. I will be quite content if you simply come to dinner once in a while."

William saw his father's face in his grandfather, saw his own. Tall men, lanky, with freckled skin. But his grandfather and father were almost completely bald, "bald before thirty."

"You're fortunate," his grandfather said. "You inherited your grannie's hair as well as her even disposition. I can still hear her saying to your father, 'Now Sandy, now Sandy, dinna fash yourself,' when he was in one of his famous tempers."

William tried to adjust to the idea of his father as a small boy with famous tempers. He must have outgrown them early.

It was to his grandfather he went first with the idea of doing part of his M.A. in Africa.

Grandfather got up and went to the piano. "Do you know this hymn, William?" William came and stood behind the piano bench. "Once to Every Man and Nation."

His grandfather turned around. "And what part of Africa were you thinking of?"

"West Africa. I could do a thesis on the lost-wax process, how it has evolved, who is still doing it etcetera."

His grandfather turned back and finished the hymn.

"Music," he said. "Music is more than the food of love, it's the soul's food—it's esperanto, it's direct without the awful barrier of language. Who would not be stirred by such a hymn? Even a non-believer like yourself." And then, "I wonder if you shouldn't pick another topic? I know Africa is—how should I say—*trendy* at the moment, a *trendy* subject. But there might be other subjects out there of equal interest."

"What happened to my parents out in Africa?" William asked.

Grandfather got up from the piano and went back to the couch. He poured himself a whisky, gesturing to William, who shook his head no.

"What happened to them out in Africa?"

"I wish I knew," his grandfather said. "They changed,

that's all. Changed completely." He paused. "Something terrible. It must have been."

William asked the question he'd been waiting all his life to ask. He tried to keep his voice steady but it wobbled.

"Something to do with me?"

His grandfather's head shot up. "Oh no! Oh never! Is that what you've been thinking, laddie? Oh, not at all."

"How can you be so sure?" The wobble again.

"How can I be so sure? Because your mother was here for the last month of her pregnancy—she lived with your grannie and me. And she remained here for eight weeks after—until we were sure she was all right and you were all right and you could have a vaccination. She was *besotted* with you, absolutely *besotted.*" He took a long sip of his whisky. "We all were."

"Then what happened. *Something* happened."

"Something happened but we never found out what. They cut themselves off from us—."

"From just about everybody, or everybody from the past. It wasn't just you, Grandfather." William told about the phone calls, the white lies. The old man had tears in his eyes.

"Thank you for telling me that," he said. "I wish Seonaid could have known. Your mother was besotted with you and so happy! Once the doctors put her on some medication for her toxaemia and she began to feel better she walked around like a queen. She said she felt sorry for all the flat-bellied women she saw on the street; she said she felt more alive than she had ever felt in her life."

"Was it Africa, then? Didn't she want to go back?"

"Oh no, it wasn't Africa and she was raring to go back. She loved to tell us stories about the school and their life there and how the women carried everything on their heads. She'd put a book or two on her head, holding them up with her left hand, standing very straight and with her stomach sticking out in front of her and walk around the room.

"'Like this,' she said, 'only maybe a huge basket of yams or charcoal and a baby riding behind. I think of them as caryatids. And they're beautiful; they hold up the world.'"

"Then what...?"

"Then what, indeed. Something went wrong, but not right away. She wrote letters—I have them for you, if you'd like them—wonderful letters about how well you were adjusting to the heat, how fast you were growing, how good it was to be back...."

"And then?"

He shrugged. "About two months after her return the letters changed. It wasn't just that they were less frequent—we expected that, what with her teaching and the new baby and all—but the *tone* changed. They were duty letters. 'Dear Seonaid and William, we are all well here. The rains are coming soon.' Stilted, almost automatic. 'Baby sends his love.' Then she wrote that they were coming home to Canada, that the climate didn't suit you after all, and that she had an offer of a job in Victoria. They never even stopped on their way through. Your father has visited fairly regularly, especially after your grannie became ill, but we've never seen your mother since we kissed you two goodbye and she boarded that army plane to take her back to Africa."

He put his hand over his eyes, then took a deep breath.

"She turned and waved and held up your little paw so that you could 'wave' as well and she gave us such a smile of pure happiness...." He cleared his throat.

"There might be other topics as interesting as your lost wax, William. Think about it hard, before you make up your mind."

William nodded, but they both knew.

At the door his grandfather said, "She had the loveliest singing voice—I expect she still has. She used to sit beside me on the piano bench, your grandmother standing behind with her hands on my shoulders and we'd belt out the old hymns and the sentimental old songs. She sang to you as well—lullabies and just wordless melodies."

"I have never heard my mother sing," William said, "or not that I can remember."

He turned his collar up against the falling snow and headed down the street to the bus stop. He knew without looking back that his grandfather was still standing behind the storm door looking out, or looking in—hearing his mother's voice perhaps, all those years ago. "Once to every man and nation, comes the moment to decide." Then, laughter and warmth and music and now, an old man, alone, turning out the lights and making his way up the stairs to bed.

What had been done to them that they could do this to him, to me?

William went to see the chair of graduate studies the very next morning, but it was several months later before he told his parents what he planned to do. And then it slipped out, by accident, thanks to Chantal.

William's mother liked to cook and she had small dinner parties from time to time—curries, groundnut stew, things she'd learned to cook on her travels. Mole. Dolmades. Flan. He was allowed to have a friend over. The masks weren't so frightening when you had a friend over, so they crept down the hall and sat near the bottom of the steps, listening.

Once upon a time his father's name was Lillian. Out in Africa, where he, William, was almost born. Where the masks came from. People laughed at the story of Lillian who turned out to be William who was really Sandy, his father, who was truly sorry he couldn't be here tonight.

Somebody said shall we keep an empty chair? Shall we set him a place, this elusive husband of yours??

The first day of school he said his full name, William Kwame MacKenzie, and the teacher said what an interesting name what does Kwame mean? Is it a family name? No, he said, I was born on Saturday, that's what it means. My father is William Alastair.

But one of the boys said Commie, it means he's a Commie and they ran across the playground towards him pointing their fingers, "Bang Bang, kill the Commie," until he hit and kicked and got sent to the principal's office. After that, for a long time, he was William K.

If a bomb ever dropped the whole world would go up in

a big bright flash. Stay tuned to the radio. You wouldn't be able to go outside; the air outside could kill you.

William's mother Pat was small, with curly auburn hair, a compact woman. She had been adopted, as a baby, by a couple in Ottawa. They had never told her anything about her birth parents and in her first year of university even her adoptive parents died within six months of one another. She said she'd had a calm sunny childhood of museums and canoeing on the Ottawa River, skating on the canal. She'd gone out to the University of British Columbia to study to be a nurse but soon discovered she was more drawn to arts and education. Eventually she decided she would like to teach, but only children who had speech problems of one sort or another. She saw an ad for COW in her senior year and rushed to get her application in.

"I seemed to have been given so much—a welcoming home, straight teeth, vitamins, summer camp, a good education. It wasn't just a yearning for adventure although that too, of course; it was a sense of obligation, of paying back in some small way I suppose. And it was different then—you could take two years out of your life, put the future on hold, in the certainty that you could come back to a job. In Canada it was mostly middle-class kids like myself who signed up. I suppose it was the same everywhere, except of course for the American boys who didn't want to go to Vietnam. We met quite a number of them."

So William pieced together bits of his mother's history. She didn't really like to talk about COW, except in a rather amused way at those dinner parties, the dinner parties that were never attended by his father. When William was in grade twelve he began to wonder if his father had a girlfriend somewhere and his mother knew about it—that the bright, amusing dinner parties took place on the nights she knew his father was with the other woman. If so, the other woman wasn't giving him any happiness, for he came home late and grim-faced, after the washing-up was done. Sometimes he went straight upstairs without even saying hello.

So far as he knew his mother never put an ad in the paper or searched for one: "Girl, born Ottawa Sept. 24, 1943, seeks contact with birth mother. Reply box———."

In grade eight his school went on a trip to Ottawa. In the National Gallery there was an exhibition of paintings by people who had been children when the bombs dropped on Hiroshima and Nagasaki. Eyeballs running down faces, a man who seemed to be trying to get rid of his gloves, but no, that was his skin hanging off. Someone had drawn a flower coming up through all the rubble. The teacher pointed it out to them. Hope, he said. Amazing to think that people who survived *that* could still have hope.

William asked if he could stay in the gallery a bit longer, please. He'd meet up with them in an hour. They had sped through the Group of Seven, through the modern stuff—he wanted to go back and take another look.

"Not a chance," the teacher said, "we have to stay together." The canal was still frozen and they went skating. He thought it would be wonderful to live in a city where people skated to work. They were supposed to take notes on the Parliament buildings and the speeches but it was so boring. One of the boys drew a big cock in his notebook and wrote underneath "The Honourable Member." They got a chance to shake hands with Mr. Trudeau, but William never met his grandparents, although he was only two hours away, by bus, from Montreal.

His grandparents sent William a set of sixty-four Crayola crayons in a box with a sharpener built in. He was six years old and learning to read a bit, but he couldn't read the names of the colours yet so his mother read them out to him again and again until he had memorized his favourites—blue-green, blue-violet, brick red, mahogany, orange-red, orange-yellow, midnight blue, violet-blue, violet-red, burnt orange, raw sienna, raw umber. He could, of course, recognize the *w* on white but the colour didn't interest him.

Last year he read in the paper that certain colours had been "retired" to the Crayola Hall of Fame: green-blue, lemon-yellow, orange-yellow, orange-red, midnight blue, violet-blue, blue-grey, raw umber. William was one of the hundreds of people who wrote in asking the Crayola company to reconsider and who made these decisions anyway? He received a nice letter from the Consumer Communications representative, saying that it was always a pleasure to hear from people who enjoyed their products, but consumers *had* been asked and new colours had been added. She enclosed a list of the replacement colours and a printed history of Crayola colours from the time they were first introduced in 1903. William was interested to note that what he had called "peach" had begun as "flesh" but the name had been voluntarily changed to peach, "partially as a result of the U.S. Civil Rights Movement." And his "midnight blue" was "Prussian blue" up until 1958 when it was switched "in response to teachers' requests." He wondered if they had done anything about Indian red and went to a toy store to check it out. (They hadn't.) Crayola now offered seventy-two colours in a plastic carrying case and some of the colours had silly names—to attract today's kids, he supposed: Atomic Tangerine, Wild Watermelon, Laser Lemon, Shocking Pink.

He opened the display package and smelled the waxy smell, breathed it in, just as he had done on his sixth birthday. Pointed and perfect in their paper covers the crayons lay like small, colourful torpedoes in their clear plastic caddy. Ages 4+, it said. Non-toxic/*non-toxique*. He wondered if the child who received these would be as thrilled as he was all those years ago.

He took his sixty-four crayons to Sunday School, which was just a block away from where they lived. His mother sometimes went to church, his father never. That day they were handed a scene of Jerusalem to colour. William opened his crayon box and selected carefully. Head down, tongue out, he got to work. He was so busy he didn't hear the Sunday School teacher when she came and stood behind him.

"Oh William," she said, "those are palm trees, not parrots or cockatoos—palm trees are green, green, green, not pink and green or yellow and blue. And I know it's hard, but you must try to stay within the lines."

"I don't want to go to Sunday School any more," he said when he got home.

"Tired of all that Jesus stuff, are you?" his father said. "It's about time."

"That's not it," William said. "I hate my teacher. She's mean and I hate her." He began to cry.

His mother talked to the teacher who said she had no idea what it was all about. William heard his parents talking about "the problem" when he was supposed to be asleep. When he was angry or upset he took out his black crayon and drew swirls and spirals on the backs of scrap paper. He couldn't understand why his teacher didn't remember what she'd done. He knew the palm trees weren't birds but they *looked* like birds. It was his picture; he could colour it any way he liked. Standing in the toy department of Eaton, sniffing the crayons, he remembered quite clearly the hurt and the fury. And the shame, he thought, the shame. He never told his parents the real reason, but he never went back. It didn't matter—his parents gave him plenty of newsprint to draw on and his teachers at school were not so fussy.

Crayons themselves, once he got down to using them, had always been a little disappointing. The richly coloured wax that showed above their paper wrappings translated into a pale, too pale, imitation—just a hint of the promised colour, except for black. He soon graduated to the stained-glass brilliance of magic markers but never liked their gas station smell (the "flavoured" ones were even worse) and you couldn't chew on them the way you could on crayons.

The attraction of Catholic churches was their waxy smell. On weekends, when he stayed in Chantal's flat above the fruit store, they made love with candles stuck everywhere—in wine bottles, on saucers, in an elaborate Georgian six-armed candelabra found in a box of junk they bid for at an auction. It was badly dented but that only made it more precious. (They made shadow puppets with their hands upon the walls.)

One night William told her about the masks, how they had frightened him as a child. Chantal did not go regularly to church but she still believed in the power of icons and images.

"They should probably never have been taken away from Africa; those things aren't toys."

"I think they frightened my father as well, and that my mother knew it, that she left them on the wall not just because she liked looking at them but because he didn't."

"Your mother sounds like a real bitch."

"No, she isn't. She's a good person, I think, but whatever is there between her and my father gets in the way."

"Why don't they split up? It's not healthy to live like that."

"I don't know. It's not like she has to depend on him financially, and I'm no longer there. I really don't know."

"It's amazing you turned out as nice as you are, all that poison in the air."

"You think I'm nice?"

"Most of the time I think you are very nice."

As he travelled through this country he remembered the names of the crayons and began to see things—the red earth, the fruit and vegetables, the market cloth, the sky, even the flesh of the people—in those terms: bittersweet, mahogany, sepia, raw sienna, burnt orange, all the greens and blues and violets, the red of tomatoes and peppers, the yellow flesh of the pineapples, the whole brilliant swirl of it all. He mixed up the watercolours in his little tin and laid down swatches of colour in the watercolour block he had brought with him.

One of the great disappointments of his life is that he cannot draw. He yearns to draw, to paint, the way others might yearn to be on the Olympic ski team or to write the great Canadian novel. He feels at home in this land of vivid colour—it thrills him the way a northern landscape never has. Is this because his first sensations were here?

A girl he once knew, a very pretty girl, told him she would give up all her good looks if she could sing like Edith Piaf—even if it was only for one day. He said he understood, but did not reveal his own obsession. Until he met his grandfather. Until they began to talk.

"It's a gift," his grandfather said. "Either you have it or you don't. Perhaps you have other gifts."

"No," said William, "I don't. I have what they call a 'good eye' and God knows my heart deserves it, but my hand refuses to co-operate."

He had Saturday morning lessons at the Art Gallery. He didn't have to beg. Years and years of lessons and they had been fun. It was fun to play with all the messy delicious materials from the world of art—clay, paint, inks, charcoal, yarns and looms. But his "good eye" told him very early on that he had no talent, not a single drop of it. It was like being tone deaf. He knew perfectly well why he had gone into art history. The next best thing.

"Perhaps something is holding you back," his grandfather had said. "Perhaps you think too much in terms of the representational?"

"No," William said, "I just don't have it in me." Yet the week before he left he had walked into an artists' supply house and equipped himself with a small black metal box of watercolours, some brushes, and a thick block of watercolour paper. But now he was simply putting down a wash of colours with a written explanation underneath: "the road along the coast," "the faded sky at noon," "mourning cloth," "Accra taxis." He kept a notebook as well and wrote in it faithfully every evening. It was a sort of one-sided conversation with his grandfather and perhaps he would hand it over when he returned. "I'm lonely," he wrote, "perhaps lonelier than I have ever been in my life (and I am by nature a solitary person), and yet all this loneliness doesn't drive me to drink or despair or thoughts of cutting short my journey or wishing I had told Chantal to stay. The first few days, maybe, I felt like that, but now I'm like a long-distance runner, I'm high on loneliness, exulting in the pain of it—all my senses sharpened because I don't have to concentrate on anything except the journey itself. And I'm 'other'—so conscious of this now that I'm out of big cities—very 'other,' the white man, the 'Bronie. I have to get used to being singled out, pointed at, giggled over. My parents went to a specific place to do a specific job so maybe they didn't feel this so acutely, but they must have felt it sometimes. Flesh colour here would range from pale yellow-brown through the darkest mahogany. My flesh is not 'flesh colour' in Africa's Crayola box. I am 'white,' like a ghost."

William's father had come to Montreal on a surprise visit, ostensibly to see *his* father but maybe to check up on William as well, meet William's girlfriend whom he never brought home. Chantal was delighted and they went to a couscous restaurant on rue Rachel. William had, so far, said nothing about his trip to Africa; he should have warned Chantal. After two glasses of wine she began to prattle on about her crazy assignment with *Elle*, how excited she was to be going to the Côte d'Ivoire.

"*l'Afrique*—such a magical word. Of course your bad son won't let me go any farther than the Côte d'Ivoire so we will part company there while he goes on but still, we will have a good time in Abidjan."

"Oh," from his father. Just that.

William picked up the ladle and poured more stew onto his plate. He was annoyed that his hand was shaking.

After a while his father said, "Well, this is a surprise."

"It's to do with my degree," William said. "I've decided to do my thesis on the lost-wax process."

"Lost wax," his father repeated, face more chalky than wax-like. He put down his napkin. "Would you excuse me for a moment?"

"Jesus," Chantal said, "I'm so sorry. I didn't know you hadn't told them. Maybe you better go after him?"

William shook his head. "What would I say?"

In a few minutes his father was back, still pale, a wet stain on his tie.

"Sorry about that," he said. "I don't think I'm used to such spicy food." He gave them a ghastly smile. "Now where were we?"

"William," Chantal said the next day, "I don't know if you should do this thing. How do you know what can of worms you will open up?"

"I'll deal with it."

"Oh yes, *you* will deal with it. Don't you care how it might affect your parents? You saw your father last night. Whatever his secret is I think you should let it alone. Why go rooting around in somebody else's past?"

"It's the past of my parents, Chantal, not just any old past. And it's my past, too. I was out there with them."

Chantal gave him one of her looks.

"There is something in you I don't like, you know. You are looking for a reason to act cold towards your mother and father, to write them off. Why do you want to do that? It's not nice."

"You don't understand."

"You are right about that, for sure."

William was summoned to his grandfather's house.

"Whatever this is all about, it's darker than I thought. When he came back last night he was like a man who'd seen a ghost. Pick another topic, another country—there's plenty out there."

"Didn't you *ask* him what was wrong?"

"I tried, but he was not forthcoming. And I cannot

demand. We were always a family for respecting privacy. And"—the old man looked at him over his reading glasses—"I don't want to lose him." The admission made his voice shake. "We lost your mother over this, we lost *you*—your childhood years; I can't lose him. Whatever happened, he has needed to come here, year after year, even if it is just to sit and stare into a glass of whisky."

"Did Grannie ever say...what she thought might be the matter?"

"We discussed it...of course we discussed it. Was it something we had done? and so on. And once, only once, she confronted him outright. Said she wanted to know *why*."

"And?"

"And it was the only time I ever heard him raise his voice to her. He said, 'It's nothing to do with you or Father and I won't come back if you are going to *hound* me about this!' Hound him! We didn't ask again. It was cowardly of us, perhaps, but we didn't ask again."

William came away from the house on Clarke Avenue thinking Chantal and his grandfather were right: let sleeping dogs lie. But the next day his thesis advisor contacted him with a list of names—a man in Cape Coast, a man at the university outside Kumasi, the name of a village in Ashanti. "The more I think about your idea, the more I like it. You might want to do a long introduction, from general to specific, on what happens when a craft is 'elevated' to an art form and becomes sought after by collectors and museums and at the same time corrupted by tourism, if it does. I hear this is what has happened with the goldweights. Good luck. Take plenty of notes and, if possible, good photographs." Two days later he heard he had been awarded a small grant.

(But no word from his mother; she said neither stop nor go. He had written to her, after his father's visit, but she did not reply. Wasn't silence a form of consent? And so he went to the art store and bought his tin of watercolours, his small brushes, his watercolour block. He began his series of shots.)

"I'm going," he said to Chantal, who was busy making her own preparations.

"Then I'm going with you."

"No."

"Yes."

"No."

They fought and made up, fought and made up, still managed to study for exams. Finally it was agreed that he would go with her to Abidjan, as originally planned. It would be good for him to get acclimatized before he began his journey. And they could be together in the evenings. Chantal shrugged. "I suppose it's better than nothing."

On the plane Chantal sat in Club Class with the rest of the fashion crew, but she came back often, to check on him. She was so excited she couldn't sit still.

"*l'Afrique!* Pinch me, William, I can't believe it!" Looking down he saw that the earth of Africa was red, a dusty red. He hadn't expected that. The descent was bumpy so he didn't attempt water-and-paint right then, but that night on the first page of his watercolour block he laid down a broad band of that soft brownish-red, like a smear of dried blood.

William was sitting in a chair by the window, staring down at the serpentine pool that undulated along one side of the Hotel Ivoire (four stars). For a while he had watched Chantal pack, but as she kept her back turned to him and seemed to have given up speaking to him altogether, he had decided simply to sit quiet and wait it out. She was wearing a piece of market cloth wrapped around her waist and William thought how beautiful her back was, the skin smooth and almost luminous; the vertebrae stood out, as she bent and folded, bent and folded, bent and folded, like the small peas in their edible pods that hung from the fence each year in his mother's garden, *mange tout* in French. He smiled, thinking of all the times that back had been pressed against his chest as they slept. But was glad she hadn't seen the smile; she was too angry and upset. Two hours ago there had been a nasty incident in the rue du Commerce but it wasn't just that. She wanted to come with him and he had said no; for the hundredth time he had said no. This past week had been wonderful but now it was time to get down to serious business. He had to go alone. He had told her this all along but she hadn't believed him. Abidjan wasn't even part of his original plan but when Quebec *Elle* hired Chantal to be one of the models on a shoot in the Ivory Coast she had begged him to come with her and then go on his "*p'tit voyage*" from there. Chantal did not believe in dwelling on the past; why spend all that energy looking backwards? And this wasn't even *his* past.

"Part of it is."

"Well, okay. Maybe a few months. But as for the rest...."

At the very least he could take her with him. He knew she thought he was a puzzle she would one day solve, a nut she would crack. They had argued a lot on this trip but still fell into one another's arms. It scared them, the way they felt about one another. "Because we are so unsuitable, William. This can only end in tears."

"All the more reason for us to be apart for a while."

He was going to have to speak soon, the suitcase was nearly full. She and the other models were going on location for three days, first to Grand Bassam and then upcountry. He could imagine the sort of spread that would come out of all this: first an idiotic title making some reference to the midday sun and then Chantal and the others lounging around in picturesque settings, rich or poor, in very expensive clothes:

"Chantal, Fatima and Denise make friends with the children of———." Mud huts and big-eyed kids staring up at these strange women, the photographer, the make-up artist.

"Chantal's long skirt by Issy Miyake, antique gold necklace by *Caravane*, eyeliner, eye shadow and mascara by Estée Lauder, Chanel Intense Sun Protector SPF 30."

"Smiles courtesy of the children of the Côte d'Ivoire."

He'd seen enough of those magazines lying around Chantal's apartment—he could probably write the stuff in his sleep. If his French were a bit better, that is.

(Their new friend Bernard had asked Chantal what she did for a living and she had said "hard fluff.")

"I'll be finished on Thursday; I could fly to Accra to join you."

"No."

"Maybe I'll come anyway. Just appear. You wouldn't be hard to track down."

"You wouldn't do that." And he knew she wouldn't dare. If she did, that would be, *vraiment*, the end.

"Chantal," he said now. No reply.

The incident with the camera had frightened them both. They were taking a coffee at a small café on the rue du Commerce, a café where William went each day to sit and observe the scene, when Chantal spied two women, still quite far down the street but coming towards them, each with a Singer sewing machine on her head. Chatting away as they walked, as though they were wearing straw hats or headcloths.

"Here," she said, "quick. I'm going outside. As those women come by take a picture of me. Only stay at the table, don't let them see you. This could be great."

"Why don't we just ask them?"

"Then they'll either say no or they'll pose. You know what happens."

She thrust the camera into his hands and rushed outside.

A young man in a singlet and khaki pants had been drinking Coca-Cola and watching them from a nearby table, or so it seemed to William. When he didn't get up and try to sell them anything or come over and ask where they were from, what hotel they were staying at, William figured the guy was just looking at Chantal. But as

Chantal ran outside the man left too, throwing some coins down on the table and hurrying out.

William focused the camera on Chantal leaning against a lamp post, pretending to consult a guide book. As the women came abreast of her he raised the camera and took a picture, then another, just to be sure. The whirring buzz seemed very loud to his ears but the women went on, not noticing the white man, sitting at his table drinking *café-crème.*

Chantal came back in, picked up her bag; they paid and left. But as soon as they got outside the fellow who had been sitting at the next table appeared in the street in front of them and began shouting. He tried to grab the camera away from William, accused them of taking a picture of him without permission. He wanted the roll of film. Chantal shouted in rapid French; William, speaking slowly, tried to explain. The man grabbed for the camera and two men rushed forward from the crowd that had gathered; a hotel security guard in a white uniform and the owner of one of the stalls that lined the street grabbed the man's arms and restrained him.

"*Allez-y!*" they shouted. "Go!"

"But we didn't..." William was still trying to explain.

"*Allez-y!*"

Just then the man leaned forward and spat directly in William's face. The spit hit his mouth and William, frantic, afraid, wiped it away with his fingers. All Bernard's warnings and obsessions came back to him.

Chantal always carried a small bottle of Evian water in her bag. He opened it, still on her shoulder, and rooted around—"William, *zut alors!*"—found the bottle, poured half of it into his cupped left hand, washed his lips, wiped his hand on his pants, poured out the rest of it, shaking.

Chantal hailed a cab and they began fighting even before the door was closed.

"Look what happened! Just look!"

"He was just trying to get some money off us. Forget it."

"You weren't the one who was spat at!"

"Tsk. Yes. But it's no big deal."

"It is a big deal. You should *ask* before you take pictures."

"But we weren't taking his picture and he knew it; he was just trying some good old blackmail and humiliation to make us pay up."

"That was awful, terrible."

"Forget it."

William hated scenes; Chantal didn't mind them.

When William agreed to go to Abidjan he told Chantal that he wasn't going to stay at the Hotel Ivoire with her and the rest of the group. She thought that was crazy. *Elle* had agreed she could have a room to herself, a room with a double bed, so what difference did it make? He didn't know how to explain without seeming to belittle something that she so clearly enjoyed doing and that allowed her to live most of her life as an ordinary student. And she had no illusions about modelling—what the images she presented did to the young women who bought those magazines. However, she needed money and she had the face and body that were currently *à la mode*. From behind she almost looked like a boy.

This was her first overseas assignment and the other two models were black. Chantal wasn't just wearing designer fashions inspired by the textiles of West Africa, she was wearing designer sunblock—a different one each day. Not that she ever really stood in the sun for more than a few minutes—big umbrellas, whisked away at the last minute, saw to that. But it was good advertising: if that pale girl can be safe in *Africa*, then I'd better buy some for the beach.

William decided to stay at the Grand Hotel. "Hmph," said Chantal, "it won't be," and it wasn't. But it was reasonably cheap and he wanted to save most of his money for Ghana. ("You mean to say," squawked Bernard when he heard about the Hotel Ivoire, "that you could be sitting in the lap of luxury—or sprawling on the bed of luxury—and you prefer to stay *here?*"

"That's what I tell him," Chantal said. "*Il est toqué*; he's crazy, a real nut-case.")

The hotel was at the very bottom of a side street off the rue du Commerce and when William walked in, after waving goodbye to Chantal and her "gang" as she called them (no thank you he would take his own taxi and meet up with them later / William why must you be so stubborn you could be robbed or murdered you don't know this city), the desk clerk was asleep with his head on the counter, although people were passing to and fro in the lobby and a lot of noise, including the sound of a television set, was coming from what was obviously the bar.

William cleared his throat. No response. He cleared his throat again and said *Bonsoir*. Said it once more, loudly.

The man behind the counter raised his head and looked at William resentfully; the whites of his eyes weren't white, but yellow. Perhaps the hotel didn't want customers (white); perhaps it was *complet*. But no. A room *avec deux lits* was available; there were no more singles. He couldn't tell if the man were lying or not but he was too tired to argue. He did ask to see the room; he had promised Chantal he would at least do that. The man handed him a large old-fashioned key and told him to go and look. When he came back down to say he'd take it the man was asleep again. He retrieved his pack from behind the counter, telephoned Chantal to let her know his room number (disappointed to be told she was not in her room but he left a message) then fell asleep as he was trying to figure out what time it was back home. If it was half-past nine here then it must be, it must be, it must be. What difference did it make? He was in Africa; he'd arrived. For the first time since he had met her he hoped Chantal was out having a good time without him. It was sleep he lusted after tonight, only sleep.

And then, just at the corner of his memory, in this small and stuffy room (air-conditioner out of order) he saw or rather *felt* himself as a small boy, being picked up: "Shh, don't wake him." Strong arms lifting and his face against wool. And so to sleep with the words (almost) on his lips: they did love me after all. An image, a phrase he won't remember when he wakens. Outside room 307 the night clicked and whirred and flapped and moved along in its dark cloak, never silent, never still. Taxis roared across bridges, beggars rearranged themselves in doorways, cockroaches scampered over things in bureau drawers, things in pantries, even breathing things in beds. Africa waited for William. Africa was used to waiting; let him sleep.

For the first two days, before he met Bernard and Susan, he wandered the city by himself while Chantal and the others arranged themselves (or were arranged) in various attractive poses. He did not go near the Hotel Ivoire even though it tempted him with its famous *patinoire*. There had been a photo-shoot on the ice; they even got hold of a hockey stick from some guy at the Canadian High Commission. Françoise, their boss, brought along copies of Canadiens sweaters.

William loved to skate; his closest times with his father had been when he was learning to skate. What he remembered first was a lack of balance, back and forth instead of side to side, and the sensation of falling, straight down, like an elevator dropping. Later thinking there must be some trick that allowed others to glide whereas all he could manage was short, choppy, hesitant *steps*. He understood (now? then? when?) that skating was about one foot, the "rear," being at an angle to the front foot, so that you could push off against the edge of the rear blade and glide along the line of the front one.

And then the exquisite moment of release when suddenly he could do it (By George, I think he's got it!) and he glided for a few minutes before he stumbled over the puzzle of how to make his back foot into his front foot. What he was learning to do, he thought now, was a new type of walking.

Mobility and freedom. The early memory of "getting

his legs" and being able to skate the length of the rink but unable to stop. (Which accounts for an interesting scar on his chin.) Once, in an art history class, he had seen a slide of a painting in the National Gallery of Scotland: "The Rev. Robert Walker Skating on Duddingston Loch." The Rev. skated with his hands folded across his chest, long legs gliding over the ice; it was exactly the way his father skated. (His father, also, skating backwards, holding out his hands. "Come on, you can do it." He'd forgotten about that until now.)

Once, during a particularly cold spell, his father (*and* his mother, yes both of them) took him to a frozen creek outside the city. The ice bumpy, not so easy to negotiate, but the wonderful feeling of being outside in the open air.

They skated, both of them, but either alone or with him between them, never together, holding hands.

He wanted to be on a hockey team but was never any good at all that cut and thrust, too slow. Hockey was like chess: you had to think ahead, be aware of what was going on all around you. They said that Gretzky could keep the whole game in his head.

Chantal liked to skate as well; they skated at Beaver Lake, holding hands, and supported the Canadiens. But a skating rink in Africa did not appeal; the Hotel Ivoire did not appeal. Maybe when he came back, on his way home.

"You are just being bloody-minded, William."

"Maybe."

After her tuition and her daily expenses all of the money Chantal makes from modelling goes directly into the bank. She wants a house and a bit of land, perhaps in

Magog or Sherbrooke. William knows that he is part of this picture and is ambivalent. What would they use for money, day-to-day money, once the land was paid for and the house was up? He does not think he was cut out to be a commuter. Chantal dreams big: they will also have a *pied à terre* in Montreal. William will teach at university two days a week and when she needs to come to the city for a job, she will. "Or we can rent one room from your *grand-père*. He would like that. He rattles around too much in that big house."

Chantal wants chickens and ducks and babies. What does *he* want?

William buys a cloth for Chantal, who can sew anything. Black pineapples printed on a soft, sandstone-coloured background. She has black hair and that ivory skin. Loves wild clothes but wants to settle down.

"Settle down." William sees a test tube in his high school chem lab—a precipitate—little bits of stuff suspended in liquid. Or the snowstorm in a glass dome his mother has had since she was a child: a small girl in a red coat and white muff, smiling. Now the domes are made of plastic. Chantal buys them for her ever-increasing tribe of nephews and nieces; she is the only sister who is not yet married. His mother's snowstorm was real glass, and heavy. "Gently William, gently." The girl inside smiled and smiled however hard it snowed.

"Settle down"—never to whirl again. Was that what this trip was really all about? A "last fling"? (Would his first fling be his last?) Before he settled down, down, down. (Job, house, wife, child, ducks and chickens. Old MacKenzie had a farm, ee-eye, ee-eye-oh.)

He felt so free these days in Abidjan, realized all his (remembered) life had been divided into school and not-school. And even during not-school there was usually some planned activity, summer camps and later, summer jobs. He felt as though he were playing hooky, sitting at a café watching the passing scene, wandering the streets. His real journey had not begun and so he was under no obligation to do anything at all. And of course he wasn't really alone; each evening, after she had showered and changed, Chantal appeared at the Grand Hotel and they went wandering together, eating at some small restaurant, ending up in bed. She could not stay out too late, because of the early shoots, so after he had seen her to a taxi he went into the bar of the hotel and had a beer. He was thirsty all the time out here. Juice, coffee, bottled water, beer. It interested him that he didn't seem to pee any more than usual—he must be sweating buckets. Most of the time, except in the first few minutes after a shower, his body was slick with sweat.

On the third night a white couple walked into the bar just as he was thinking of going upstairs to bed. The man was in his fifties, wearing a black tee shirt that said *African Queen*. It was a bit too tight, so that his round belly pushed up against it, as though he were hiding a giant bagel underneath. The woman was just a bit younger, with a money wallet on a string around her neck and a thin, disappointed face. Susan and Bernard, not a couple—in the "couple" sense—as it turned out, but both staying at the Grand Hotel. Bernard, an editor for a New York publisher, on his way to a *salon du livre* in Mali but having a holiday both before and after; Susan a former Peace Corps worker, nouveau agronomist, who had spent the last twenty years working in various parts of Africa.

"We've seen you before," Bernard said, "but you were occupied with your lovely wife?...girlfriend? Anyway, now that we've found you alone let me buy you a drink. *Trois bières!*" (In a dreadful accent.)

They raised glasses. "Welcome to the land of scratch and sniff," said Bernard. A few beers later and they were old friends.

Chantal liked Bernard right away but wasn't so sure about Susan.

"She is full of funny stories, you notice, but they all end badly. She is *cynique*; I don't like that."

At a restaurant three blocks away, set back on a side street and the sign easily missed (Chantal and William had missed it), they spent the next evening eating brochettes of beef and frites and swapping stories. Bernard had brought along a beautiful young man in a tangerine silk shirt. The man—the boy really—ate little and said less but William was sure, in spite of the half-closed eyes, that he was paying close attention.

Susan said once, when she was in the Peace Corps, one of the volunteers, who'd been told not to swim in the river, did so and was eaten by crocodiles. Later they decided that if they had taken bets on who was most likely to be eaten it would have been him, hands down.

"Hands off, don't you mean?" Bernard said. "Was there anything left to send home to Mom and Dad?"

For a minute Susan's face changed, remembering. No joke now. What had they found?

"Not much," she said. "Bernard is more afraid of mosquitoes than crocodiles, aren't you? He has a large drawing of a female anopheles taped to the wardrobe, don't you Bernard?"

He was not embarrassed.

"I do, I do. Did you know they stand on their heads when they bite? *And* they don't whine when they come looking for you. You might not even know one was in the room. They—all of 'em—can carry dengue as well as malaria."

"I wonder why they can't carry AIDS," Chantal said. "Isn't the mosquito's stinger just like a syringe? So if it bites someone with AIDS and then bites you, wouldn't that be like using a dirty syringe?"

"You'd think so, wouldn't you?"

The young man was looking puzzled so Bernard turned to Chantal. "Can you explain to him what we're talking about?"

Bernard confessed he had lied in order to come on this trip; he told his boss he spoke perfect French when in fact he couldn't speak a word. Well, maybe one or two.

"The last time I spoke French was in grade eight. Our teacher always seemed on the edge of a nervous breakdown. She wore one stocking with a seam, one without. Or maybe she was trying to make some kind of statement, who knows?

"Anyway, all I remember is *J'entre dans la salle de classe* and a bit from some poem, very beautiful, François Villon I think:

> *"Il pleure dans mon coeur*
> *Comme il pleut sur les toits"*

So Chantal explained. "SIDA. Is there a lot of it here?"

The boy shook his head. "Plenty," he said in English. "I am afraid too much."

Bernard grins at all of them, shakes his finger at William:

"Beware/Beware the Bight of Benin
There's one that comes out for forty goes in."

Chantal looks at William, her worried look. On the way back from a photo session at Yamoussoukro ("Chantal, Fatima and Denise feed the sacred crocodiles....") their van passed a man sitting by the side of a wrecked car. His face was streaming with blood. A policeman was already on the scene so they didn't stop, but now she has a new worry to add to the others. What if William is in an accident and needs a transfusion? Back home, at this very moment, there are men and women dying because of tainted blood they received more than fifteen years ago. How much greater the danger here!

"Chantal," he said, "I am going to be very very careful, but I can't worry about all this. You've been infected by Bernard's paranoia. He's the one I can't puzzle out, what he's doing here. He acts as though he's gay, as though he wants us to be sure and notice that he's gay, yet it would be madness for him to go on the prowl here. Madder than in New York."

She shrugged. "Maybe he is already infected?"

"And would go around infecting others? That's a terrible thing to say."

"No no. Not go around infecting others. Just go on a holiday. The opportunity presents itself—the *salon du livre* in Bamako—and he decides to get away from New York City and go on a little tour. His companion was black."

"What do you mean was? What do you mean black? Who told you this?"

"Bernard. He told me."

"You've only known him a few hours."

That shrug again.

And now here he was with the boy in the tangerine shirt. If you felt that way—about men—how did you restrain yourself? Women too. Would a white man—did a white man—go to a prostitute out here? Any more? Did sailors simply buy their condoms and take their chances? When you stepped off the plane you smelled it—Africa. The air was thick with the hot sweet breath of sex. You felt that women would fall open in your hand, like ripe fruit. If Chantal weren't here to protect him?

Sitting at the café, walking along the streets or in the markets he was aware most of all of women, women in those wonderful cloths, women with headloads, women with babies slung behind, women walking, women getting on with the business of life.

"Aren't you lonely during the day?" Chantal asked, sitting up with their bedcover, tiger-striped, tucked over her breasts.

"No," he said truthfully and perhaps a little too quickly. "It's all so new. I'm just a sponge soaking it all up."

She reached across him to the night table, one of whose legs was shorter than the others. They had corrected this with an old *roman policier* some former occupant had left behind. Lit a cigarette and stared at the wall.

"When are you planning to leave?"

"Sunday, I think. I want to take the bus along the coast."

"I'm not finished until next Thursday. Françoise has decided we should have a few shots up-country, so up-country we shall go, heigh-ho heigh-ho. I hope we don't see any more accidents. But of course I could join you by the Saturday."

Silence from William, who was wondering if the *Guinness Book of Records* listed the size of the world's biggest cockroach.

"Okay," she said, "*parlons d'autre chose*."

"Chantal... Listen. Most of my luggage seems to be a medical kit. I'm not going out in the bush, you know."

"What medicine have you got for your *head*, William?"

He chose not to understand her.

"Tylenol. And a straw hat if needed. Sunglasses. Sunscreen."

"Oh! *J'en ai marre de ton idée fixe*. What if you find... well...something really terrible? Will you feel better then?"

"What if I don't find anything at all? What if they are just an ordinary middle-class married couple who happen to dislike each other intensely."

"They must have loved each other once."

"That's the point. They must have loved each other once."

"And you think the answer is out here?"

"I think so. Was it the Plains Indians who were sent out into the desert and forbidden to come home until they'd had a vision?"

"Jesus Christ! Is this some sort of test of your *manhood* then? Something you have to pass because your parents failed? You are really crazy."

They hadn't realized they were shouting over Bernard's knocking until he stuck his head around the door.

"Ah, heterosexual love! I knew it was okay to come in because what you were shouting wasn't endearments. Would you like to go to dinner in, say, half an hour and then to a nightclub in Treichville? It's Susan's last night in Africa."

Chantal had the bedcover so William, who had been lying on his back while Chantal berated him, sat up quickly and brought his knees up to his chin.

Bernard smiled. "I spy with my little eye...."

"William," Chantal said after Bernard had left, "we are not finished with this conversation; it must be continued."

And now she was closing and locking her case. A final check of the bathroom, under the bed, to be sure nothing had been left behind. Except William. She had left William behind. Stood in the doorway in black cotton billowy trousers and a black jacket lined with the pineapple print. She had had the outfit made up in one day and it suited her. Her skin was the same pale ivory as when she arrived. What would night, what would life here, really be like when she was gone?

"Have fun on your trip up-country."

"*Bien sûr.*" Her eyes were full of tears.

"I'll call you as soon as you are back in Montreal. You won't forget to mail the letters?"

She shook her head.

"I wonder...." She swallowed, started afresh. "I wonder if I will ever see you again."

He didn't remember moving but now he was kissing her, kissing her, stopping not only her mouth but his, so that the words wouldn't come leaping out, "Chantal, don't go."

An impatient Françoise came striding up the corridor. "Chantal! We are waiting on you. Come."

That night it was William who knocked on Bernard's door; Bernard would love to go out to dinner but was otherwise engaged. Time for a drink, however. There was always time for a drink.

It was true about the drawing of the female anopheles mosquito. There she was, scotch-taped to the closet door. Bernard began to read in a melodramatic voice what he had written underneath, copied out from a pamphlet on malaria.

"'She enters your room at night. You may recognize her by the way she rests on the walls—she stands on her head with the tail end of her body tilted upwards, protruding into the air like a rocket on a launching pad. She is your enemy....

"'Attracted by the warmth of your body and the carbon dioxide you exhale—'"

Bernard checked his face in the wavery mirror. "Hard to believe that anything would be attracted to this, isn't it? Must be my sparkling wit."

The *ascenseur* was out of order so they walked down the stairs and into the bar. It was still too early for anyone to be dining in the restaurant and they watched a man scatter water on the floor, then push it around in lazy circles with a mop.

"The blessing of the linoleum," Bernard said. He raised his glass. "'Sunset,'" he said, "'the hunt for human blood begins....' Would you like to hear me expound on bilharzia, yellow fever, river blindness? Seems amazing to me there's anyone left walking around at all. And now this—this AIDS business. Susan told me when she was someplace in Central Africa—Zaire I think—the people accepted the condoms gladly and gratefully but then cut the tips off because they believe intercourse is a sacred mingling of the male and female fluids. And another place where they hung the condoms up, like fetishes, over the sleeping mats. Maybe this is it for darkest Africa, lights out, finish. What a cruel joke that would be."

Bernard waved to the boy in the tangerine shirt, who stood in the doorway, in no hurry, looking quietly around the room.

"In the meantime / in between time...." He finished his drink and went out.

William had a pineapple, half a loaf of bread and some groundnuts up in his room. He bought a beer to take up with him; it wouldn't hurt to get an early night and he didn't feel hungry enough for a proper meal. He had a book as well—several books. What more could he ask for?

The man who weighed the baggage on a big, old-fashioned standing scale had enormously swollen thumbs. They weren't like thumbs at all, really, but they were in the thumb-place and had deeply embedded and barely visible nails at the end. William was glad that Bernard wasn't with him; he'd be scanning his dictionary of tropical diseases to try to figure out what the fellow had and whether it was catching. His farewell gift to William had been a book called *Where There Is No Doctor*. Since the incident on the rue du Commerce he was more aware of his own hidden, pushed-down paranoia, but rationalized it by saying that if someone spit in his face back home he'd be upset, too. *And* worry about germs or worse. That was only natural. If the fellow with the thumbs (was there a slight ooze around the edges of one nearly hidden nail?) had anything infectious he wouldn't be there, handling bags and bundles, writing out chits to show how much your baggage weighed and how much you had to pay the cashier. Nobody else seemed uneasy; nobody even gave those thumbs (they looked as though they would burst at any moment) a second glance.

He was one of the early ones and sat now on a bench, next to two sisters from Togo—there was trouble in Togo, big trouble—watching the scene, his daypack and a large bottle of NAYA water at his feet. Somehow—when?—Chantal had been alone in his room before she left and had sewn a large patch on his big pack. A red maple leaf and the word CANADA. This did not seem to mean much to the sisters, who asked him where he was from. It embarrassed him nevertheless to be so labelled. No doubt Chantal saw the badge as some sort of talisman—who would shoot a Canadian?—but he intended to take it off as soon as possible. There might be big trouble—"plen-ty"—in Togo, and he'd already read about the trouble up north in Burkina Faso, but where he was going there was no trouble at all. Or not that kind of trouble; just the usual poverty, disease, unemployment. Nothing you'd shoot a stranger for.

And he wasn't a woman. Susan told them she was leaving Africa primarily because the farmers wouldn't listen to her but also because—the last straw—a Peace Corps girl had just been raped, in Niger, a Muslim country, at knifepoint.

"She wasn't dressed in a provocative way but she was walking alone past a deserted building. She ran a small literary program for women and had simply taken a new way back to her house. The man came up behind her, clapped his hand over her mouth and dragged her into the building. She thought they liked her in that town.

"The truth is, they don't like us—they want what we have but they don't want us. I think they despise us; they think we're ugly and smelly and immoral."

"You're talking about women, here, right?" said Chantal.

"I'm talking mostly about women, but I don't think they like any of us. They want our expertise and our money but they would prefer we mailed it down."

"Is that true?" Chantal asked the boy in the tangerine shirt. "*C'est vrai?*"

"*Oui*," he replied, looking down at his plate, "*en général, c'est vrai.*"

William had tried to be pleasant to everyone, even the sleepy, sullen desk clerk and the boys who wandered the streets of the Plateau, cheap watches up and down their arms, or ran between the taxis and cars, draped in neckties, lottery tickets, waving *Le Figaro*, *Le Monde*, French editions of *Time* and *Newsweek*. And several times he had chatted with the night watchman after he had seen Chantal to a taxi.

The telephone in his room was on the wall, just above his left ear. After Chantal left it began to ring in the middle of the night. The first time he said, "Wrong number," half asleep, but he had no sooner hung up than it began to ring again. A man's voice, hurried, a tumble of words in French. You must help me, my wife and child, you promised, you promised.

William was sorry again, you have the wrong number. *Vous vous trompez le numéro.*

"*C'est Guillaume?*"

"*Oui. C'est Guillaume.*"

And again the rush of words. You promised you would help me.

"Who *is* this?"

"You know who it is," the man said.

"Leave me alone," William said, "or I'll call the police."

He thought he recognized the voice of the night watchman but he wasn't sure. It would be easy for that man to get his number. But he had promised nothing. Had he been misunderstood? Was this some kind of blackmail? The phone rang again and again until finally he had let the receiver hang, and the dial tone buzzed like an angry insect for the rest of the night. In his dreams someone said 'allo, 'allo, 'allo?

What was the French word for blackmail if he had to

go to the police? He wished Chantal were there; she had a way of dealing with hassles and an amazing vocabulary to go with it. The first time he saw her she was walking backwards up rue St. Denis, yelling at a man in the doorway of a bar. Did he think she was his *chien de poche*? Is that what he thought? People were smiling and laughing while William, new to the city, stood there astounded. She was making a scene and enjoying it! Amazing.

Then she backed right into him, a pretty woman in a black leather jacket and black-and-white polka-dot leggings. "Oh," she said, startled. And then she laughed and fell in step beside him, giving her waiting companion a smile and a dismissive wave of the hand.

That was the beginning; he wished that she were there now. She'd get rid of this guy quick. He wrapped the thin bedcover around him and went to the window. Down to his left he could see taxis still speeding back and forth across the bridge. Even the chic people went over to Treichville, to the nightclubs there. No doubt Bernard was still dancing the night away with his friend in the tangerine shirt. Nothing here got going until about eleven.

All alone by the telephone, only the last thing he wanted it to do was ring.

No calls came the next, his final, night. And now he would never know who it was who had phoned him and whether, inadvertently, he had promised something...to a desperate man.

At the bus depot William was surprised to see that most of the travellers were women and more and more women were arriving all the time, followed by men straining to balance enormous headloads done up in cloth or burlap. He began to see why baggage was weighed and taxed.

"*Les marchandes?*" he asked his companions.

"*Oui, les marchandes.*"

Powerful women, petty traders. Two days before, the market women had gone on strike and brought Treichville market to a virtual halt. They felt the duty they paid at the airport was too high, that pockets were being lined at their expense. It would be intimidating to be confronted by a crowd of these women, particularly the older ones. There was lots of loud talk and ordering about now. And the petty merchants of the bus trade were arriving as well: women with large enamelled pans filled with packets of biscuits, cigarettes and matches, oranges, loaves of bread, handkerchiefs, groundnuts—things you might need for your journey. They looked to William like queens with fantastic crowns. He wanted to take out his watercolour block but felt shy. Instead, he stared and stared. He watched the way the women held themselves, and the way they talked back, the way they laughed, hee hee hee, or shook their fists, babies asleep on their backs. One group was obviously talking about him, laughing no doubt at his pale, freckled skin, his general thinness. To them, he must lack substance. They did not know about *Elle*, that thin was beautiful. They wouldn't think much of "her voice was ever soft, gentle and low...." The men (most of them) cowered when the women spoke.

It was 8 a.m. and already the ground was steaming. He tried to imagine all of this crammed on a bus, even a nice bus like this, a State Transport bus on which, to his surprise, he was even to have a numbered seat, a window seat, and it looked as though the windows opened.

He felt as though he were in the middle of a giant box of crayons: red, orange, orange-red, tangerine, melon, blue and blue and blue, every imaginable shade of green, of violet. And brown. The gradations of brown. He felt as though he had been blind all his life and now the bandages were off—he could see. How colourless the world was going to seem, back home.

The bus driver honked his horn three times.

"*Allons*," said one of the Togo sisters. "Let's go."

After everyone was seated, five abreast with a jump seat folding down as each row filled up from the back, the driver's mate asked for identity papers, which were to be handed up to the front along with 2,000 CFA, for "*le péage*." This seemed like a lot of money—how many tollbooths could there possibly be between here and Accra? And surely that would be included in the price of the ticket?

No one but William seemed surprised at this demand. The mate examined each piece of identification carefully —some were simply folded pieces of paper—counted the money and placed it in a leather purse. When he came to William's passport he looked at it for a long time, then put it with the others.

The driver said something to the mate.

"*Canadien*."

"Ah," said the people in the first few rows, "*Canadien*." The word was passed backwards, *Canadien*, *Canadien*,

Canadien. Someone called out "*Beau pays!*" There were smiles all round.

The bus pulled out of the depot with a few small boys running alongside. It turned left and headed for the coast road. Now he felt as though his journey had begun. Abidjan was a holiday. Fascinating, but a holiday. *This* was the real thing.

By the time they reached the border the bus had been waved down thirteen times, sometimes by the army, sometimes by police, always by men in uniform. It was all very low-key and friendly. The mate got down with the leather purse and went around the side of the bus. The luggage bays were opened then quickly shut. The mate got back on the bus. William, dozing, expected he would soon get used to it.

Then they were hours at the border. First, Immigration —"You are a student?"

"Yes. I want to study the lost-wax process and see a bit of the country while I'm here."

"You are a tourist?"

"No. Not really. I am a student."

How different this unsmiling woman was from the other women he had encountered so far. He sensed that she didn't like him and for two cents she'd send him back where he came from.

"You have put Mrs. Owusu-Banahene as a reference. You know this woman?"

"My grandfather knew her, when they were children."

"You have never met her?"

"No. But I have a letter for her." He took out the letter but she waved him away without looking at it.

"I can go?"

She didn't even bother to answer. He wanted to say, What's your *problem*? but of course he didn't. No talking back at borders. And there was still Customs to get through. A uniformed man and a woman were opening bundles and baskets, taking the lids off containers of palm oil, unrolling bolts of cloth to see if something might be hidden inside. William's medicine kit, with its syringes, swabs, sutures, was right at the top of his pack. That was really dumb. They'd see all that stuff and think he was some kind of drug addict. The woman at the Immigration desk had probably given them a signal to search him thoroughly. Did they go in for body searches here, sticking fingers up your ass, tongue depressors down your throat. These inspectors seemed harsh; some of the traders had already been sent off to pay fines, muttering to one another about the unfairness of it all, saying insulting things about this country.

William had bought two dozen pencils printed with the red maple leaf. He smiled as the male inspector moved towards him.

"Are these your things?" It sounded like your tins. Are these your tins? He had been about to say no.

"Yes, that's all."

"Please, where are you from?"

"Canada." William held out a fan of pencils. "Would you like a pencil from Canada?"

The man smiled and took two. He put them in his pocket and X'd the pack with yellow chalk.

"Canada," he said. "Fine country."

A small part of William was disappointed that he seemed so harmless, not worth bothering about. Only a small part; the rest of him was glad he had got off so easily.

It was high noon now and he needed to get out of the sun. Mad dogs and Englishmen? He went around to the far side of the bus, where there might be some shade, and his eyes (he'd been squinting against the glare) did not at first register what he saw. When he did see he stammered, blushed violently and fled. Women were sitting in the open, now empty, luggage bays nursing their babies and chatting. Their blouses were open or their cloths were down around their waists. The women stopped talking when they saw him but the babies sucked on; he could hear their sucking noises, slurp, slurp, slurp, a soft lapping sound. Little grunts and moans.

He could hear the women's laughter as he backed away and moved quickly around the back of the bus and down to the line of people who had now been cleared to cross over to the other country. In the grass and on the walkway there were dozens of dead and dying insects, dark brown, almost black. They were grotesque—something Edward Lear might have invented, about three inches long and with a small horn like a rhinoceros. What were they dying from? Why were they here?

"Beetle," a young man said. "You like one?"

"No," William said, "no thanks," putting his hands behind his back. "Interesting, though. Why are there so many? And why are they dying?"

The man shrugged and smiled.

"Perhaps it is God's will."

They gave off an angry, clicking sound.

On the other side of the fence that separated one country from the other, the money-sellers waited.

"You want cedis? Name your price. Cedis Cedis Cedis."

William drank two bottles of Fanta orange, one right after the other, then walked away a bit and did as the few other men were doing, peed against a wall.

William had never slept with anyone before Chantal. He had "made love" to a few other girls but he had never stayed the night. It came as a shock to him how pleasant it was to sleep with someone else beside him in the same bed, to wake up and touch her back or her thigh and have her turn to him, her eyes still shut in sleep. To be touched by her. He looked at couples in a new light. It wasn't just sex, then, that kept them together but cosiness—an old-fashioned word but that's how he felt, cosy—for the first time in his life. And for the first time felt sadness for his parents who, as far back as he could remember, had never shared a bed or even a bedroom.

Once, when he was about seven years old, he had gone for supper to a new friend's house. The other boy had taken him on a tour and when he showed William the big bedroom with the big double bed and said, "This is my Mommy and Daddy's room," William couldn't take it in, couldn't understand but was too shy to ask "which?"

He had not moved in with Chantal but he spent every weekend with her. She wrote messages on his back with her fingernail, sometimes in English, sometimes in French. She sat up in bed drinking coffee, completely naked except for one of her collection of old hats. What it was, William thought now, was this: she loved life. She found being alive a very interesting experience; she found other people interesting. She really listened. Had anyone ever really listened to him before?

She threw her arms around him in the street. He would be a fool to give her up just because he didn't want to live in the country and raise chickens. And why didn't he? What was wrong with chickens?

One of the young girls from the village next to the border (more a collection of shops and stalls—the owners probably lived with their families somewhere else, out there in the bush) ran up to him, urged on by her friends.

"Please, where are you going?"

"To Accra." She wore what was obviously a school uniform, a bright blue cotton dress trimmed in white—her friends wore the same.

"When you come back this way I will marry you!"

She ran back to her friends, laughing. William wished he didn't blush. Did Africans blush? Would it show if they did?

The night before he and Bernard had had a few drinks together, quite a few. At one point Bernard thumped his chest. "I want to fly!" he cried to William and the world in general. "I want to fly—before my feathers fall off."

All afternoon they drove along the coast. Later, when he thought of that first day on his own in that country, he remembered it as a waking dream and always the dream started with the babies sucking at those full brown breasts, their little snorts and snores of contentment. Comfortable in his window seat, one of the Togo sisters next to him asleep with her head against the back of the seat in front of her, the endless buzz of conversation from the back of the bus, the landscape unwinding like a diorama outside, coconut palms and small villages, mounds of small glittering fish for sale, taxis and lorries with slogans painted on the front or back: "Psalm 100," "I'd rather have Jesus than Silver or Gold," "Except God." ("Except God what" he thought sleepily, too tired to try to figure it out.) The Don't Mind Your Wife Chop Bar, The Last Chance Café, Super-Lotto, women and children, especially children, waving.

Earth the colour of flower-pots, glimpses of pale sand and a sea like a plate of those sparkling silver fish.

Once the bus swerved violently to avoid a snake. (William didn't see the snake but those in front who had seen it passed the word back—an enormous snake, *BIG*.)

From time to time people sang hymns: "Rock of Ages," "Abide With Me," "The Old Rugged Cross." "Amen," they said. "Praise the Lord." His grandfather played those hymns on the piano. His mother had a lovely singing voice. Did she join in when she travelled around on buses? A young woman, almost as young as he was now, almost as young as Chantal, off to see and save the world. Had he ever been on a journey like this, with her? Had she sat under the makeshift awning of the luggage bay and fed her infant with the rest of the women, her full white breast an object of great interest. Would the milk taste exactly the same? The driver put on a tape: *Jeal-ous-y / Jeal-ous-y / Jealousy is the root....*

The sun moved slowly down towards the cool waters of the sea; he fell asleep.

And when he woke up they were stopped. Cape Coast, and it was dark. He could smell the acrid charcoal fires and the darkness was thick and heavy with moisture—a thick black cloth across his face.

The "depot" was really just an old two-storey building with a canteen on the ground floor. The canteen was closed, boarded up, and William looked around for a place to pee. He'd drunk all of his bottled water and had eaten four oranges during the afternoon. He tried to see where the men were going but they seemed to have moved off towards a bigger street. Probably looking for drinks.

William asked the mate how long they would be stopping. Not very long, they were late. Were there toilets near by? The man pointed around the corner of the building, but there were no toilets, only darkness. When in Rome.... He didn't want to stay out any longer than necessary with no repellent on.

He peed at the very end of the building and right away from some bushes (he saw them only as squat, furry, shapes) as Bernard had discovered there was some awful thing that could go right up your pee and into your body that way. It sounded far-fetched but one might as well be careful.

He was just finishing, shaking himself, when he heard a noise, a kind of croak, and a hand reached up to grab his cock. He was so frightened he cried out.

The hand, an old hand, more like a claw, shook him and let him go. It was an old woman; he had almost peed right on her where she slept. He could see her now—a bundle of old cloths.

"I'm so sorry! I didn't see you. Please—"

She laughed at him and said something in another language. Laughed again, the cackle of all the witches in his childhood fairy-tales, the witch with a curse or a knife.

The driver honked his horn. William threw some money down and ran.

Pitch dark in Accra. Susan had told him to stay at the "Y," so had the *Lonely Planet*. But the incident with the old woman had unnerved him. The "Y" might be the cheapest hotel in Africa but he wanted to catch his breath; he wanted lots of hot water and a room of his own. He didn't want to have to talk, to explain anything more today. And so a taxi took him to a hotel, where for vastly more than the twenty-five cents he was told he would pay at the "Y" he had a room with a private shower. He stood for a long time under the lukewarm water, scrubbing and rinsing, scrubbing and rinsing until he couldn't believe there was a parasite left anywhere on the surface of his skin. He took out a roll of masking tape and mended a small tear in the window screens and then got into bed.

He thought about Chantal, thought about the old woman, remembering the feel of her hand upon him. Like being grabbed by a bird. Was surprised to discover the memory made him hard. Began to pull gently at himself, no urgency and yet he felt comforted by his own clean fingers, his familiar fingers, moving his flesh up and down, up and down. Imagined Chantal instead, her hand there, her mouth there, the way she ran her tongue up and down the inside of his.

Yes. Oh yes, that was better. Sleep now. No dreams.

The next morning he awoke to the sound of a rooster and crying babies. And then a splashing outside the far window as though it had started suddenly and violently to rain.

He got up to look. Water was falling in a stream from the balcony above him. But not rain. Someone was having a morning pee. He laughed and went back inside, hoping there was no late riser, curled up against the building, down below.

William was early for his appointment with Serena Dedman, field officer for COW. He had explained on the phone that his father and mother had been COW people; he wanted to get in touch with some of the volunteers who were here now. When he was very small, when he had first heard the name, he had imagined some sort of monstrous hybrid, half human, half cow, knowing nothing then of the minotaur, of centaurs, but frightened to think his parents had once been such creatures. Who turned them back?

When he asked, his mother laughed and shook her head.

"What a funny little boy you are. COW is an abbreviation, like when Grannie and Grandpa send you a parcel and it says Wm. MacKenzie instead of your whole name. COW stands for Canadian Overseas Workers—we were volunteers who went to work, oh, all over the world. People called us 'the COW people.'" She paused. "I wonder if anyone else ever made your mistake?"

Much later he read a story called "The Pig Man" and understood the little boy's terror. Children were literalists. They expected words to mean what they said.

He didn't mind waiting. He sat alone, in a small lounge, and read old copies of *West Africa* and *The Catholic Standard*, *Canadian Forum*, *Newsweek* and *Time*. He had been on the move all day—to the High Commission to register his name and pick up any mail (just one letter, from his grandfather, still unopened in his pocket but just the knowledge of it lying there a comfort), to the bus depot to check on buses to Kumasi, to the bank, which had closed by the time he got there, to the post office. At first, after Abidjan, the city seemed drab and dusty, badly maintained. Taxis—the same mad drivers—and crowds everywhere. Signs—DON'T URINATE HERE. Dust and decay.

At the post office the first thing he saw was a notice advising clients not to seal their letters with tape. "Such letters may be opened." He had sealed all of his envelopes with tape because the glue wouldn't hold. Had he written anything inflammatory to his grandfather? to Chantal? His message to his parents was on a postcard he bought in the

Ivory Coast, a smiling market woman with a load of bananas on her head. HAVE ARRIVED IN GHANA. LETTER SOON. LOVE WM. Would it be inflammatory to describe the dead and dying rhinoceros beetles, the traders arguing with the customs officers, the "road taxes"? Yes. Probably. Oh yes.

But surely they didn't open letters to Canada? Any threat to the Chairman would come from the opposition here. It wasn't like the IRA with its Irish supporters in New York and Boston.

The only stamps available were scorpions. Four scorpions (when he looked closer he saw they were goldweights) for a postcard, five for a letter. It didn't look terribly friendly—all those scorpions lined up across your mail.

Serena Dedman was a very good-looking woman from, originally, Sierra Leone. She did not get up to greet him, but came around from behind her desk and sat on the sofa, patted the cushion beside her.

"And what brings you to this country?"

"What I said on the telephone. I want to visit the brass villages—some of them anyway—and I'd also like to contact some of the volunteers."

"We call them co-operants now, like the French. What have the co-operants to do with your interest in the goldweights?" She lit a cigarette but did not offer the pack. Rothmans. "You will be disappointed with the goldweights—it's mostly rubbish now, but I can put you in touch with a woman in Kumasi who is famous for her collection. She might know of a village that hasn't caved in to the demand for key rings and the like. You may be disappointed with the co-operants as well. There were four and now there are only three. One went home recently."

"Why?"

"Why not?" She exhaled a long ribbon of smoke. "You know, years ago, when COW first started up, this was the country everybody wanted to come to. Land of hope and glory, if you will. A new dawn breaking. Now people don't come. Ghana? *That* place. *That* failure. I suppose one might say, also, Africa? *That* place, *that* failure."

She turned her head quickly and looked at him.

"Tell me, how do you like it here—so far."

"I've been here less than a day."

"And?"

"And Accra seems rather drab after Abidjan, less colourful. But that's a hasty judgement. I like the people."

"Ah yes—the people. You don't count with these people you know. They've seen so many white people come and go—you are all just one face. They smile at you but they forget you the minute you pass by." He had a feeling he didn't count with Serena Dedman—that's who he didn't count with. It made him prickly and he wanted to change the subject before he lost the chance to get the names of those volunteers.

"As I said on the phone, my parents were with COW in the late sixties. Up past Wa."

"Did they like it here?"

He decided to be honest—or partly so.

"I don't think they did. They liked it at first but then...but then they didn't."

"A not unusual reaction. You see, you can't save a

world that doesn't want to be saved, that doesn't even know the meaning of your 'saved.'"

"They know it in the religious sense."

"Oh yes. They are a deeply, genuinely religious people. And proud. When people come over here with 'solutions' it implies that only those people understand what 'the problem' is."

"Well, what is the problem? Do you know?"

"Disease. Lack of education. Fatalism."

"Why do you stay if you feel so negative about it?"

Another long puff of smoke. "Because I am a pan-Africanist. If this place goes under there's always somewhere else."

"That sounds more like a cynic than anything else."

"Tell me, did you enjoy reading the newspapers?"

"The local papers?" He smiled. "Well, the English is sometimes amazing, but I'm surprised at how many there are."

"Oh yes. Most of them have only recently reappeared—for the NAM conference in September. The newspapers reappeared and the crazies disappeared. They were rounded up and put away. Soon the situation will reverse itself. We have freedom of the press, indeed. The freedom to praise."

"Are most of the mad people men?"

"Why do you ask that?"

"In Abidjan I saw only men who were mad, naked men who walked down the middle of the streets."

"Hmm. Perhaps they feed the ladies to the crocodiles. Perhaps that is why." She made a tent of her perfectly manicured hands and placed it over her nose, then turned to him again, stared.

"Have no fear. You will see plenty of crazy women too, *plenty*. Be patient. They will come."

He couldn't wait to get out of there and he left as quickly as he could, declining her offer of a lift. But at least he had the names of some villages and the names and addresses of the three co-operants. Also of the woman who collected goldweights. He was surprised to see that it was Mrs. Ethnay Owusu-Banahene.

"We used to sit around at night," Susan had said, "and make up letters to our parents. How so and so had been stung to death by soldier ants or murdered by savages. We never sent them, of course, but it was great fun."

"Did anyone in your group die?"

"In my group just the boy who was eaten by crocodiles and I was away when that happened. But there were volunteers who died. Road accidents mostly. One person in Nigeria from malaria encephalitis. Several were sent home pregnant or mildly crazy—what they call 'bushed.' 'He go for bush.'"

Bernard put down his fork. "*What* is malaria encephalitis? I haven't heard of that."

"A kind of malaria that swells your brain. You go mad and then you die."

"You go mad and then you die? Is there a cure?"

"I don't know." Susan smiled. "I don't think you always die."

"Well thank God for small mercies. But what am I

doing here, when I could be safely in New York reading Arsenio Hall's autobiography and dealing with the normal dangers. I must be mad to have come here."

William thought of the Cheshire Cat; *Alice in Wonderland* had been one of his favourite books. We're all mad or we wouldn't be here. On the way back to the hotel (he'd move tomorrow, what difference did it make) a child on a billboard screamed for some new drink—Ma——Mee!—while a ragged man knelt down to drink from a gutter. He liked the city better as it grew dark and the lamps were lit behind the small stalls that lined the road near his hotel. He felt, even if it were untrue, that he did not stand out so much in the dark; he was just a hand pointing, I'll have some of that and some of that. Serena had told him many of the food-sellers and taxi-drivers were recent graduates from Legon. Was this true? The pepper sauce burned his mouth; his lips felt stung and swollen but whatever it was tasted good. He got a beer from the bar and went up to the covered verandah on the second floor which overlooked the street. A large television was set up there and comfortable tables and chairs. The bartender told him the news came on at seven.

He was the only one there. Too early, perhaps. This seemed to be a hotel for businessmen, many of them German. No doubt deals were still being made in offices and bars. What did this country have left that anyone would want? Lumber? Gold? That morning, looking for somewhere to have a bit of lunch he'd searched the area around the post office and come to a supermarket of sorts, more a department store, the GNTC, which advertised a canteen. He had a coke and a sardine sandwich in the small dreary canteen and then wandered around the store. There were virtually no customers and little stock. A man on a ladder was putting up Christmas decorations and a sign urged him to try the lay-away plan.

Fans. Some cooking utensils. Thermoses. A small section of tinned foods.

Upstairs the furniture section contained heavy plush furniture wrapped in plastic. He couldn't imagine sitting on such stuff in this heat. Perhaps they kept the plastic on?

But there was also a section, up there, of books and school supplies. He bought some lined exercise books, with a map of the country on the back of one, weights and measures on the back of the other, a language guide to Twi ("N'tontom: Mosquito") and a guide for young people called "When We Are Married." Not that he had any intention, but he was curious to see what sort of advice would be offered.

Coming back out onto the street was a shock—the heat and noise and bustle. Why would anyone want to patronize that sad place behind him? It would probably be bankrupt if it weren't government-owned. Now, waiting for the TV to come on, he opened the language guide.

It rained yesterday
It is raining
It is drizzling
Rainclouds have gathered
The weather is clear

"What will the weather be like today?"
"The harmattan is near."

"How are your wife and children?"
"They are fine."

"Does the path go through a forest?"
"Is the river wide?"

"Don't cry."
"The baby is crying."

a as in gather; *e* as in hate.

He put the book away when the national anthem came on. Pictures of happy farmers, market women, children, policemen, all singing praises to their homeland.

And then the newscaster, in the traditional, toga-like garment (his in greens and yellows), one shoulder bare. His co-anchor wore a dress and headdress of market cloth as well. William imagined Peter Mansbridge or Peter Jennings, one pink shoulder showing, reading the news.

The broadcast was in English, with videotape to illustrate. Chairman Rawlings pressing the button which signalled the electrification of yet another village. Let there be light. The Minister of Transport examining a great trench across the highway in the Western Region. The past rainy season had been particularly hard on the unpaved roads in the north and west. An awards service at some famous school. Fighting and unrest in Togo. And now for the rest of the world.

Then the weatherman came on, quite ordinary and dull in loose shirt and slacks. "You're welcome," he said and took his pointer. The farther north he went, the hotter it got. 31°, 32°, 34°. William had spent two summers in Montreal. Would it be so very different? Plenty of water, salt tablets if necessary. And he was taking it slowly—his eagerness to get up there seemed to have slowed down considerably since the winter day when he had looked out his window and thought, "I must go back there, but how?"

Over the years William's mother had sponsored foster children around the globe. Sent cheques and wrote to them faithfully, sitting at one end of the dining-room table while William did his homework at the other. They both had desks—all three had good, sturdy desks in their rooms—but somehow William and his mother usually ended up at the table while his father went for long walks with the dog or read books in the living-room.

The children wrote back—Esme from Greece, Maria from Mexico, João from Portugal—and sent photos taken by the group worker in that area. At Christmas time, even though it was frowned upon, they went shopping in Chinatown for pencil sharpeners shaped like kittens and ducks, paper snakes that wound cleverly up and down a stick, paper streamers, puzzles, lovely useless things to accompany socks and underwear. Sometimes William wrote letters too, told them about his dog Harry or the new songs he was learning at school. His mother had taught him not to talk about things like bikes or new hockey equipment. New skates.

"These children have nothing."

William tried to imagine nothing, tried to imagine not even enough to eat. But in the pictures his mother stuck around her mirror the children were smiling—Maria, Esme, João. Why were they smiling if they had nothing, not even enough to eat?

Never any children from Africa. You would think those would be the ones she'd help first.

Sometimes she even went to visit them. In the summers, while William was at camp. She did not seem happy when she came back from these trips. One year William asked if he could go as well—she was planning a trip to India to see a boy near Bombay.

"No," she said. "I don't want to be worrying about you when I should be worrying about him."

"I would be good, I promise."

"That's not the point."

"You never let me go anywhere with you!"

"Not on these trips, no."

He stood there, glaring at her, then ran away to his room.

She liked those other kids better than she did him. It wasn't his fault he wasn't starving in India. Why didn't she just go to the Third World and stay there if she liked it so much. Just go over there and live in a cardboard box. He'd send her letters and treats once in a while—if he remembered. He had done a drawing for Ranjan; he took it out of the bottom drawer and tore it up. It wasn't very good anyway. He tried and tried but he couldn't make his dog look like a real dog, look like Harry, couldn't make anything look like what it really was. It wasn't just because Harry wouldn't sit still, it was something else. Even at that age he knew he didn't have it and the knowledge stung.

"Does Daddy have any foster children?" he'd asked once.

"No."

"Why not?"

"Ask him," she said, but the way that she said it meant don't ask.

He wished he could remember what it was like to suck at his mother's breast (those snorting, satisfied grunts and squeals from the babies on the far side of the bus). Had any man, grown up, dared to ask his mother, "How was I, at the breast? Did I grab hold and suck you dry? Did I fall asleep so that you had to tickle my feet to wake me?" (a detail from Chantal about one of her sisters' children). "Did you like it?" There was some famous writer—he couldn't remember the name now—who hadn't wanted to give up nursing, screamed and yelled for the breast well after his second birthday had come and gone. His mother painted a demon face on her breast and the next time he asked for it she opened her blouse and "cured" him in one night.

Of course he had licked and mumbled Chantal's small breasts, firm as tomatoes. He liked that and so did she. Just thinking about it now gave him an erection. One breast and then the other and then she would say, "Turn over, William," and slide her face down his belly.

Did babies have tiny erections as they sucked the milk from their mother's breasts? Did husbands say to wives, "Let me, he's asleep; it's my turn now."

It would be warm, that milk. Remembering once, on a school trip to a farm, watching the farmer attach the milking machines. Surely the cows would prefer the farmer's hands? That intimacy gone now, except on small farms or in other countries. (A *National Geographic* article on Denmark, the barn cat being given a treat—the milk squirting directly into its mouth, the cat leaping up, the farmer smiling.)

What did it feel like when the milk came in? Sometimes painful, at first (Chantal again, the sole source of his breast information), but after that? Did both yearn for it, mother as well as child? He loved to have his cock sucked and that thick, heavy feeling as it grew big. Did it feel like that, for the mothers—oh yes, oh yes, there you go. Lovely.

(But the women on the far side of the bus, like Chantal's sisters, laughing and chatting, paying no attention—so far as he knew—to their sucklings. He was probably romanticizing the whole thing. Still, he would like to know. Dear Mother, something has come up I'd like to ask you about....)

Semen wasn't at all like milk, more like glue—the glue that stuck the egg and sperm together, making those babies, all those babies, sucking all over the world.

Two things happened to William the following day in Accra: he handled a weapon for the first time in his life (cap guns and cork-poppers and water-pistols didn't count) and he saw a saint.

He woke up early—his watch on the bedside table said 5:45—not just because of the cockerel's crowing and the babies crying, the sound of someone sweeping, sweeping, sweeping, not just because he'd turned the noisy air-conditioner off and was covered in sweat, but because of a dream he'd had.

Not once had he dreamed of Africa or black people since he arrived, but last night he had dreamed of his dental hygienist, a woman from Haïti. She sat on a stool by the side of his chair, as she always did, wearing those thin white rubber gloves they all wore these days. His head was back and the overhead light made him uncomfortable. He tried to tell her this but found he'd been given some kind of injection so he couldn't move or talk.

She grabbed his jaw in one hand and picked up a pair of pliers in the other. "These will all have to go," she said.

He was trying to scream when he woke up.

The dream was so real that he ran his tongue around his teeth several times, just to be sure they were all there.

No point in going back to bed. He got up, took a shower and went in search of breakfast. There was a woman who sold pineapples just a few yards from the hotel; perhaps she would be there already. His favourite breakfast was now half a pineapple, which he cut up with his Swiss Army knife, cut up as he would a grapefruit, so that the shell remained intact. He speared cubes of pineapple on the tip of his knife, ate a piece or two of the soft, spongy, too-sweet bread, drank half a bottle of water and was ready to face the world. Today he must put his life in order: bank first, then the cloth market, a good look around the city, an early night. Kumasi tomorrow, then Tamale, Bolgatanga, finally Wa.

"Wa Wa Wa," he said to himself. The muted sound of a trombone (or the crying of a baby). Although there was a telephone in his room, there had been no phone calls in the night, no tumbled words, you promised, you promised, you promised. Only the dream. "These will have to go." Probably just a way for his subconscious to remind him that it was time to get a move on.

Two young women were selling poppies, the same kind as back home, at the entrance to Barclay's Bank. Was it really November? Mothers would be getting out mittens in Victoria; shovels and bags of salt would be selling briskly in Montreal. That is, if back home really existed; there was never a mention of Canada in any of the papers. Those who questioned him, "Please, where are you from?" invariably said "Fine country" when he said "Canada," but did they have any idea of where it was, what it looked like? Because of the COW people, perhaps they thought it was a country of the young. No one here, except the been-to men, the politicians and their wives, a few students, no *ordinary* person, had ever seen snow. Would not be able to imagine cursing the cold.

Did they suffer terribly when they ended up in London or New York or Montreal? Did they ever feel warm enough? Nine a.m. and he was sweating heavily. He might look foolish, with his long, pale legs, but he'd have to start wearing shorts. Then the children would have something else to point at—"'Bronie, 'Bronie, 'Bronie!"

Dozens of people were already at various counters and windows; he had to look around to find the foreign currency section. Dozens of people there as well, including a few whites who stared at him indifferently.

He waited his turn, presented his passport and cheques, sat down on a bench and waited some more. His passport was added to a pile on the desk of a man in a pink shirt. Mr. O.B. Boateng, said a small plaque. Mr. Boateng didn't seem to be in any hurry.

An hour later William stuffed the money into his day-pack, leaving just a few thousand worth of notes in his moneybelt. The notes, most of them, were as thin and worn as the sheets at the Grand Hotel, the kind his mother turned into rags for cleaning. There were even fifty-cedi notes. Equal to what? Fifteen cents? Amazing. Some people had brought carry-alls. It must have been like this in the Weimar Republic.

As he was leaving he noticed a tall, handsome policeman, who sat on a chair in the corner nearest the doors, his long legs sticking out in the aisle. He held a machine gun or submachine gun in his lap. Held it very casually, William thought; perhaps it wasn't loaded and was just for show.

The policeman caught him staring and smiled.

"Fine morning," he said. (*His* polished brown legs looked excellent in shorts.)

"Yes, it is."

William moved closer. "This is going to seem a stupid question but is that thing loaded?"

"Oh yes." He held it out to William who had to fight

the urge, once again, to put his hands behind his back. It was heavy and smelled of oil.

"What is it? I mean what kind? I don't know much about guns—weapons."

"AK-47." He pointed his finger at the crowd. "*Puh-puh-puh-puh-puh.* Where are you from?"

Just holding the gun made him nervous, fearful. How did you ever learn to fire it without shaking? He held it a little longer, just to show an interest he no longer felt, but then a strange thing happened: the longer he held it, the more he liked the feel of it in his hands. (*Puh-puh-puh-puh-puh.*)

The policeman-guard came from a town on the border; French was his first language. William, in French, asked if he had ever had to use a gun.

"Not here. *Pas dans la banque.*" He smiled.

He had trained in Cuba, six years. Finally his family said come home, we need you. So he quit the army and joined the police. Now he was—"how do you say it?—*ennuyé?*"

"Bored."

"*Oui.* Bored. But my mother isn't crying."

William wanted to ask him *when* he had used the gun. Who (how many) had he killed? What did he think of Commander Jerry John? Wanted to say, come for a beer when you get off duty. He had never talked to a soldier (ex) before. Mostly it was sailors he saw in Victoria but he hadn't talked to them either. There were hundreds and hundreds of men about his age who lived, who had *chosen* to live, in a world he knew very little about. And the little he did know—the soldiers at Oka for instance, the ones he'd seen on television—didn't inspire him. He supposed it was a job, like any other, but it was a job that let you kill people, trained you to do it. Bang Bang. Was he a coward? Would he ever know? He handed back the gun and walked away. It would be stupid to ask questions. He might get the man in trouble (he might get himself in trouble, end up in jail). Someone somewhere here was nervous, else why the warning in the post office: letters sealed with tape may be opened. He put his fingers to his nose; they smelled of metal and of oil.

He had been wandering around the cloth market for quite a while, bargaining for designs he liked, twice making the mistake of wanting a piece of what turned out to be mourning cloth, once, something else, a lovely scarlet, which made the market women scream with laughter. He couldn't stay away from the cloth. He wondered if his Sunday School teacher was still alive. How he'd love to send her a piece with acid-yellow starfish on a blue background or navy-blue huts and palm trees on pale orange. For years he had blamed her public criticism for his inability to draw and even now, when he knew that wasn't true, that he had no talent, he still blamed her for her narrowness of vision. "But William, palm trees are green." Well fuck you, Mrs. Corey, palm trees are any colour you want to make 'em. Here's a present from West Africa; wish you were here.

Swirls and whirls of colour. He was spending too much money. He didn't care. All those pizza deliveries, all those tables waited on, plus a big fat cheque from his grandfather, made him reckless with the money. He bargained, of course, that was part of the game.

"Last price."

"Last price."

"Name your last price."

But they knew a sucker when they saw one.

He was just thinking of heading somewhere for a cool drink and something to eat when he spotted something going on at the end of the street. Even as he began to walk back more people appeared, then more. At the junction with Nkrumah Avenue a crowd was gathering fast. He asked three schoolgirls what was going on.

"Mandela," one said. "Mandela is coming by here."

"Any minute," said another, and then the inevitable please-where-are-you-from?

"Although I knew by now," William wrote to his grandfather that evening, sitting on the verandah, everything packed up for the morning's journey, "that any minute now didn't really mean any minute now, I wanted to stay, even if all I saw were motorcycle cops and the whoosh whoosh of black limousines speeding past, their official flags flying. I wanted to see how the crowds would react. I wanted to see this man who had spent twenty-seven years in prison and still believes some day his people will be free.

"Was this Mandela's first visit to another African country since his release? I didn't know. What did he think of a country that had been independent for thirty-four years (longer than he had been in prison), a country no longer ruled by Whites and yet a country that seems, at times, so inept at keeping itself going, so split apart by tribalism and factions. (Listen to me, the instant expert, but I have been reading the papers!) Ghana is so much freer than anything Mandela has experienced and yet there is no constitution, no parliament.

"The crowd grew and grew. Schoolchildren, given a holiday no doubt, in the brown-and-cream uniforms of the state schools, noisy, excited, waving small flags—the red, yellow and black of Ghana, the brown, green and yellow of the ANC. Workers, older students, market women, young men with nothing to do, mothers with babies on their backs. A man began selling eyeshades that said WELCOME MANDELA; a policeman and a policewoman began turning away traffic, sometimes joking with the drivers, sometimes shouting if the drivers gave them any trouble.

"Hundreds now, maybe thousands, six, seven, eight deep. The sun beat down. A madman wearing an old, soiled pith helmet covered in plastic and carrying a Bible moved through one section of the crowd, saying the end of the world was at hand. A boy sold FAN ice cream from a huge cooler balanced on his head. One of the schoolgirls asked for my address in Canada. This happens all the time.

"And then a murmur, a shout, but it was only half a dozen young army men, with submachine guns (I handled a gun today but that's another story) roaring up to the junction, leaping out, waving their guns and shouting 'back, back.' The crowd surged backwards and I was nearly knocked to one knee. I thought they might start shooting or hitting us over the head but having shown they were fearless protectors of the State, they jumped back in their jeep and sped away. The crowd pushed forward again, shouting insults.

"But now it was the real thing—yes, here came the motorcycle outriders, what seemed like dozens of them, and then a film crew, aiming backwards towards the second vehicle in which, standing up (the vehicle going slowly, slowly) was Nelson Mandela in an open-necked sport shirt. (I could see his eyeglass case and some pens in his shirt pocket.) He was waving, smiling, no, *beaming*, raising his clenched fist in the famous salute—we *shall* overcome! Next to him, by his side, the Chairman of the PNDP, Flt. Lt. Jerry John (they say his father was a Scot who slammed the door in his face when he dared to visit) dressed in army fatigues and dark glasses, giving a sort of military wave from his temple.

"The crowd went insane. 'Man—day—la!' 'Man—day—la!' It's the closest I've ever been to a scene of religious ecstasy. All along the avenue as they passed: 'Man—day—la!' 'Man—day—la!' And *he*, standing so straight there (I thought later how we had to look up and thought about religious processions and icons passing through a crowd), an ordinary-looking man, 'a man of sorrows and acquainted with grief.' Almost everyone was weeping."

Later, in the cold drinks store on the corner, sitting on an upturned crate and drinking a Fanta orange, he realized he'd been holding his breath the whole time the procession passed; he'd been waiting for the shot.

He watched it all over again on the news at seven. The motorcycle cops, the army, the open vehicle, Mandela with his arm raised, Rawlings, the flags, the cheers, the cries. William leaned forward as they passed the corner where he had stood. Was that a white face, a 'Bronie face in that sea of brown faces? Was that him? Quick. Yes. No. Maybe. It didn't really matter; he was in there somewhere, part of that moment. He didn't know if he would come across such a moment again.

When they stopped at Nkawkaw the beggars appeared at the bottom of the steps, almost blocking the way back into the bus. One was an old blind man with white eyeballs, one in an antique wheelchair, one missing a hand. There were four altogether, thin to the point of emaciation, in ash-coloured rags and with Muslim caps on their heads. They stood singing, or whining in a sing-song way. If he closed his eyes he could imagine them as a swarm of insects—*hmmm, hmmm*—or someone playing a kazoo. Almost everyone, bladders empty and stomachs full of stew or roasted corn or fish (William had his usual sardine sandwich and something called Pee Cola since there was no Fanta or Coca-Cola left), almost everyone dropped some money into the tin held by the man in the wheelchair. Each time a coin or note was offered one of the men said a single phrase. After an encounter in Accra, where a Muslim man had said to him, "Give me some money so I can bless you," William assumed that some sort of blessing was being given.

The man with the missing hand had an arm that ended in a knob.

William was used to beggars—or as used as one ever gets. These days there were beggars in Montreal, beggars in Toronto, beggars even in Victoria, B.C. Old, young, drunk, sober: every city had its share of beggars. (Once, in New York, out from what they had thought was a heap of old clothes, a hand had appeared with a cardboard sign: DYING OF AIDS. HOMELESS. HELP ME.) Some beggars were runaway kids; some were old women. Some said "Have a nice day" even if you gave them nothing; some cursed you; some bowed.

In Accra the schoolchildren followed him, "'Bronie, 'Bronie, 'Bronie, you give me *pesewas*!" but that was more a game than an earnest plea.

Why should these old men worry him so? Because they truly believed they could bless or curse? Because he'd heard so much about the extended families here that he couldn't imagine old people with no one to look after them? No one shooed them away; almost everyone gave them money.

They continued their song as the passengers resettled themselves and were still chanting as the driver honked his horn and drove away. This was a regular rest stop; another bus, more lorries, would pull in soon. They had, William thought, nothing else to do. And it occurred to him then, as the bus continued on the road to Kumasi, that perhaps these men were the sole support of several families. Could this be? If so, what were the families doing while these skeletal creatures stood singing in the blazing sun?

Hark, hark, the dogs do bark.... He had never liked that rhyme. Tried to set against this new image, as he closed his eyes and settled back in his seat, the image of his grandfather in the sitting-room on Clarke Avenue, a glass of single malt whisky on the table beside his chair, reading a book, a woodfire, perhaps the first of the season, snapping and crackling in the fireplace or, perhaps, reading and rereading the first of the (almost daily) letters from his grandson out in Africa. He had given up on a journal. The letters would be his journal.

"I'd ask you to stay here"—Mrs. Ethnay Owusu-Banahene smiled at him—"but the house is chock-a-block full. You should have let me know you were coming." She and William were sitting on a rug in the big second-floor lounge, hundreds of goldweights spread out between them. She was busy turning them right side up and sorting them into groups. William could hear children playing in the downstairs hall:

> I am Zacharias
> I am Number One
> Number One Stole the Meat from the
>   Cookin' Pot
> Who, me?
> Yes, you.

Thump Thump Clap Clap Thump Thump Thump.

The watchman was talking to someone on the verandah; the cook was shouting out the back door. His hostess did not seem to be aware of any of this as she sorted the goldweights.

"Your grandfather should have written me!"

"I think he wanted me to have complete freedom from any parental or grandparental interference."

She reminded him a little bit of his grandfather. They came from the same village and her voice, even after fifty years in Africa, still sounded like the voice of a Scot.

"A lot of these figurative ones have proverbs attached." She held up a rectangle made of six small star shapes, the sort of stars you could make with a cake decorator.

"'Even if I am but one star among many,'" she said, "'I still have need of the sky.' But I like the abstract ones best myself—the designs are very old; they have a kind of formal beauty I don't find in the figurative weights."

She showed him stepped pyramids, incised bands, scalloped circles.

"I can see where these could become addictive."

"Oh, aye. It's certainly an addiction with me. John courted me with goldweights—as well as the blather and rhetoric the Ghanaians are famous for. I joined the Afro-Asian Society at university—there were a lot of overseas students, mostly the lads, in Scotland then, taking their degrees. I danced with all of them but it was John who told the best stories."

"Desdemona and the Moor." He hadn't meant to say it out loud and blushed.

"Something of that, surely, but I'd travelled a bit and read a lot—a much more sophisticated Desdemona. And his honeyed words were all about politics, the future of Africa, not about 'cannibals that each other eat, the anthropophagi, and men whose heads do grow beneath their shoulders.'

Oh yes, the parallel was pointed out long before *you* saw the light of day, and we read *Othello* at school.

"My father was nothing like her father either; he and my mother were both delighted with John. However, there were enough Iagos around, both male and female.... Ah well, that was a long time ago. But the Scots have always intermarried, you know that. Look at your own country. Look at all those Orkneymen who worked for the Hudson's Bay Company. I didn't do anything so unique—from a Scot's point of view."

(Except that you were a woman, William thought. It was the men who intermarried, not the women.)

"Did my grandfather ever meet John?"

"Your grandfather had gone off to Edinburgh, to study law, but we kept in touch. Scots can be rather tribal, like this lot here. We'd grown up together in a village of three thousand souls and we knew each other very well. If your granddad hadn't met Seonaid and I hadn't met John.... But he came to my wedding; that's the only time they met."

She sat up and brushed off her skirt. The rug was dusty.

"Now tell me all about William and all about yourself. And meanwhile we'll see about getting you a place to stay."

She went to the door with the tea things and exchanged her soft voice for a bellow.

"Kobena / Ko—ben—a!"

A young girl was passing in the hall.

"Auntie?"

"Mary, after you've got rid of that ironing, would you mind going down to the kitchen and asking Kobena for fresh tea?

"Do you like jollof rice?" she said to William.

"I don't think I've ever had it."

"Well stay for supper and try it. Kobena can ruin most dishes but he makes a good jollof rice." She sat on the sofa and William sat next to her.

"William's grandson! It's hard to believe. He used to dip my plaits in the inkwell. We corresponded for years after John and I came here and he went off to Canada with your grannie. And then… I don't know. It became a letter at Christmas time, then a card, then… nothing. You look like him, you know, except for that shock of hair. He'd begun to lose his by your age."

There was a small silence; the children were still playing their jumping game.

> "Number Two Stole the Meat from the
> Cookin' Pot!"
> "Not I, Not I."
> "Then Who?"

William cleared his throat. "Did you know that my parents were in this country, over twenty years ago—with the COW people?"

She looked at him, then got up and left the room, returning with a book bound in faded green leather. She leafed backwards through the pages then handed it to him.

There they were:

January 20, 1966

Sandy MacKenzie
Patricia Kelly

"Thank you for all your help and hospitality."

He stared at their signatures; his mother had written the thank you.

"They seemed such a nice young couple and he, of course, being William's son.... I told them to come back any time but they never did. I just put it down to their being so involved up north. They probably wanted to see as much as possible in their time here. One visit back to Kumasi might have been enough.

"William wrote they were getting married—I believe we got an invitation but were in England that summer—but I think that's just about the time our correspondence was dropping off. And so much was going on here! One tends to get very casual; I suppose I should have kept in touch with them. I suppose I thought they'd turn up if they needed me. Did they never mention their visit to Kumasi?"

"No, I don't think so. They don't talk much about their Ghana days."

"I've always wondered if perhaps I did something to offend them—I can be quite abrupt. Young people are easily offended."

William shook his head. "I don't think that was it. Something happened up there. Something bad."

"It couldn't have been *too* bad or I'm sure we'd have heard of it. Ghanaians love to gossip. The news would have filtered down, eventually, if there'd been something dreadful."

"They changed. That's what Grandfather said. And they came back early; they didn't finish their tour. They *said* it was because the climate didn't agree with me, but he doesn't believe that and neither do I."

"William," she said, "have you never heard of culture shock?"

"Of course."

"Well, maybe it's as simple—or as complicated—as that. They suffered from culture shock—lack of privacy maybe, that's a hard thing to get used to, or the flies on the babies' eyes, the lepers, who knows? The north is very different. Maybe they suffered from culture shock and then felt ashamed because they gave up and went home. And after a woman has a baby, she changes. Things that maybe didn't bother her before start troubling her. Is that dish really clean? Did that boy with the open sores brush up against my child? One can become obsessed, out here, about hygiene. By the way, wash your hands a lot and always, if you can, before you eat. You'd be surprised what can be under your fingernails!

"And she might have been feeling poorly herself. It takes a long time to heal—out here."

"Do you think that might have been it? Culture shock?"

"It might have been."

He thought of his reaction to the spit on his face. It wouldn't be hard to imagine going over the edge into a paranoia about cleanliness. And with a baby. Maybe something did happen that had to do with him? Then what he saw as hate was really mutual shame?

Which one failed, then? Which one received the blame?

Mrs. Owusu-Banahene ("please call me Ethnay") fixed William up at a rest house on the Old Lake Road and gave him the name of a man to see at the university, gave him an open invitation to dinner ("Do you like fou fou and stew? Dinner is always very simple here, too many mouths to feed"), gave him, just as he was getting into the taxi, a goldweight. "Just so you'll keep in mind what the real thing looks like; you're bound to see a lot of rubbish."

The weight was in the shape of a bird with its head looking backwards.

"Is there a proverb with this one?"

"Aye. That's the Sankofa bird and the saying is 'Had I Known.'"

Later William thought that Ethnay Owusu-Banahene's house was like a pop-up book. A door opened and another person popped up. Her son. Her grandson. Her granddaughters and their friends; it was they who had been playing games in the hall. An old man suddenly appeared in the lounge. He'd had his cataracts removed and came to thank "Auntie." Some members of John's family arrived with legal papers that needed to be signed. Empty chairs at the long dinner table were suddenly filled. An Englishwoman, very pregnant, drifted in halfway through the meal. Her husband was away and she would stay here until she had her baby.

As well as jollof rice, there were a large bowl of fou fou on the table, looking like a pan of yellow bread dough on the rise, and a bowl of stew, which they called soup. A small granddaughter showed William the correct way to eat fou fou with his fingers: "Don't chew! Don't chew!"

There was talk of fairies—of the little people. One of the granddaughters said the little people were especially fond of Fanta orange. If you left a bottle of Fanta out they would drink all the goodness in the night and in the morning you'd be left with nothing but clear water.

"And the cap still on the bottle!" said another.

There was a leaf you could rub on your eyes and then you could see them, the little people.

William smiled; his hostess saw him smile.

"You will have to revise your ideas on reality, William. Here there are spirits all around you."

After supper they watched television. "Good evening. Here is the news at seven."

In his bed at Violet's Rest House William couldn't sleep. Had his parents sat at that table, surrounded by children, relatives, visitors? Were they asked if they believed in fairies? Had they made love in the guest room upstairs, now occupied by the pale young woman whose baby was due any time? Had they sat up into the night talking, talking? John Owusu-Banahene had been alive then. He'd once been imprisoned by Nkrumah. Their visit was just before the coup. Did they talk about that, about the government, about new hopes for the country?

He heard the first rooster crow and then another and another. Why had he thought of Africa as a quiet place? It was noisier than back home. So much of life was lived outside and even when inside the open windows let in the sounds of the taxis, the radios, the voices of people passing.

He had loved the evening at "Auntie's" house. How quiet his own house always was. Was that one of the reasons he liked Chantal, because she wasn't afraid to raise her voice? It seemed to him that he had spent his childhood in a house of whispers. Not true, of course. They spoke in normal voices, but it might as well have been whispers. As though they didn't want to wake something sleeping in the other room.

Cock-a-doodle-doo! Why did they do that? Territorial? King of the Castle?

Mrs. O-B had told him one of the proverbs about the cock:

"The hen too knows that it is dawn, but she leaves it to the cock to announce it."

No doubt that one was thought up by a woman. Cock-a-doodle-doo.

He put the pillow over his head. He could grow to dislike roosters. And the babies would start up any minute.

William arrived at the Technical Training Centre at 8:30 a.m. He was told to please wait, the man who would accompany him to the brass village had not yet arrived. So he sat and waited in an outer office, staring at shelves piled higgledy-piggledy with large brown folders. Last year's notices were on the notice board. Were people too busy or too tired to straighten things up? Had it got to the point where they didn't know where to begin? Even as he watched a large pile of folders slid to the floor with a crash. A woman opened the door of the inner office, looked out, closed it again.

At half-past nine the same woman came out and said the man he was waiting for would not be coming; he was in jail. The director had gone down to try and get him out. The woman seemed to think this was a big joke. She ignored the fallen files.

"What's he in jail for?"

"He has not been sending his regular payments to his wife so she came to town and had him locked up." Hee Hee Hee. "As for this man, he is no good at all."

William smiled politely. "Then there is no chance of going to a brass village today?"

"Oh yes. Yes. Yes. Yes. It is all being arranged. Mr. Amponsah is coming and he will take you himself. There is no problem."

He felt he couldn't sit any longer watching files so he asked the way to the art department. A student was sent to show him.

"Please—"

"Canada," William said. "It's a fine country." He was discovering that his temper rose with the sun.

A teacher appeared and William was handed over. Did he want to take pictures?

"I'm afraid I didn't bring a camera," he said, lying. He wanted to save his film. He tried to think of something pleasant to say as they walked along past low white buildings, windows and doors open to catch any possible breeze.

"Our director is away in Accra. He would have been very pleased to meet you. Our director is having a show in the capital. He is a very famous man."

"Is he a sculptor?"

"Oh no no no. He is a painter. He sells his paintings all over the world. He is a very big man. He has work in all the major cities."

In the courtyard outside the art studio there was a larger-than-life sculpture of a woman in a grass skirt—it looked like grass—holding a machete in one hand and a rifle in the other. It was the only piece he saw that had any movement in it at all. Most of the stuff was lumpish, uninspired. Who was that, Mother Africa? Or this country's equivalent of Marianne?

"Yaa Asantewa," the man said, "the woman warrior. She is our greatest lady. She put the English in their place."

"I can believe it," William said.

It was too bad, he agreed, that he didn't have more time. Perhaps he would be able to come again?

"Yaa Asantewa," he wrote in his notebook. "Look up."

Transport took another twenty minutes to arrange. They assumed he'd brought his own, were surprised that he didn't have a car or a jeep or at least a motorbike. Eventually a pickup truck was found and Mr. Amponsah invited him into the front seat while a group of people, including the director's secretary, the woman from the inner room, scrambled for places in the back.

"The women brought chairs, which they sat on, like queens, as we bumped our way along the red and dusty roads. Do you remember the giant Crayola box you and Grannie sent me once? I'm living in it: brick red, apricot, bittersweet, mahogany, burnt orange, sepia, raw sienna. Purple bougainvillea against a white-plastered tutor's house, green-yellow fan palms, the washed-out blue (blue-grey) of the sky, scraps of black which are the vultures always circling. The brown skin: the brown skin needs a whole new box of crayons by itself. Swinburne called Christ 'the Pale Galilean' but he wouldn't have been so pale, would he? I'm the pale one, I'm Crayola's 'flesh,' now called, for political reasons, 'peach.' I feel like a ghost, a negative. Are African ghosts white? If they are, why is that? Why aren't they just a paler version of the Africans themselves. (White, by the way, is the colour of victory here.) I love the skin here, keep wanting to reach out and touch it. They touch *me*—or the women and children do—but I don't have the nerve to do the same."

He didn't tell his grandfather that he not only wanted to touch, he wanted to taste. He didn't tell him that.

To Chantal he sent a postcard of two young women in bright cloths and adorned with beads. "Two northern beauties," it said on the back. "I think I am the only tourist in the country," he wrote, "but I'm loving every minute of it. XXX." He had tried to call her from the post office but all he got was the answering machine. "*S'il vous plaît, laissez un message.*"

After about forty minutes they came to the brass village, just an ordinary-looking place, small, a couple of paw-paw trees, houses with sheet-metal roofs. It wasn't until they got down from the truck that he saw the kilns, the rows of grey blobs like misshapen wasp nests of some kind, the smiths sitting under the trees, working.

The men obviously knew Mr. Amponsah and came out to greet them, except for one man, who was intent on moulding a small figure from wax. William wanted to go straight over to him but his guide said he planned to buy a few new pieces for the TCC so they were shown into a small house. The driver and the rest of the group had disappeared; it seemed they had just come along for the ride.

The house was very hot inside, even before it became crowded with men. William felt a bit sick from all the bodies and the closeness of the place. He wondered if he was going to throw up. He and Mr. Amponsah and five or six others crowded together on a cracked vinyl sofa, while in front of them, on a low table covered with a cloth, piece after piece was displayed, some large (hunters in battle dress with flintlock rifles, shea butter pots with seated figures on the lids, leopards, crocodiles, a wonderful antelope with horns laid back against his head and what looked like a big grin on his face, a man playing some sort of xylophone).

Mr. Amponsah bargained for some of the larger pieces, including one that William coveted—three men in a boat. He wondered how many people came out to this village; he doubted he would have found it on his own. Did they take their pieces to town to sell at the Cultural Centre or did they ship them to Accra to be sold at tourist shops? Ghanaians wouldn't buy them, would they, except to sell again? Nobody weighed gold dust any more. They had served a purpose once, were useful as well as beautiful. It was surprising, really, that they were still made at all.

Most of the small pieces were not very well finished, crudely modelled in the first instance perhaps and made worse in the casting. He was glad he'd seen Mrs. O-B's collection first. And many of the smallest "weights" had brass circles attached, so they could be used as key rings.

It was clear that the men expected him to buy some of these if nothing else. He shook his head; they didn't interest him.

"Name your price."

"No price."

"Four hundred cedis. Last price."

He saw how easy it was for people to scoop up stuff in the Third World and bring it back to sell at inflated prices. It paid for the cost of the trip. What if he said, I'll take it all? Did dealers do that? Come out here and say I'll take it all?

In the end he bought the cheerful antelope, a direct cast of a groundnut in its shell and a small brass box, not much bigger than a matchbox, with an abstract zig-zag design on the lid. It reminded him of Mrs. O-B's abstract weights.

"For gold dust?" he asked, holding it up.

"Oh yes. For gold dust. In Gold Coast time." They laughed.

A young man slid into the group, placed something in front of William, said nothing.

"Did you do this?" William asked, delighted.

The man nodded. He was not much more than a boy. He can't speak, the others said, he has no tongue.

What William held in his hand was a miniature chair, about an inch and a half in height, a brass-studded chair fit for a lilliputian chief or nineteenth century governor. William had seen one like it in a book on Ashanti art.

"It's beautiful," he said, "how much?"

One of the older men answered. Eight hundred cedis. Less than three dollars.

Didn't they know? Couldn't they see the difference? He glanced at Mr. Amponsah for help, but he was very busy talking to someone else.

"I'll take it," William said. "Does he have any more like this?"

The young man shook his head no, no more, but began unwrapping a faded piece of cloth. William waited. What new treasures lay inside?

A woman's head with spiky hair, crude, with a ring at the top. Small dogs, also with rings.

"Yaa Asantewa," said the men, pointing to the head. It was exactly like the others on the table.

"Did you do this as well?"

The boy nodded. William bought the head; he bought two. "I wish you had another chair," he said.

No one had another chair.

"I still don't understand it," he said to Mrs. O-B the next evening. "Why was there only one? The boy's an artist."

"Or a thief? This could be old. It looks old but that's not too difficult to fake. Would you like me to find out for you?"

"But he sold it for peanuts!"

She smiled.

"You know what I mean. If it were stolen, wouldn't he have the sense to sell it for a lot of money? Wouldn't the other men have raised the price or sold it to a dealer?"

"I agree. It's a mystery. It's quite possible, you know,

that he didn't see any difference between this one and the rest of the stuff."

"But the other men?"

"Perhaps the other men as well."

"How could that be?"

"It has no ritual value and no useful purpose—except to sell to someone like you. What did Mr. Amponsah say? He knows good work when he sees it."

"He said, 'Lucky you.'" William held the little chair in his hand. "Supposing the boy's an artist?"

"If he really is, then they know it and are keeping his stuff back for some reason."

"Why, then, would he show me anything at all?"

"Pride. To see your reaction. I don't know. Don't try to reason everything out while you are here. You'll just give yourself a grand headache. I'll find out more if I can but it might be better just to keep it by you and consider yourself lucky. It's as nice as anything I've seen in the last while."

"I feel I've cheated him."

"The village didn't seem to think so, did they? Ashantis—Ghanaians generally—are very good at sticking up for themselves. They love arguments and legal brawls. I could tell you stories!"

It wasn't until he got back to the rest house that he realized he'd forgotten to ask why the boy would have no tongue. William was discovering certain things about himself, things that he felt a psychiatrist would trace back to his childhood but he wasn't sure, had a feeling he was like that from the start, one of which was that he didn't mind being alone, that it didn't bother him when there was no one around to talk to. But not to be able to talk—that was another thing. Whatever that boy wanted to communicate—love, hate, despair—it would all come out as a series of *ah ah ah ah*'s, like when the doctor examined your throat.

Was he born that way? Was it cancer? Could it have been—surely impossible today—a punishment? He was to spend an entire day at the village, with an interpreter, on Thursday. Perhaps there was some way, without being rude, that he could find out more. But when he went back he was told the boy had travelled.

"One of the smiths was making a series of birds. He bit off a lump of dark green beeswax, softened it in warm water and rolled it in his wet hands into an oval body. Then he pulled out a neck and formed a lump for the head. He moved quickly, pinching here to form a beak and a crest, rolling legs, cutting claws, attaching small rolls for the back claws. He took up some fine wax thread, made a spiral, cut this in half and arranged the half circles as wings. Then he added a stylized tail. The man did not look up at me or my interpreter or the village children who had gathered around him and were competing for my attention. 'Take my picture! Take mine!' Under a tree, on a flat board between his legs, he rolled and pressed until a bird, just over an inch in height, stood perched there, waiting to be entombed in clay, waiting to be melted, to be 'lost' only to rise again like the phoenix, only this time as a shining bird of metal. (There's a poem by Yeats we took in English 100, something about wanting to come back as a mechanical bird. Your friend Mrs. O-B just might have it—you should see her books!! All with a musty smell and strange things fall out from between the pages but she is a *reader*; I wish I could have met John.)

"Perhaps I am just in a poetic mood, but don't laugh at me, Granddad, if I say it was as if the smith had made the soul of the bird first and then the soul having vanished (but leaving its imprint behind) the body took on its shape.

"'This is a foolish bird,' my guide said.

"'What is it called?'

"'Hornbill. It is an idiot bird.'

"After the model was completed the man turned it carefully in his hands, looking for flaws, smoothing out roughness with a wetted bamboo tool. Finally he set the bird to one side.

"'When he has ten birds he will move to the next step. This is only the beginning.'

"All through the long morning I watched this man and took pictures. Because they knew I was coming I think they had chosen their master craftsman and so I spent most of my time with him; but there were others making hunters, women with loads on their heads and babies behind, a miniature world of men and women, birds, beasts and fishes. Most of the figures had proverbs attached to them; I used my notebook as much as my camera. I saw another version of the hornbill as well, this time with a snake—a very elaborate snake, covered in rings for scales—attached to the bird's breast.

"'What's going on here? Another proverb?'

"'Oh yes. You see, the snake lent money to the bird but she wouldn't pay it back. Then one day the bird was drinking at the pool and the snake catch her. We say "the snake on the ground has caught the bird in the sky.'"

"'Meaning what?'

"'Think and you will see it.'

"My friend Bernard, whom I've already told you about, would probably say it means 'Don't drink the water'!"

The sun rose higher. William walked around, watching the men at their various tasks, asking the names of tools and vessels. The grey blobs he had thought of as wasps' nests were the clay moulds, each containing at its heart, like a sweetmeat, a small wax model. Tomorrow the kiln would be heated up and the lost-wax process would begin. William asked if he could come back yet again.

He watched the girls and women plaiting one another's hair, pounding yams, washing clothes. The children were sent down the road to Janet's Cool Shop for cold drinks and groundnuts. One of the charcoal ovens, which had been cooling overnight, was cleared out.

William asked, towards the end of the afternoon, if he could try. Now he was the man with enormous thumbs, only clumsier. The children laughed at his efforts to make a bird and even the smiths smiled. A snake, head up, ready to strike, was finally managed, although it refused to stay erect.

"You must master the rolling of wax," the guide said. "You must master the use of tools. This man has been doing this thing all his life."

Out of his pocket he took the figure of a hunter with a gun and a dead animal, some sort of antelope, on his head.

"Do you see this gun? This gun had fifteen wax parts." The gun was barely an inch long.

"I suppose all this will eventually die out," William said, as they drove back towards Kumasi.

The man shrugged. "That depends on many things. Fathers teach sons and sometimes they go to other villages as well. And the world is interested now—the art world. That man went to a craft fair in Austria last year. I went with him and two of the other men. They were a big success."

"That man sitting under the paw-paw tree? He went to *Austria*??"

William's romantic vision was slightly offended by this. He had been seeing these men as primitives, never leaving their village except to go to another village or, at the very most, to carry a load of weights to the shop at the Cultural Centre in Kumasi. Now he learns that three of them have been to Austria, of all places! They've flown in airplanes, stayed at hotels, perhaps experienced snow! What was it like, coming back to the village from all that?

His guide was laughing at him, at his surprise.

"Did they like it—Austria?"

"We were all very cold. We are not used to such things, even I am not, who studied in London and ought to be used to anything. But it was nice to be taken seriously—as craftsmen. We didn't take key rings, no fear!"

"Did the boy go?"

"What boy?"

"The boy who has no tongue?"

"I don't know him."

Austria! He couldn't get over it.

He sat on the edge of his bed for a few minutes—he'd arranged to meet two of the COW people in the bar of the rest house—and smelled his hands, that waxy smell. He used to open his box of crayons and inhale deeply before he chose a colour. He had asked for a small piece of the beeswax. They said it came from wild bees. That the men who collected wild honey used to throw it away until Mr. Amponsah made a deal with them.

His hands didn't look clumsy; why wouldn't they do what his brain told them? All his hands were good for was holding a pen or a pointer. There was a late-night movie he saw once, about a musician who'd injured his hands and had them replaced with the hands of a dead murderer. His roommates, English majors, said Malcolm Lowry had used that movie in *Under the Volcano*. Sometimes he felt as though he'd been given the wrong hands.

Austria! He hadn't even been to Austria.

He bought another goldweight that afternoon. A girl with a swollen belly, someone pushing her from behind. When he asked for an explanation the men told him that if a woman did "bad things" with a man before she was married she and the man would be driven from the village and made to stay in the forest for a certain length of time. Then a sheep was killed and the blood smeared on the woman and the man. "After a certain time" they could return.

"Does this still go on? Today?"

"Oh yes."

William thought of the ethnographer Boas and how

the west coast natives often told him what they felt he wanted to hear.

"You want to buy this? What price will you give me?"

He could stay. He could go back to the village and say teach me, teach me, agree on a price for an apprenticeship. Under the trees, rolling and kneading and spinning the wax threads, the sharp smell of the charcoal fires, the women pounding fou fou, the laughter of the children. His thesis could be part history, part record of his own apprenticeship. He would learn to model that foolish bird, the hornbill, learn to make the small boxes, learn to use his hands, to make them do as they were told.

Wax. The smell, the feel of it, excited him.

And he wouldn't have to go any farther. Dinners at "Auntie Ethnay's" when he felt the need of company, days at the village (he could get a second-hand moped) unless they would let him stay there. Would they let him stay there? No need to go up to the north where it was hotter still, no need to do anything but turn into truth the reason he had given for coming here: "An examination of the lost-wax process as it is practised today in Ashanti." Dear parents, I have decided not to go up north. The hell with the past.

He decided to let the birds decide. If he dreamed of the hornbill (surely the proverb meant everything comes to him who waits?) he'd stay here; it would be foolish to go on. If he dreamt of the Sankofa bird, with its head looking backwards ("had I known"), he'd go north and find out what went wrong all those years ago.

When he came back to the room, at midnight, he concentrated on the goldweight and then on the simple sketch of the snake with the hornbill in its beak. Concentrated hard, first on one, then the other.

He dreamt of neither; he did not dream at all.

The neighbourhood cock woke him as usual: even the pillow couldn't keep out the rusty cry—*ark-ark-ark-a-oooo*. Bloody bird. Off with his head and into the stewpot with him.

And then the goats
And then the taxis
And then the babies.

It was worse than the Bremen Town Musicians.

He gave up and began a letter to Chantal.

The back cover of William's exercise book contained the multiplication tables, length (in millimetres and centimetres), all sorts of useful things he couldn't imagine ever having need of.

The Volume of a Cube:
10 cm x 10 cm x 10 cm = 1l (litre)
1000 ml = 1l
1000 cm3 = 1l

All very serious and straightforward.

But then, with the temperature, a joker had taken over.

degrees Celsius

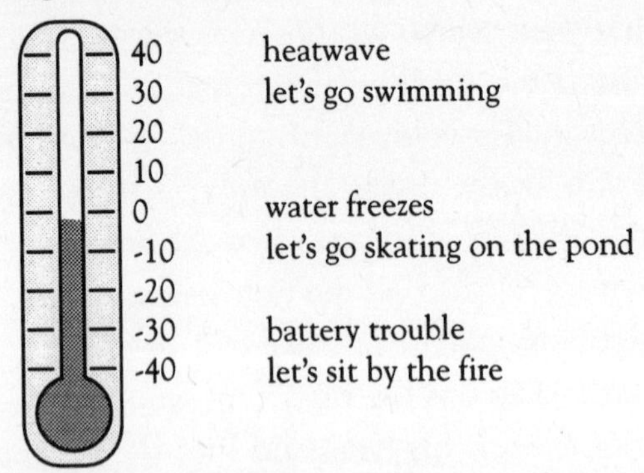

Later, when he was delirious, he started reciting all this, unaware that he had given it more than a passing glance.

William had been a little disappointed in the COW people, the younger one in particular. He was very cynical about the whole thing. "We're here in Ghana because we have to be. COW is funded by the number of people placed, so there have to be COW people placed. Serena would prefer it if there weren't any co-operants; we're too much hassle. She especially doesn't want females. I can't wait to go somewhere else where I'll have real work to do."

He intended to work in all five continents. He liked the word co-operant better than volunteer. "Volunteer" sounded unskilled, unpaid or underpaid ("like the Peace Corps").

"So COW is now seen as a career move?"

"There's no need, any more, for enthusiastic kids who've never taught before to come out here and do badly what they've never even done at home. Your parents wouldn't even be considered now. Well, maybe your father would—he spoke some French as well as English. He might be useful somewhere. You have to have two years in your field now before you are admitted."

(But he had been impressed during his orientation week in Accra because Serena sent him around with a Ghanaian who was given a big pile of money. They ate at the finest restaurants.)

The other was older, more reflective. He said the problems of the farmers here were the same as the problems back home. He also wanted to work in five continents; both had girlfriends who would join them. William showed them a picture of Chantal just to prove... Just to prove what?

The last night in Abidjan, after falling into a drunken sleep, William woke up to a banging on his door. Woke up afraid. Was it the man who had phoned him? Please, you promised. He decided to keep quiet. Then Bernard's voice. "William! Wake up! I know you're in there!"

William jumped up and removed the chair from underneath the doorknob.

"What's the matter?"

Bernard punched the light switch. "I've been bitten," he said, and sat down on William's bed.

William thought snake, thought scorpion.

"Where? Where? Shall I get a doctor?"

Bernard pulled off his tee shirt; his chest and shoulders were covered in dark hair.

"Near my left shoulder blade. Or I think so. Look, will you?"

William was waking up now. "Bernard, did you come banging on my door because you've been bitten by a *mosquito?*"

"It's not funny. It was a malaria mosquito, I'm sure of it. See if you can find the mark."

William hesitated to touch Bernard's back; it was all sweaty.

"Hurry up."

"I don't see anything, Bernard."

"You have to feel, then. Feel around. There'll be a bump."

Still William hesitated. Then Bernard's voice, hurt, amused, sarcastic: "It's all right, William. You won't catch anything by touching me."

William couldn't find any signs of a bite and it turned out Bernard wasn't even sure. He'd been having a nightcap in his room when he saw a mosquito standing on its head. When he killed it, it was full of blood.

He put his tee shirt back on. "Ah well, some other unfortunate, not me. Unless the bite shows up later."

"Go to sleep, Bernard."

"I guess so." At the door he paused. "Why have you barricaded your door, William? Not against me, I hope."

"No."

"Sure?"

"Positive."

"You're very pretty, in your fashion, but you're not my type. Too tall."

Then called through the keyhole.

"Just kidding."

Outside the big market in Kumasi there were piles of second-hand clothes and shoes. One of the granddaughters was with him; he wanted to buy more cloth, he couldn't get enough of it.

"You know what those things are called?" Pointing at the jackets and dresses, the high-heeled pumps. "'Bronie wawu'—a white man has died."

Once inside he was glad the girl had come with him. Such a stew of smell and sound; open-air, yes, but the hundreds of people and the various things on offer created such a fug it was hard to believe that blue up there was anything but a sheet-metal roof painted to look like sky. He felt claustrophobic, wanted to say, "Look, it's all right, I've changed my mind." He knew that if he'd been alone he would have bolted. It was like being flung face first into a compost heap and the paths they were walking on were littered with rinds and other debris. He had sandals on; what if he cut his toe?

She had moved ahead, a basket over her arm, assuming he was following her. And for a moment he was lost, terrified, just as he had been years ago at The Bay, when he and his mother became separated in a Christmas crowd. When he finally spotted her coat (her back was to him as she bent over a counter) he ran up and flung his arms around her from behind.

The woman who turned round was not his mother.

He could still hear the loudspeaker: "William is waiting

for his mother at the Information Counter on the Main Floor; William is waiting for his mother."

But there she was—the granddaughter, whose name was Alice—laughing at him, beckoning.

"You must not dawdle or you will get lost."

He was so relieved to see her he almost kissed her. And was charmed by the way she said "dawdle," surely her grannie's voice speaking there?

"I will do my errands and then we will get your cloth."

She was only a young girl, but she knew how to bargain. Standing there in her school uniform (not a state school; she must go to a private school somewhere), hand on her hip, she gave as good as she got. The older women treated her seriously. Sometimes they said something about him and he *thought* (he was not very far into his introduction to Twi) that she said he was her cousin. But then, these terms were used very broadly here—sister, brother, auntie. She seemed quite pleased to be with him but when he offered to carry the basket, now heavy with tomatoes, shallots, a big piece of yam, a pineapple, oranges, she shook her head.

"Then you would be my servant."

He liked the cloth stalls the best. With their shutters open and the bolts of bright cloth inside, they reminded him of the doors on Advent calendars. What fresh surprises awaited him inside?

One of the patterns, which came in many colour variations, had black webs printed all over it.

"Anansi," she said. "Do you know about Anansi? My hair is also Anansi."

He could see that now. The other night the granddaughters had been doing each other's hair in elaborate patterns—using black thread to tie off an end here, create a loop there. Now that he took a closer look he could see that her hair had been turned into a sort of web.

"Do you have to undo that every day?"

"Not at all. It can last...maybe one month. But I might get tired of it before then." She shrugged a very adult shrug. She was almost a flirt, he thought, but not quite.

He bought Anansi cloth in navy blue over magenta, black over brilliant green. Long ago his mother had read him Anansi stories. Anansi was always trying to get something for nothing and he giggled as she read, but what he liked best was that Anansi could turn himself into anything he liked—a stick, a sleeping mat, a piece of yam. He was very good at getting out of tight places.

A little procession came at a slow trot down the lane where they were shopping. The man in front had the sort of signboard on a stick he had seen once in a posh hotel bar. But this sign advertised some prophet. His little band of apostles, men and women, hopped along behind him singing a hymn. One of them paused to hand out invitations to a rally.

"Are you a Christian?" Alice asked.

"No. Not really."

"Do you not believe in the Afterlife?" The two women who ran the stall, plus Alice, all staring at him.

He intended to say "No," firmly, in a manner that would show he was not in the least intimidated by those large, incredulous eyes.

"I'm not sure," he said. That was good enough. They smiled again, urged him to go to the rally.

He took Alice over to the police canteen for a Fanta.

"When my grandfather died," Alice said, "all the women shaved their heads. I'm glad I wasn't old enough." She sucked up the last bit of Fanta with her straw.

"Did your grannie shave her head?"

"Oh no, that wasn't necessary. But there were lovely funerals, all kinds. We like funerals, here."

"You *like* them?"

"Oh yes. We are sad when somebody dies—we were *very* sad when Grandfather died, he was a famous doctor—but we like the funerals. If anyone dies while you are here I'll see if we can get you invited."

"What do you like about them, Alice?" He pointed at her empty bottle, did she want another? She shook her head.

"The singing and dancing. The orations."

(It was so strange, listening to her talk. Singin', dancin'. Her "African" voice, right up against "do you not believe" with its faint overtones of Fife.)

They parted outside the post office where Mrs. O-B's driver was to pick her up.

"One of the women," she said, "back there in the market. She wanted to know if you were Grannie's other son."

"Dear Chantal, *Wo ho te sɔn?* How are you? I bought this air letter inside the main post office and now it is being typed up by my new friend Alexander, the youngest of the public letter-writers who sit in an arcade to one side of the post office building. Alexander says he does not get as much work as the old men because he is not trusted as much to turn clients' thoughts into elegant sentences but he likes the work and soon some of the old men will die. Most of his work is business or legal but he says he can write a very good love letter, full of passion, if called upon. Many people are lined up on benches, waiting their turn, so I will keep this short. I am heading north tomorrow so the next note you get will be from Tamale or Bolgatanga. I met two of the three COW people here, nice enough but a bit of a disappointment. I think they were rather contemptuous of me just travelling around with very little purpose in mind. As I said in my postcard, I think I am the only tourist in the whole country! I am going to find some lunch and then take a look at the fort where a queen mother called Yaa Asantewa kept a group of Europeans holed up—virtual prisoners—at the turn of the century. From everything I hear about her, you two would have gotten along well.

"Goodbye for now, my honeypot,
"William

"P.S. Alexander added the honeypot—it was his idea. He wants me to take him to Canada. I told him he'd have to get in line."

The pieces of cloth weren't going to fit in his pack. He'd already sent one lot home with Chantal, mailed more from Accra. Perhaps he could wrap them up in one of the garbage bags he carried with him and strap it to the outside of the pack. He really didn't want to part with them. Or not yet.

Mrs. O-B said the Ghanaians had no aesthetic sense, but William didn't agree and was surprised to hear her say it.

"No sense of colour, I mean." She was wearing a dress made of market cloth, rather subdued, brown print on pale blue. There were animal heads all over it. It had a proverbial meaning, she said: "When you see the animal's head in the soup, remember your own."

Back at the rest house William took a shower and lay down on his bed wrapped in the magenta Anansi cloth. *Not* his colour, definitely, but he liked it nevertheless. He would give it away when he got home. Meanwhile....

On the low wall outside his room two lizards with orange tails were doing prehistoric pushups. It seemed to him too hot to do anything so athletic. The COW co-operants had invited him to be their guest at the university pool: "A group of us gather there on Friday afternoons. We swim and then have a meal at the canteen." Too hot to do that too. Get up and get dressed, take a taxi out to the university, sit with a bunch of white people discussing where they'd go next, like foreign correspondents.

Unfair, unfair. He just wanted an excuse not to move. He'd have a sleep and then, after supper here (Violet had a Chinese cook, a good one—delicious smells were already floating down the corridor and under the door), he'd write up his notes on the brass village.

The market cloth had been wrapped in out-of-date

Dutch newspapers. One piece was obviously the entertainment section. William was startled to see a picture of John Candy dressed as a policeman.

In Accra, he'd bought some roasted corn off a stall and that had been wrapped in an old writ from the High Court of Justice:

"Elizabeth the Second, by the Grace of God, of the United Kingdom of Great Britain and Northern Ireland and our other Realms and Territories Queen, Head of the Commonwealth, Defender of the Faith, TO...." It was dated in the year of our Lord 1959. Where had it been all this time?

Something about cutting down timber, "435 trees wrongfully felled."

He saved it to show his grandfather.

Two geckos were half hiding behind the mirror, waiting for flies. He decided to sleep on his stomach. The granddaughters had told him that if a gecko falls on your mouth while you are sleeping, you will die.

He dreams that Alice is holding a large lizard over his mouth.

"Swallow it," she says, "don't bite it."

Recipe for a Happy Marriage
1 cup consideration
2 cups milk of human kindness
1 gallon faith in God and in each other
2 cups praise

1 reasonable budget (with a generous dash of co-operation)
1 cup of contentment
3 teaspoons of pure extract "I am sorry"
1 cup confidence and encouragement
1 cup blindness to the other's faults

Never serve with a cold shoulder or a hot tongue.

"The last sentence is pretty good, don't you think, grandfather? I've been reading a book, booklet really, which contains this 'Recipe for a Happy Marriage.' It's by the same guy who wrote 'Flamboyant English Treatise.'

(Been and Being:
Kofi is being funny these days.
Ama is being taught how to type.
When I was going to school this morning, the house was being painted.
I been to school today.) There are occasional lapses.

"He might argue that he wasn't illustrating agreement of subject and verb so 'what do it matter' but there are others. What, for example, is an *allergory*? Sounds like something you might find in a swamp, smeared with your lost companion's blood.

Works by the same author:
O'Level English Bombshelled.
English Vocabulary Galore.
Bonanza Time in English.

"I think his heart is in the right place, however. Some wonderful stuff in the first book on what he calls 'bungalow girls'—girls who live at home with their parents, who have servants and don't cook, wash their own cloths and so on. One horrible example is cited of a bungalow girl who didn't know how to clean her own teeth or wash her own panties! (Lots and lots of examples of wrong behaviour, but we do that in our self-help books as well.) I suppose bungalow girls should really marry up with 'verandah boys' (you see a lot of them about), then each would get what s/he deserves.

"Actually, I like the 'mistakes' that are made in English. (I enclose a few newspaper clippings for your enjoyment.) And the signs: The Don't Mind Your Wife Chop Bar (Annex); The Hotel de Bull; Yao Adouboor, physician; MBChB (Failed). Does he get any patients?

"When I first arrived I couldn't get used to the crowds; it looked as though the whole city was on the move, that some sort of grand evacuation was taking place. Now I'm used to it (more or less) although the big market—over 10,000 licensed traders and God knows how many outside, around and about—is hard to take. You just have to plunge in. If you stop and stare either you'll be trampled on or a small swarm of children will collect around you giggling and asking for money.

"Mrs. O-B says there's a big increase in children begging, parents sending their children out to beg. She would love to hear from you—will you write her? She showed me an old guest book with Mom and Dad's names in it before they were married; it made me feel strange, almost sick.

She has no information re what might have happened up in Wa.

"I'm writing this under the three-bladed fan in my room, all packed ready for tomorrow's new adventure. The fan doesn't really do much good but at dinner I heard some distant thunder and was told it might rain. I thought the rains were over but they say sometimes there are small rains at the end of the season. The thunder is closer so I hope it does rain. If it does I think I'll go out and dance in it, like a kid.

"Has the first snow fallen? Has Chantal been over to see you? I hope there *is* a *poste restante* at Tamale; if I'd known I was going to stay this long in Kumasi I would have suggested you send a letter here.

"XX William

"P.S. Two American women at dinner, one a nutritionist doing a survey for a flour company (!) back in the States, the other a nurse, who is waiting for her house to be readied. She'll be here two years and has just been in Micronesia. Calm, competent, intimidating.

"'And what are you doing here?'

"The nurse tells me someone threw a sick cow in the river last weekend and now there are four (known) cases of cholera in Kumasi. Shall I read you the symptoms of cholera, out of Bernard's book? I wonder what he's up to?"

Violet had taken a liking to William and she arranged for her van and driver to drop him at the bus depot at 5:30

a.m. for the 7:00 a.m. bus as she wanted him to be sure to get a good seat. She also gave him a thermos of tea and a packet of sandwiches. William vowed to send her a special calendar from home as soon as he got back.

She needn't have worried, as not that many had decided to go to Tamale on the early bus. Lots of people were going to Bekwai and Wa and he knew he should probably go straight up there but everyone said, see Tamale, see Bolgatanga. And the COW people said, you *have* to go to Bolga and meet Johnny—he's the Crocodile Dundee of COW. William wasn't sure what that meant but it sounded interesting. Did crocodiles eat cows?

A man came and sat down at a bench near by.

"Good morning. Welcome to the STC bus depot."

William thought he must be an employee, perhaps chief cashier (the ticket window wasn't open yet), but no, he was selling English lessons—pamphlets one to six. He kept up a long spiel in Twi. There were occasional anecdotes at which everybody laughed. Several people bought the pamphlets, which were really nothing more than lists of errors in English.

(Do not say "I am going for typewriter," say "I am going for the typewriter.") The woman next to William was reading a grade one reader (THIS IS ABENA. ABENA HAS A CAT.) She told him the man came regularly to the bus depot to sell his pamphlets. William wondered if perhaps Canadian poets, and writers generally, should do that. Hang around bus depots, airports, wherever people had to sit and wait. There were probably laws against it. All those bookshops and newsstands would complain.

William's French teacher in Montreal had told the class that one of the best ways to become fluent was to read children's books in French. Here was a woman, her baby asleep, doing just that. Not shy about it either, no pretending it was really for her little boy at home.

It was a good morning to travel, cool and misty after the brief thunderstorm, and William felt happy to be on the road again. People moved over on the bench so he could sit down. They smiled.

"Fine morning."

A woman came to pray with them. No one was rude to her or laughed when she asked them all to bow their heads. Afterwards she blessed them and asked for money. William was surprised at how many gave to her, even a policeman who had come to chat with the security guard. Mostly coins, but still, they gave. William put in a hundred-cedi note. One man shouted that she should only bless those who had given money. All laughed.

"Safe journey," she said, touching his arm. He could see that she was mad, just a little bit, harmlessly, gently mad.

From his window he watched her shuffle away. Was the money all for her or were there others dependent upon her, someone without legs or a nose just around the corner?

He watched two young men go across the yard, hands loosely linked. They didn't have to be lovers; they might, out here, just be friends. The only man I have ever held hands with, William thought, is my father.

They crossed the Volta River around noon. Mrs. O-B, Auntie Ethnay, said it was a shame in a way that he couldn't cross by the Yeji ferry, as they did in the old days. Then he'd see how much was flooded when the great hydro-electric scheme was finished. Trees sticking up like dead men's hands—uncanny feeling about the place. And the ferry itself was almost as old as the *African Queen*. Lorry drivers fought to get on; it was always overloaded so maybe it was just as well.

This crossing was merely a trickle—hardly a stream. He could have walked across it. William took a picture. He would label it "Crossing the Mighty Volta."

A young man got on the bus with a basket of medicines and began a harangue as the bus bumped along. Once again there were anecdotes and a sprinkling of English words as well as some very graphic gestures: "tapeworm twenty-seven feet long!" "digestive problems," "mix with something containing sweetness." One powder seemed to cure anything. When William raised his hand and asked to see it, the man said, "Brother, I will come back and tell you in your language," but he was doing a brisk trade in his own and never did.

"Nostrums," William thought. A good old-fashioned word. Mrs. O-B might be a Christian but she believed in miracles and the laying on of hands. Would she believe in these powders or were they all a fake, "snake oil." How did you get a tapeworm anyway? Twenty-seven feet of worm inside your gut! No salads, William, and wash your hands, wash your hands, wash your hands. He liked street food, liked buying things out the windows of the bus, but after that guy he was grateful for Violet and her corned-beef sandwiches.

It must make a difference, he thought, where you are conceived. And if, like me, you were conceived in the tropics and then, before you even stuck your head out, yanked into a northern latitude—Montreal in winter, for God's sake!—where you do make your appearance and are brought home from the hospital bundled up like a child of the Michelin man and you open your unfocused eyes on whiteness, all that whiteness as they hurry you from the car and up the steps, into the house, where you are unwrapped and ooh oohed over and put to bed in a snug cot in your mother's (temporary) room. Outside the window the snow is falling, falling like something out of a story by James Joyce and your unfocused ears cringe at the sound of the snowplows, the sirens. You want to cry out, This is not my element!—but you don't know words, you can only bawl in frustration, shit your diaper and wait for comfort from the one constant in all this, your mother's body, your mother's smell. You have not yet heard the voice of your father except through the drum of your mother's belly.

Then, *then*, no sooner are you beginning to figure things out (if I cry, she'll come or one of those other voices, the soft one and the deep) and your body is used to the heavy feel of blankets, your eyes are used to the cream ceiling above your cot, then you are taken away from cold and back to heat, down the steps of the airplane and into heat, which your cells, somehow, remember (how could they?);

you stop crying and are as good as gold.

Strange awkward arms hold you, hairy, slick with sweat. Your father. That voice.

I had been back and forth across the Atlantic, had flown over more countries than I have actually set foot in, before I was twelve weeks old. So thought William as he lay on his bed in the catering rest house in Tamale. The water was off so he had been supplied with two bucketsful. A "boy" of about fifty brought them in and set them in the shower stall.

Several mosquitoes had pushed their way in with the water-boy so William lit a mosquito coil and wondered if any of the "Silent Service," as he had decided to call the bad ones, had come in as well. His grandfather had talked about the silent service—were they the guys in the submarines? They must have been. ("They're *all* bad," Bernard said, "they can give you dengue, cholera, you name it. Don't let any mosquito near you.") He laughed at Bernard but wouldn't mind, tonight, having that fancy collapsible net he carried with him. However, the fumes from the mosquito coil seemed to be doing the trick.

He opened the rickety night table and there was a Bible—no, not a Bible, the Koran. He was definitely in Muslim country now. Like most of the students he knew, he had attended rallies in support of Salman Rushdie, but he knew nothing about the Koran, little about Muslim art, the Muslim world.

He'd read parts of *The Satanic Verses* and thought they were funny. What would it be like—to be so outraged by them you'd want to kill? A kind of patriotism, only religious and directed at just one man.

"In the name of God, the Compassionate, the Merciful: *A lif lām mūm*. This book is not to be doubted."

There was a movie on in the hall beyond the bar: *Kickboxer II*: "A Brutal Action Film." He'd seen the sign outside the restaurant door.

In Accra, in Kumasi, wherever he went he saw notices written on blackboards, nearly always for Brutal Action Films. These seemed to have taken the place of westerns, at least over here. Hey, what about back home, with Chantal's nephews and nieces going around doing Ninja Turtle kicks at you and at each other. Better than guns, maybe. He had thought about going to the film, just to see who showed up, but he didn't think he could sit up any more today. Why not lie here and learn something?

He flipped to the section on women. Weren't they terribly hard on women?

"Forbidden to you are your mothers, your daughters, your sisters, your paternal and maternal aunts, the daughters of your brothers and sisters, your foster mothers…."

The light flickered and went out; the fan stopped. He could hear shouts of disappointment from the moviegoers. He waited a minute or two, and when the electricity did not come back on he reached for his flashlight and felt around in his pack until he found the emergency candles.

During the long hot day they'd gone limp and now looked more like old-fashioned lamp standards or shepherds' crooks. He could straighten them, carefully, but they'd probably do it again. Well, didn't he read by flashlight when he was a boy? "…your foster sisters, the mothers of your wives, your stepdaughters who are in your charge, born of the wives with whom you have lain...."

He clicked off the light. Tomorrow he'd look at it. Too tired, too tired. Christ it was hot! Allah! Well, there was one thing you could do, alone, in the dark. But it turned out he was too tired, too tired. Tomorrow.

He walked into town to get some fruit and find the post office, find the bank. Those bundles of cedis disappeared very fast. Just before the main road a woman and her child got up from the dirt and confronted him. The woman wore faded pink rags and looked wizened and old, but he had a terrible feeling she was the child's mother. The child, in a ragged grey dress, was about five.

They stood in front of him and gestured, scratched their palms and put their fingers to their mouths, scratched their palms and put their fingers to their mouths, over and over, wordlessly, staring at him.

"Oh God," he said, "here. Get something to eat." He knew they would be there when he came back, that this was probably their regular station. They didn't thank him, just wrapped the money in a piece of cloth and moved back towards the verge. He had given them enough money for a good meal, more than enough. The woman looked ill; her eyes glittered with fever.

They didn't move because this was the time of day people left the rest house; they couldn't leave yet, not yet. That must be it. Cars had to slow down because there was a junction. They would wait a little longer; their life must consist of waiting—it was their "occupation," with occasional breaks for food.

Where did they sleep?

The walk into town refreshed him, cleared his head. He bought three bananas from a young woman standing under a tree. (When he tried to lift her load, just to see how much it weighed, he could only get it to his shoulders; much laughter over this.) He bought oranges, hard-boiled eggs. Everything fitted neatly into his daypack.

At the post office there was a letter from Chantal, a letter from his grandfather and a postcard from Mali, a Tuareg and his camel. The message on the back had been made with a rubber stamp. Having a wonderful time / wish you were here. But the signature was Bernard's. He liked Bernard, in spite of all the dramatics, some of which were surely an act?

The market was big and open-air. It wasn't market day so there weren't the usual crowds. He knew now that aside from a few strings of beads, a few souvenirs, he would always head for the cloth.

He noticed, on his way to the cloth stalls, quite a number of white women choosing vegetables and greens. There must be an aid project near by.

At noon the muezzin's call went out over a loudspeaker. William had seen a mosque last night, when he arrived. It didn't seem to be finished and so he could see right inside, rather like a multi-level car park, row after row, layer after layer of men kneeling with their heads bowed to the ground. Now, in the streets, he saw men stop what they were doing, and kneel. You would always know, in this town, which way was east.

He had a wicked desire to stand there and shout

"Rushdie!" or "I am Salman Rushdie" and see what would happen.

On the way home some boys in a field called him to play football. He set his pack down carefully, where he could watch it, and joined in. They played rough and he got the wind knocked out of him twice but it was the heat—and hunger—that made him give up.

They all wanted to be his friend; they all wanted to come to Canada.

They were playing barefoot! He hadn't even noticed. Did they dream of playing in the World Cup? His heart was pounding from all that exertion in the heat. Time to get back to the rest house, aptly named, have a snack and a cool drink, pour one of those buckets of water over himself. A third of a bar of Lux soap had been provided, just as it had been at Violet's Rest House. Who spent hours cutting up these bars? Lux might have some grateful customers if they made their bars one-third of the standard size.

He washed—oh he'd show the world that he could make a bucket of water go a long way; he even washed his hair, first, and the red dust ran down his body like rust. The Tin Woodman takes a bath.

No letters from his parents. None. Well, had he expected any? They probably called his grandfather to get news. They didn't want him here so they wouldn't write to him here. No doubt his mother was too busy writing letters to her foster children. No, take that back. She was a good mother; he was a good father. Did they ever abuse you? Did you ever go hungry?

On the way in he had given two hard-boiled eggs and two oranges to the beggar woman and her child, when they stepped in front of him, scratching their palms, touching their lips with their fingers. He was sure they didn't remember him.

On the table cum desk under the window he spread out his lunch: groundnuts, a hard-boiled egg, bread, an orange, bottled water. He had packed a small cardboard salt and pepper before he left home; the salt was nearly gone. No doubt he could buy salt in the market, work the top off, fill it up, tape it back on again. He wanted a tomato but wasn't sure, even if it was peeled. But this was a good meal nevertheless and tonight he would ask in the bar where he could go (other than the restaurant here) to get a bean stew and some fried plantain.

"William," he said, "you're a lucky lucky lucky man," propped his pack under his pillow and lay down to read his letters.

"*Mon cher, Tu me manques, tu me manques, tu me manques*. I worry so about you I cannot sleep...."

They said—the ubiquitous "They"—that African men did it from behind. Did they mean anal intercourse or just from behind, the way he and Chantal did sometimes, her leaning across the bed, propped up with pillows, he standing, knees bent, entering her that way, one hand touching her, the other steadying himself against the bed as he went in and out. But he didn't really like her facing away from him, in spite of the beautiful curve of her *mange tout* back.

(Why would they go to all that trouble with the clitoridectomy and the other awful thing, if they only did it in the ass? But don't be silly, he told himself, you don't get babies that way.)

But no clitoris to touch and thrum until she cried out with pleasure. And what would it be like on the first night, the breaking and entering, like some vicious burglar—the terrible pain.

One night Chantal said, "Turn over on your stomach."

"Why?" he said.

"Just turn over, you will like it."

"Like what?"

"You talk too much. Turn over and put your hands around your cock."

She fumbled in a drawer for a minute and then he felt a small gloved finger enter him, a gloved finger covered in some cool jelly, lovely, no pain, no pain at all, just a mounting sense of pleasure with Chantal straddling him from behind and this lovely sensation, don't stop, don't stop, don't stop.

"Now do it to me," she said. "Be gentle."

After that they kept a supply of the thin, white, powdery gloves, the same kind Chantal and her friends used when they hennaed their hair, in the small drawer of the night table.

"Say: 'Enjoy your unbelief a while; but the Fire shall be your home. Can he who passes the night in adoration, standing or on his knees, who dreads the terrors of the life to come and hopes to earn the mercies of his Lord, be compared to the unbeliever? Are the wise and the ignorant equal?'"

That evening, as he rode in a taxi to the recommended restaurant (there was a seat-belt fastener but no seat belt and no window on the passenger side), he saw, in the darkness, groups of men everywhere, in a sort of wave-like motion, standing up and kneeling down to pray outside their houses. It was hard for William to imagine religious ritual as an active part of one's day-to-day existence. He had given up daily (nightly) prayers around the time of puberty. Chantal's mother was religious, she went to mass every day and at Grandfather's house, even if it were only the two of you sitting down, you said a brief grace. He hadn't been inside a church, except to look at art or architectural details, in years. Yet when "religion" was one of the blanks to fill out on a form he always put Protestant. Why? Was he hedging his bets a little?

Did these men, kneeling out there under the stars, really *believe*? Or was it like brushing your teeth? Well maybe it was like brushing your teeth—to keep the soul healthy and disease free, rid yourself of spiritual plaque.

What did the women do while this was going on?

When he came out of the bar at the rest house an old Range-Rover was just pulling away. He was sure he saw the COW symbol on the side as it turned into the road, the logo of a cow with a maple leaf branded on her rear. He went to the desk to enquire.

"Oh yes. Mr. John Phelps. He is with COW."

"Is he staying here?"

"Two nights only."

William left him a note. But was delighted to see the same Range-Rover parked outside the Alhambra Hotel and, yes, there was the cow.

He was the only white person there, head down, bent over his food.

"Mr. Phelps?"

"That's me, son. What can I do you for?"

"...And so tomorrow I set off north for Bolgatanga with Johnny Phelps. Someone—if not God—is surely looking after me. Johnny was only here for two days, to answer an emergency call to fix a computer that was down. Something to do with a project partly funded by COW, where loans are given to women (small loans, or small in our terms, $50 to $200) so that they can improve their small farms—buy seed, fertilizer, etc. and be more independent. Time to do the accounts and the computer wouldn't work. So, rather than fly somebody up from Accra or over from Togo (there's a Canadian COW worker in Togo who is a computer whiz) Johnny came down and fixed it in an hour. He's spending today showing them how to fix it themselves next time!

"I suppose the fact that he's clever at fixing things, sees a problem and solves it, is why the others call him Crocodile Dundee. He's also a bit of a renegade—has no time for Serena and her cynicism. Or her brand of cynicism—he says he has plenty of his own. I'm looking forward to getting to know him a bit. Ate what he was eating—bean stew and fried plantain: delicious.

"The market is much smaller than Kumasi, but quite spread out. Stall after stall of men making the striped northern-territory smocks (Nkrumah wore one of these, Johnny said, when he became first black head of the country—to prove he was a man of the people; now think about Mulroney, his Gucci shoes) on ancient Singer sewing machines, same kind we saw in the markets in Abidjan, same kind those women had on their heads when I was spat at. I am going to get one for you, Grandfather, maybe one for myself.

"There is always something to look at or something to listen to. Did I tell you I now hate roosters? They don't crow when it is dawn, they crow whenever they feel like it. Testosterone build-up or what?

"I'm sitting in a gazebo-like structure, very small, with a thatched roof, like most of the houses up here. A boy is sweeping the red earth in front of the main building with a handleless broom. A rather futile exercise as the big tree in the parking lot is shedding its leaves. Three guys are sitting in front of me, on the other side of the table, having a spirited conversation in Dagboni. I think they work here; every so often I hear a word in English—'the manager,' 'head office'—mixed in with all the other sounds.

"This place is very run down, no running water, electricity that comes and goes, a general air of having known better times. Except for spotlessly clean sheets and pillow cases the place is dirty, not filthy but dirty. We're provided with a thermos of drinking water each day but I don't like the looks of it and buy bottled water—I can get NAYA as well as others for 450 cedis, about two dollars for one of those two-litre bottles. I wish I had one of those clever blue cups of Bernard's; I drink huge quantities of water. (I pour the thermos water into the bucket so 'they' won't be offended. Ridiculous.) The rest house has been sold, but 'the Castle' (the government) is reluctant to finalize the deal because a powerful chief who wanted to buy it is very angry.

"Sunday School is going on in another pavilion near by. One of the boys has a plastic trumpet. He has just been told off because he keeps tooting it. There is also a church service in the hall where the brutal action films are shown. Lots of people, all dressed up, both in cloths (the men) and in Western clothes. They've been singing and clapping their hands and I'm about to get up and go over, to sit quietly in the back. The church is called by the locals 'Brother Charles' Church' but it is really the Something Miracle Church—I can't quite read the banner from here.

"P.S. Johnny is the oldest co-operant in all of COW. About my father's age, I'd guess, with grey hair and black, black eyebrows. Shorter than I am but not short and he looks very fit. He could probably have lifted that load of bananas with one hand. English accent, cockney maybe; I'm not good at accents—regional."

William did not add another P.S. that just after he entered the hall and sat down quietly at the back, the minister began to pray. Suddenly first one, then another, then another began babbling away louder and louder. Was this speaking in tongues? He thought it must be, but it was terrifying, as though, through all that confused sound one voice was struggling to come forth—HEAR THIS. NOW

HEAR THIS. He was afraid to go, for fear they—it—this collective thing would turn on him, cast him out, or worse. He felt the same atavistic fear he had experienced in the upstairs hallway when he was a child. He was confronted by the Other, the Unknown—he was a voyeur and not a believer. Ho! Boy. You can't fool us. Go back where you belong. Infidel! He sat there, shaking, until gradually the sound died down to a murmur, then a gasp, a whimper, then the pastor, Brother Charles, wiping his face with a white handkerchief calling out "Praise the Lord!" and the exhausted congregation sobbing "Amen."

He went back to the same restaurant that night but Johnny wasn't there. He probably had lots of friends in Tamale. The beans and plantain were good but not quite so good as when you had someone to talk to. He had so many questions, too, questions Johnny might be able to answer—if he weren't too busy fixing other things.

In his room he put everything back in his pack except an orange and some biscuits for the morning. He began to see the true meaning of the word pack. That's what you did, pack your pack and unpack and pack the pack again. More cloth to go in the garbage bag, dirty clothes here, clean there. He'd do a wash when he got to Bolgatanga.

The electricity was on so he read for a while, not the Koran, although he would read the whole thing through when he got back home, he promised. It didn't seem so bad, what he'd looked at already. Lots of Thou Shalt Nots just like the Bible, lots of stuff about the division of property. He made a crude drawing of his room—bed against the wall, table, chair, fan, louvred window, just to remember how things were. Coloured it in: grey-blue walls, grey blanket on the bed, red covers of the Koran on the night table, the solitary orange. His watercolour block was about three-quarters full of swatches of colour, each one annotated. Would they be of any help, later on? He mixed the grey-pink of the beggar woman's cloth, the dull brown of her hand. But he couldn't draw the hand, or that gesture, or the church choir in their purple robes and white surplices. Would colour be enough, later on, to enable him to bring back shape? If there were a way to put down sound and smell!

He took the green lump of beeswax from where it was wrapped in a handkerchief (he had bought two from a boy in Accra and wore one around his neck, to pull up, bandit-style, when the dust got too bad. The harmattan season was coming and the wind had begun to blow). He softened the wax in his hands, rolled out a rope and coiled it, raised up the end to form a snake. Even the worst of the work at the Cultural Centre was better than anything he would ever do. He had asked Ethnay Owusu-Banahene about an apprenticeship, or some opportunity to work with the men in the village.

"If you really wanted to do that I could enquire. It might be possible to arrange. You'd have to stay on or come back later. Would that be your thesis then—a description of some sort of apprenticeship?"

"Yes."

"Would that get you an advanced degree—just doing that?"

"No. There would have to be a lengthy introduction.

I'm not an artist, I'm going to be an art historian, teach art history."

"A pointer pointing at an image of an image?"

"Well, writing as well. I'll admit it's a second choice. Your granddaughters can draw better than I can."

"My granddaughters are not inhibited by such things as *rules*, William. They draw well—if they do—because they don't let their brain get in the way. We northerners have too much brain."

"Where is their mother, by the way?"

"Their mother is dead."

Suppose he learned to make a perfect snake, what would that prove? He would always be yearning to make the little gun, with its fifteen separate parts, and that would take years—a lifetime. Did he really want to spend a lifetime here just to prove he could do something clever with his hands? It was not as though he came from a family of artists; he was not the equivalent of the footballer's son who isn't any good at football. Why did he feel such a failure because he couldn't do this one thing? Why this *idée fixe*? Just because a small boy liked the smell of his Crayola crayons when he was six years old, that same boy, grown up, didn't have to make it as an artist.

Yet he felt, and this he would never tell anyone, that there was something in him that was longing to get out. Thinking of that church service today he saw this *thing* as something like a shout. Not a command, nothing like that. A statement about the way he (literally) saw the world. Was that too much to ask? He wasn't much of a talker, went shy in groups of more than three, used to bend over and pretend to tie his shoe in grade school, hoping the teacher wouldn't notice him. What did shy little kids do, now that there was Velcro?

He could stand up in a darkened room, with a pointer. He'd done it already and knew that, *professionally*, he could do that and answer questions, mark assignments. But he always knew he would never be a great teacher, would never be able to plunge in, without notes, to "work" a class until they too understood every brushstroke on every feather of the angel's wing. His students would say to other students, yeah, take his course—the slides are great. He's okay too—kind of stiff, but okay. Did he want to be okay, just okay? Would they wonder how he ever got hooked up with that gorgeous wife of his? She's a real character. Yeah.

He couldn't be okay, just okay, because his father was just okay, if not perhaps not okay. His father was a failure—in his own eyes, in the eyes of his wife, maybe in the eyes of his son. His father sat in a lab all day looking through a microscope at bits of tissue and blood, typing up reports. Positive. Negative. Needs re-examination. Needs ultrasound before diagnosis can be made. He came home from the hospital each day smelling faintly of green soap and something else, something generic—"hospital smell."

He had wanted to be a real research man, to find a cure for all sorts of things. He was brilliant enough, William's mother said. God knows he was brilliant enough. But then he got sick. She meant he'd had some sort of a breakdown. William knew that early on but he didn't know how he knew. Some sort of loss of vision, failure of will. He was kind and conscientious but he wasn't really there. When you talked to him, and over the years, William tried, it was like talking to someone wearing a Walkman; he was listening to something else.

William was hoping Johnny would offer to put him up but he was expecting two volunteers on a visit from Burkina Faso so he dropped William off at the Hotel St. Vincent and sped away, saying he'd be back to pick him up tomorrow night, if he felt like it. Bit of a get-together at the only hotel with decent food. If you've got other plans by then, don't worry about it. "I'll drop by around six."

Johnny had been quite forthcoming about himself on the trip. Yes, he lived alone, more or less, but there was always somebody coming or going. He had a wife but they'd agreed to disagree sort of thing. Still friends, mind you. She was coming out to visit in April or May.

He said he was a "practical man"; he said it more than once. William imagined he would want it on his tombstone. Here lies a practical man.

"There are solutions to some of the things that are troubling this country but the country itself gets in the way. Petty chiefs, tribes, obligations. Doesn't pay to be a success in this country, you'll end up carrying your uncles and your cousins and your aunts; much better to sit under a tree and chew kola nuts. Ambition? Forget about it. And most people are sick with something or other—fever will knock the ambition out of you pretty bloody quick."

"So why are you here?"

"I ask myself that question nearly every day. Maybe I get a kick out of what I'm doing. Making do. Making something out of nothing or next to nothing. Teaching the locals to do the same. At the moment we're making enormous water pots, concrete over chicken wire. They're the traditional shape but they don't break like the clay pots and they keep things just as cool."

"But they have to have the concrete."

"Concrete is already available. My God, they *love* concrete! Start all kinds of projects that are never finished, concrete forms and re-bar sticking up everywhere."

When he was born, his father, an engineer, had taken one look and buggered off. But he'd been out here at one point in his chequered career. Johnny remembered letters with wonderful stamps. "It was the Gold Coast then of course. But he never sent for us, just letters with bank drafts inside and a photo every now and then. Him and his mates standing by some dam or water hole or something. I suppose I'm a bit like him, really. My mother says I've got his eyebrows."

They stopped for brochettes and beer. At a stand-pipe Johnny took off his tee shirt and poured water all over himself. There was a long scar below his ribs and a small but equally nasty scar where whatever it was had come out his back.

"Boo!" he said to the children. "What d'you think you're looking at?"

William found himself telling his story, the COW people, his parents.

"So you're on some kind of quest, are you?"

"I suppose so."

"All this goldweight bullshit is just more or less a cover to find out where Mommy and Daddy went wrong?"

"More or less. I *am* going to write my thesis on lost wax."

Johnny laughed. "Remind me, some time, when we're sitting over a cool beer or a gin and tonic—I love gin and tonic, should've been a nob in India when the jewel was in the crown—remind me to tell you about my experience with lost-wax casting."

"You know how to do it? That's wonderful."

"Oh I know how to do it all right. Me and my late brother-in-law, bless his soul, we were into lost wax in a big way. Remind me to tell you."

"Why not tell me now?"

"We're here."

An old Muslim man got up from the bench where he'd been sleeping.

"Ah. Mr. Johnny." Smile. Missing teeth.

"Here's a friend of mine, Yusef. Give him a nice room, okay?"

"Certainly."

"I have breakfast at the Wayfarers' Inn on weekdays, early. If you're up, come and join me."

"What ti—?" But he'd turned the truck around and was gone.

The old man picked up William's pack and led the way through an arch and across a dark inner courtyard, along a dimly lit corridor full of snores. Unlocked the door and handed William the key, touched his forehead.

"Shouldn't I register? Sign something?"

"Tomorrow," the man said. "In the morning."

So tired he simply took off his shorts and sandals and fell full-length across the bed, causing unseen scurryings in the corners. Should he get up and turn on the light? Forget it. You've seen one giant cockroach, you've seen them all.

He woke up the next morning to someone knocking on his door. Knocking and at the same time announcing himself: "Kock—Kock—Kock—Kock—Kock."

He got up quickly, grabbed his shorts and took a look at himself in the mirror. The bedcover he'd been lying on was embroidered and now one side of his face was covered in pink indentations. And he stank of sweat.

"Kock—Kock—Kock—Kock."

A man with a purple plastic bucket. "Please, the water will be turned off until three. So the builders can work. This bucket is for washings."

William took the heavy bucket, thanked the man (should he tip these men? was this like room service?), closed the door. He had about half a cup of bottled water left. Should he drink it or brush his teeth? He had to brush his teeth, but he felt like taking his chances, drinking the whole bucket, what the hell.

In the bathroom there was a third of a bar of Lux—pink this time—and a meagre towel. He was glad he hadn't jettisoned his beach towel in order to make more room in his pack for cloth. He'd make sure he was back here right at three. Even with a good scrub, even under the sweet smell of Lux (or one-third Lux) he could smell himself. He wanted to be a clean boy for the sort-of party tonight.

Everything in the room was labelled Hotel St. Vincent, or rather H. St. V., in black letters: one leg of the wooden bed, the back of the chair, the table, the mirror (the bucket, the towel), even the embroidered bedcover, made in China but the property of the H. St. V. Perhaps he should get out his sewing kit and write W. McK. on his beach towel?

He put on the last of his fresh clothes over his unfresh body, made a bundle of all his dirty clothes, and locking the door behind him set out to find the manager, somewhere—or someone—to do laundry, some breakfast and something to drink. His watch said 9 a.m. Johnny would be long gone from the Wayfarers' Inn, but at least he could find out where it was.

The inner courtyard was full of men holding ladders, standing on ladders, carrying buckets (H. St. V., H. St. V.) up to the beginning of a second storey. The manager, in a white shirt, stood at the doorway of his office, chewing on a chewing stick and watching.

"We are expanding," he said to William. "There will be a gala New Year's Event to celebrate the new addition. A lucky draw. Party hats and snacks. Drinks."

(Wasn't this Muslim country? Who would come?)

William couldn't say how long he was staying; he was really on his way to Wa but wanted to see Bolgatanga. Two or three days perhaps?

"Stay as long as you like. Stay for New Year's Eve!"

William paid for three days and was given directions to the Wayfarers' Inn. He could have had breakfast at the H. St. V. if they had known. Now the cook was gone to market. His laundry, yes, yes, leave it, leave it, would be done by Isaac when the water came back on.

A man in a black car drove up just as William came through the archway. He heard loud greetings being exchanged with the manager and the office door closing. The Hotel St. Vincent seemed a happy, friendly place; he was glad Johnny had dropped him there. He never would have found it by himself.

William walked along the red dirt road feeling alone yet not alone; he had a friend somewhere in this town. In fact, he'd been lucky all the way along. It was like one of those old tales where a guide takes you just so far and then turns back. But you have the talisman or know the password and a second guide appears. Who would guide him up to Wa? He and Johnny would meet up again this evening, maybe; after the sort-of party they'd come back to the bar of the hotel for a quiet drink.

He wondered about the hotel, what sort of people stayed there. Was business so good they could afford to expand? Who came and drank from the glittering bottles behind the bar? The people he passed on the road, the people passing him, with their headloads, their black made-in-China bicycles, their dusty feet, did not look like people who frequented bars, let alone hotels.

He was so thirsty that when he saw a girl with a load of oranges, he stopped her and asked her to peel him two, right away, and he sucked them dry, one after the other, as he walked along. He thought of the green lawns of Victoria, the long showers he had taken, the way he brushed his teeth with the tap running. How many *gallons* of water did his family use a day, himself, Chantal, their friends? He would never take water for granted again, or the freedom to drink what came straight out of the tap.

Sweat soaked the underarms of his shirt. Sweat ran down his back, tickled the crack between his buttocks.

Drumming somewhere in the distance. Lorries breathing out diesel fumes. The smell of an open sewer as he came round a corner: DO NOT URINATE HERE. A shuttered house, the shutters flung open to reveal people inside making baskets. DISABLED WORKSHOP. The Why Worry Pharmacy. He stopped to copy that one down for Bernard. A painted sign advertising haircuts: The Dollah, The Seven, with an illustration , the Cocaine. "Family Planning. Think about it." Immaculate's Ladies Dress Shop. More and more people joining the crowd, moving towards the main drag and the market.

Was it really more comfortable, once you got used to it, to carry things on your head? It left your hands free, yes, but only to carry other things or hold the hand of a toddler. These women didn't lift their feet like European women; they shuffled. They walked from side to side.

"Good morning."

"Fine morning."

And it was.

At the Wayfarers' Inn, a small café consisting of one long table, near one of the main entrances to the market, the woman behind the counter told him, as he had guessed, that Johnny had eaten hours ago.

Did they know where he worked? Out by the edge of town. She asked the men sitting at the counter; no one knew precisely. A lively discussion followed; he didn't understand a word except for "Yanni, Yanni, Yanni."

"Please," said the woman, "are you his son?"

"Me? Oh. No. Does he have a son?"

"He has two sons. Not here."

"Oh." A wife had been mentioned, a wife with whom he had agreed to disagree. No mention of any sons. Were they on the outs or were they sons "by the back door" as Mrs. O-B told him the Ashantis say. "No, I'm just a friend."

"He will come tomorrow. He takes his breakfast here."

William sat down at the counter. He had milky tea, a poached egg, several slices of bread and margarine. Four cups of tea before he felt he had restored some of his body's water.

The cup was made of a soft, heavy plastic; so was his plate. The other men stared at him, not impolitely, probably because of the Johnny connection, but they did not speak to him. The woman behind the counter had spoken to them in dialect so perhaps they didn't speak English.

People came in with enamelled cups with covers, small enamelled pails. Went away with tea or stew. The Wayfarers' Inn was a kind of take-away as well. The woman moved slowly, almost as though in a dream, but the orders got filled and the customers didn't seem to mind waiting. The place, with its long counter, its sleepy "waitress," its solitary cook (who was obviously her husband), its domed cover on the enormous platter of fried eggs, its "regulars," was like an old-fashioned diner or luncheonette, like the one at Woolworth's on Mont-Royal Avenue. He half-expected to look up and see the advertised specials: bean stew, chicken chichinga, kelewele, palaver sauce.

He lingered, not quite sure what to do next. He could try to find Johnny at his work; it would be interesting to see him in action. Or he could wait to see him until the evening. He didn't want to seem pushy.

His breakfast had come to just over a dollar. He paid the woman and said he'd be back the next day.

The men watched him go, turning in their seats. They were all old, with long bones, long faces, small pointed beards. Pale robes, some with elaborate embroidery at the neck. Muslims.

"Between them and the cities we have blessed, we placed roadside hamlets so that they could journey to and fro in measured stages. We said: 'Travel through them by day and night in safety.'

"But they said: 'Lord, make our journeys longer.' They sinned against their souls...."

Were the owners thinking of this, which he had copied down in his notebook before he left Tamale, when they called their place the Wayfarers' Inn? The woman didn't look like a Muslim, but what was his idea of a Muslim woman? A hurrying figure, veiled from head to toe? This woman looked more like a gypsy with her black blouse and faded skirt; her husband, the cook, looked like a cartoon cook, only black. He wore a singlet and a cloth apron around his middle. And infidels seemed to be welcome, so who knows?

Perhaps, here, it was only the men who wore Muslim dress.

Bone structure, shape of head, lips—so different. They looked like a blend of Africa and the Orient. And they were quieter, more self-contained than the tribes to the south. It was hard to imagine these tall old men, with their slow, dignified walk, their contemplative air, whipped to a frenzy by someone like the late Ayatollah. William had read of Timbuktu. The men who passed him, some wearing the conical leather hat of the Hausa tribe, but most in the small, round, ordinary Muslim cap, were the types he imagined walked the streets of that fabulous city in its golden age, when it was a centre of learning. The sort of men who wrote elaborate verses and invented complex mathematical constructions. He thought they were beautiful, mysterious, remembered again the old man in the Accra market: "Give me some money so that I can bless you."

A woman who looked about his age passed him, going the other way. She had a baby on her back and was led by the hand by a small girl. The woman was blind. And then, as if to bring him straight down from his romantic visions, a long string of old, blind men, holding onto a rope, a small boy leading them, begging, beating against a tin can with a stick. When he was a little boy himself he had always hated the UNICEF cans at Halloween, the steady chant of Trick or Treat, Trick or Treat and holding out the tin. He didn't like begging, shaming people so that they kept big bowls of pennies by the door along with the apples and candies. He didn't like teachers telling him how lucky he was. He still felt that he was right, but when he saw the girl, the little boy, his eyes filled with tears. The girl wasn't begging but he gave her money anyway, thrust it at her, ran after the boy. And almost immediately he had his little crocodile of children following behind—'Bronie, 'Bronie, 'Bronie! You give me *pesewas*!

Why did the Pied Piper lead the children away? Of all the childhood rhymes that was the one that terrified him the most. "Because they wouldn't give him his money," said his mother, "because the mayor and the corporation didn't stick to their bargain, remember?" Her face was pale; he could tell she didn't like that poem either.

What he remembered was "out came the children running, all the little boys and girls," who followed the Piper through the door in the mountainside. All that was left of the children was a lame little boy who couldn't keep up with them.

"Don't read that any more Mommy, I don't like it."

Now his whiteness draws children to him and they follow him down the busy street and into the busy market.

"One thing I'll never get used to," says Johnny, very chic in a kind of jumpsuit of market cloth, "is their casualness about shit. They simply do not want to deal with it."

"Why not?" says a new girl, a Peace Corps worker. They have all moved away from the table and are sitting in an alcove, twelve of them plus Johnny who holds court as a kind of wise old man, a role, William thinks to himself, that Johnny enjoys playing. VSO, Peace Corps, the two COW girls from Burkina Faso, a group of Japanese volunteers. Most are teachers of one sort or another, with a few health-care workers thrown in. They are polite to William but he's not really one of them; he isn't doing anything to help the world.

"I was at a meeting in Tamale, at the courthouse, or what passes for the courthouse. Someone I knew was in trouble with the law and I thought I'd come down and see if I could help. Parked my car in the shade of a tree and couldn't understand why all the other cars were parked out in the blazing sun. When I came out—I was late getting there—I found out why. Piles of shit under the tree.

"They don't want to think about it. Contrary to popular belief these chaps are obsessed with cleanliness. Shit is too disgusting to contemplate. The idea that we would actually have a place *in our houses* where we shit is almost too much for villagers to understand. Why on earth would we do that? No way José. You need a latrine at the edge of the compound, right away from where you eat or sleep. This carries over when you come to the city; no matter how much of a big shot you become, it never really leaves you. So you shit whenever and wherever you feel the need. Then you walk away. What? My shit? That coil of stinking stuff? Nothing to do with *me*.

"There was a girl here a couple of years ago—VSO I think, nice girl. You all know by now about the right hand–left hand business? Right. Well this poor girl fell and broke her arm the second month. Her right arm. People were sympathetic, tsk-tsk all over the place, but nobody wanted to shake hands with her and her students didn't like to watch her eat.

"Very awkward. Turnaround on that bit in the Bible. Here the right hand doesn't want to know what the left hand is doing! I can talk about hygiene until I'm blue in the face—flies, disease, you know the drill. From their point of view they *are* hygienic. The district health nurses try but it's an uphill battle. Or a dung-hill battle."

Everyone laughed. More beer was brought, more stories told. One Japanese teacher said he was on strike; nobody paid attention to him anyway. The boys wouldn't fetch his water and the girls read fashion magazines while he stood at the blackboard, trying to teach world history. The VSO group talked about a friend who had gone mad and tried to kill himself. He'd been taking one of the new malaria medicines and had a severe reaction. However, he was going to be all right.

Tales of dysentery, dengue—everybody trying to outdo everybody else.

William, feeling a little guilty, told them about Bernard and the mosquito. Everyone laughed.

Then someone asked about AIDS. Asked the wise old man.

"AIDS is the least of your worries here, but it *is* here and it's increasing. My advice to you lot is be careful, don't take chances. I don't and neither should you. I wear me rubbers in the rainy season, oh yes. Any season actually."

"You know," said one of the girls who had just come down from Burkina Faso, "many people still say it is a Western disease, or that it doesn't exist here. SIDA:

'Syndrome Imaginaire pour Décourager les Amoureux.'"

"Or, if it exists," said the other girl, "it's the creation of white homosexuals. *No* homosexuality in Africa, of course."

William thought of Bernard and the young Ivoirian. Why couldn't a gay man just be friends with another man? He'd never seen him so much as pat the hand of the man in the tangerine shirt.

In William's medical kit, made up by himself with too much help from Chantal, there were five BD3CC syringes (sterile, destroy after use), Pepto-Bismol (24 chewable tablets, revised formula), an Optrex Eye Mask (Refreshes and Soothes Tired Eyes: for TV Eyes, for Tired Eyes, for Sun-Strained Eyes, for Hayfever Eyes, for Morning-After Eyes), several 5 cm x 5 cm (Type VII) gauze pads, assorted sutures in a sterile package, IV tube in ditto, tweezers, alcohol wipes, Dristan, Neocitron A, Caladryl Cream, Aloe Vera Dry Skin Creme, Gravol, Ace ankle bandage, Senokot (ten tablets), adhesive tape, Polysporin, Tylenol, Lariam, Halozone Tablets, Moleskin, Quinimax, Dr. Fowler's Extract of Wild Strawberry Tablets, the humble Band-Aid. A snake-bite kit had been rejected because the new wisdom was that these things simply aren't effective. All this in a see-through Rubbermaid box with a big red ✚ painted on the front with nail polish. William had also sent twenty dollars for a membership in IAMAT and had received, in return, an international directory of doctors and several charts about malaria and other diseases plus a coded list of which diseases are endemic in various tropical countries. (Almost anything you could think of, in the country to which he was going.)

"Where's the quick-acting cyanide?" he said to Chantal, but she didn't think that was funny.

Although William suffered, at the usual times, all the usual childhood diseases, he still had his tonsils and appendix. He had been stitched up once or twice but that was in a doctor's office; he had never set foot in a hospital, not even to have a look round the lab where his father worked, not even to visit someone else. He knew he had been very lucky, and something about all these preparations against disease and disaster made him very uneasy, as though he were asking for trouble. He wasn't stupid—the shots were important and he faced them bravely—but did he really need all this other stuff?

"Take it," Chantal said. "You never know." Then she added, face turned away from him, head bent over one of her endless lists of THINGS TO DO, "Are you going to take *des capotes?*"

"Of course not."

"Better safe than sorry."

She doesn't realize why he laughs at this.

"It's no joke William."

"No, no." And then he explained. Condoms had not occurred to him until she mentioned them. He couldn't imagine, any longer, wanting to sleep with anyone else. Now that she had brought the subject up he wondered if he should stick in a package, just in case. No. Never. (But asked himself was it fear of AIDS that finally made up his mind for him, rather than sexual loyalty? Or even fear of Chantal going through his pack some night in Abidjan. "Here! What's this. Oh Monsieur Hypocrite. What a sneaky pig you are. Well now we know where we stand.")

William spent all the next day—what was left of it when he finally woke up—at the market. He'd finally been the one to say "no" last night—Johnny dropped him off last; he and the girls were all for making a night of it, but William couldn't keep his eyes open. They were to meet up again at a bar near the Wayfarers' Inn.

He bought a pair of sandals made from an old tire, bought a leather charm to wear around his neck, a string of groundnuts done up in little twists of plastic, an expensive way to buy them but useful when he got on the road again. He sat on a low wall and played with the orange-sellers' children.

How could Mrs. O-B dismiss their aesthetics? If some oranges were purchased the pyramid was built up again. Boxes of soap were stacked as neatly as in a supermarket; spices were arranged in coloured cones. Even yams, which were not like the yams at home but more like grey-brown limbs of trees, with pale yellow flesh inside, even the yams, which you could hardly say had eye-appeal, were stacked as neatly as cordwood.

N.T. smocks were strung on ropes between shade trees and danced in the slightest breeze. William asked if he could take photographs; there were more yeses than nos and he faithfully copied down addresses.

He was offered injections, groundnuts, leather hats.

At the ju-ju stall he saw birds' feet and lumps of stuff he couldn't identify, herbs, coloured threads, red, black, white. He wondered what the ju-ju man would say if he asked for a potion to make him an artist. He couldn't think of an enemy he wanted to poison or a girl—other than Chantal—he wanted to woo. The ju-ju stall didn't look all that different from the herbalists' windows in Chinatown.

"What is this for?" he asked the old man behind the stall. William held up a lump of something tied with string.

"Oh Master, that is medicine for old men!" Hee hee hee. He laughed even harder when William blushed, called out something to his neighbour selling amber beads and bows with wicked-looking arrows. More laughter. He decided not to ask any more questions there; Christ knows what he might pick up next.

Order. In all this seeming chaos there was order everywhere. And beauty. He thought of Elizabethan England, how he imagined it, and a phrase he had heard once but couldn't remember where—"garlic and sapphires in the mud."

He bought small boxes of matches that said "Aladdin" with a picture of a lamp. He bought a piece of blue cloth printed with green thumbs, perfect for his mother, the gardener.

"Master! Master!" But no one shoved anything in his face or blocked his way. There was a lot of laughter and calling and what he assumed was exchange of gossip and anecdote.

Whirr whirr went the treadle machines as the tailors bent over the strips of blue-and-white cloth.

In spite of the babble of voices, the shouts, the constant movement, William felt curiously at peace. His headache had disappeared; his stomach was full; he stepped out of the market to have a Fanta at a cool bar near one of the gates (the woman shoved one of her children off a crate, dusted it, offered him a seat). The child looked at him, sizing him up, then stuck out his hand for some money. Instead William gave him his last stick of chewing gum and the boy went away dragging a long piece of unwound cassette tape behind him, tied to an imaginary cow.

No one in the whole world knew exactly where he was. Johnny could probably find him if he wanted to, but nobody else. He began to understand, he thought, about wanderers—all those people throughout the centuries who just packed up and left, just wandering, just looking. No responsibilities. No papers to mark before Tuesday or chickens to shut up before dark. And later on, when you were too old, too "long in the tooth" as his grandfather would say, you had all that stuff stored in your head! No museums or art galleries—the real thing. And the sense of being other, an outsider, an observer.

He was surprised to see that people were packing up—surely it couldn't be time for the market to close? His watch said four o'clock; it would be dark by seven. He lingered just a bit longer then moved with the crowd towards an exit, one that would put him out near the road back to the hotel. People streamed towards the gates. A little girl, ten years old at most, running because the load she was carrying was too heavy. It was a wonder their heads weren't driven down into their shoulders.

But just as he was about to leave a man stepped in front of him, a man in rags, a filthy man with matted hair and wild eyes. He grabbed William's arm and jabbered at him.

"Let me go."

The man's grip was fierce. He was so close William could smell his unwashed smell, his breath. He raised William's hand aloft, jabbered some more. A few people stopped to watch but most pushed past them to the exit. It had been a long day; they wanted to get back to their villages.

"Let me go," William said again. He tried to pull away. He was angry and afraid. He pulled sharply downwards and was free and running, or running as best he could, through the archway and into the crowd. He didn't look back to see if the man was following him until he had run a long way and had a sharp pain in his side.

The man was gone. Just a poor mad creature, no one to be afraid of. But the incident had unnerved him and he spent a long time under the shower, reckless with the hotel's precious water. So much for good intentions, he thought. Lay down on the coverlet. What time was it? Plenty of time, *plenty*, for a nap.

He never heard the alarm, which was very faint, so there he was again, hot and sticky, with the imprint of the embroidered bedcover on his face. He put on his clothes (long trousers, long shirt), grabbed his flashlight and set out once again for the town. He'd had no dinner but there would probably be something at the bar. It was as hot as any summer night in Montreal, but a dry hotness, unpleasant, like breathing in air from a hairdryer. Johnny had said the Muslims were smart to have Ramadan during the dry season, when you couldn't even spit between sunup and sundown. Who would have the excess moisture to spit?

No. It was more like having your face pressed into a

wool blanket, suffocating. He was walking very fast, trying not to imagine a madman waiting for him someplace, in this shadowed entranceway or around that dark corner. Someone laughed, quite near, and he jumped.

There were drums in a village near by. Dadadah dadadah dadadah dadadah. Granddaughter Alice had said she liked funerals and he ought to see one. Was there a funeral going on out there?

Johnny and the girls called to him or he would have passed them by. They were sitting at a table out in front of a small bar strung with coloured lights.

"I heard drumming as I came along," William said. "Would that be a funeral?"

"It might be," Johnny said. "God knows there's enough of them. My boys keep taking time off for funerals; one of them has certainly buried his father three times in the last year, and he's older than I am. But people do have a habit of dying in this country. Here today, gone tomorrow."

William drank two beers in quick succession; he knew he was getting a little drunk—these were big bottles—and should go get something to eat.

"Tell me about your sons," he said.

"How did you know I had sons?"

"The woman at the Wayfarers' Inn. She asked me if I was one of your sons."

"Did she now? Can't see any family resemblance, can you?"

The girls laughed at the idea of tough, tanned, black-eyebrowed Johnny being the father of tall, pale, skinny William. ("Doesn't anyone ever call you Bill?")

"Nothing to tell, really. We get on fine when we see one another, which isn't too often. One's an actor and the other's studying of all things law. They're both in Toronto and I'm here so I haven't seen them for a few years. This is my second tour."

"And he's just applied for a third," the dark-haired one, Marie-Claire, said. "He is absolutely crazy."

They were both flirting with Johnny.

"He jumps out of planes," said the other, Janice. "For fun."

"*And* goes all the way home, last year, to help out a friend who was in trouble." She smiled at Johnny. "Oh yes, we heard about these things."

"That's enough, that's enough," Johnny said. "I pay them to do this, of course."

They giggled.

"No, seriously," said Marie-Claire, "he is wonderful. He invents things. All the time. His latest invention is a stretcher with two wheels and it hooks onto a *bicyclette* so the sick person can sort of lie down when they have to come in from the village."

"*And* a new kind of bellows."

Johnny held up his hand. "Let's have less talking and more drinking."

He called to the woman inside the bar.

"I'm starving," William said. "Does she have any food?"

"I don't think so, but we'll ask."

When the woman came out with more beer, Johnny asked about food. She said she would send a boy for brochettes. How many?

"I'd like at least two," William said. "I'm so hungry I could eat a horse."

"It will probably be a goat," Johnny said. They all found this remark hilarious. As the woman passed their table she passed her hand across the top of Johnny's head and smiled.

"Thanks, love," he said, but he didn't look up.

"You were going to tell me about lost wax," William said.

"Lost wax?" Johnny stared at the bottles on the table. "We're all lost, aren't we? Didn't somebody call us lost?"

"A long time ago, not us."

"Well we're lost too. Why are we out here solving—ha!—other people's problems when we can't even solve our own? Oka crisis, Quebec separatists, Mulroney's shoes, can't drink the water, drive-by shootings. Why are we here?"

"You have something to offer."

"I could offer it back home."

The blonde girl said, "Education is important—the most important thing—if you want to change things. I know why I'm here."

"Good for you. Forgive me, but maybe I'm just getting old."

"Lost wax?" William said again. He didn't want to see Johnny drunk and cynical.

"You really want to hear about it?"

"Of course." The girls nodded.

Johnny grinned, then guffawed. "Well, it is a *rather* amusing tale. Once upon a time, when I was much younger and living in England, my brother-in-law and I dreamt up a scheme for some easy money. We were both tinkerers—he was even better at fixing things than I was, rest his soul. I hope maybe he's up there in Heaven trying to fix the wheel of Fate. I can't remember who had the idea about lost wax; I think it was me but I'm not sure. I'd heard about it from a girlfriend who was at art college and I knew, basically, how it worked. So we decided to go into the antiques business, you might say, produce antique spoons and pistol mounts, silver crosses, that sort of thing, set ourselves up in Portobello Road with a tableful of dodgy antiques.

"What you need first is a pattern-piece; you must have something to copy in the first instance; that's the first thing to remember. We borrowed a Celtic cross—one of those small silver ones...no, that's not right, we did toy soldiers first, but never mind, let's suppose you're going to make a pile of Celtic crosses."

William found it hard to follow. Johnny's narrative became more and more elaborate and sometimes he slurred his words. He was drunk; they were all drunk. If the wax was the right temperature...his brother-in-law, bless him... "You pull away the rubber and there you are, Bob's your uncle, there is one perfect green wax Celtic cross. You stick it on a little blob of wax and you do loads of them, a whole tree of them...." He ordered another round of beer. "The casting," he said, "now that's another tricky part...." The table was covered with big green bottles. Ten green bottles, standing on the wall, ten green bottles, standing on the wall.

"Shh," said the girl called Anne-Marie or Marie-Anne, he couldn't remember which.

"Sorry," William said. He hadn't realized he'd been singing out loud.

"The first time we did it we used lead—for the soldiers. We were experimenting and didn't know how much lead was going to be used, how much metal. We put in what we thought was a moderate amount of lead to make our soldiers—*molten* lead, you understand? My brother-in-law, poor soul, he's standing on the workbench and I'm down the room on another workbench—we didn't really know what was going to happen—and kicked the switch with a broom handle. All this lead went flying around the room, we'd used far, far too much—as well as the lead that went into the mould. The centrifugal force flings the metal right into the farthest recesses of your cunning little set-up. What happens then is you wait, and you calm down and you take the bits of molten lead off your face and then you have to get your soldiers out, liberate the poor buggers. It's hot, bloody hot; you use callipers and plunge the tin into a bucket of cold water—*SSSSS* and other blacksmith sounds—and then out it comes and you bang your tin, the plaster falls away and out come these little grey things. It's always grey, even gold is grey. You clip them off the sprue, the little stalks, click click click, you clean them and brush them up, get rid of any seams and shine them and ladies and gentlemen, what am I offered for this genuine antique found in a dusty tin box under the bed of an ancient gentleman recently deceased?" He held up the stick from his brochette.

"But it is amazing; you can make the most intricate, the most incredibly intricate stuff that way. Making the mould is by far the most difficult part.

"Of course we used to weather them up a bit, crack the surface with a bunch of keys (my sister used to paint the soldiers; they were a lot of work), rub them with dirty acorns, all that stuff. We really got into it in a big way. I mean, the basic tackle wasn't much but we found out you could cast anything. We got into some quite interesting things." He laughed again. "Funny as hell, sticking things in the oven and then cracking them with keys. Wouldn't have fooled a real collector, but a tourist on a Saturday morning on Portobello Road—great fun."

Johnny smiled over at William. "Forgery, it's a weird life. However, there you are. The lost-wax process as practised in London in the Year of Our Lord Nineteen Hundred and Fifty-Five. Is that any help to you?"

Actually, it wasn't. A great story but hardly something you could put in a master's thesis. He thought of those men in the brass village, patiently making each wax figure by hand. What would they think of Johnny's method of lost-wax casting? A new project for COW? Bags of plaster of Paris instead of flour? Would it catch on? Would that be any more tacky than goldweights for key rings or the image of Yaa Asantewa made over and over with a ring at the top of her head? What do you do when you have a traditional skill that is no longer needed?

"Actually," Johnny broke in, "lost-wax casting is used in modern industry—or a form of it. With fibreglass moulds. The plane you came on probably had dozens of parts made that way. Might be an interesting way to start your essay."

He pushed back his chair and stood up. "Bedtime," he said. William tried to count the number of bottles on the table. Did Johnny drink like this every night?

"I'm taking the girls to one of the villages tomorrow to see some solar ovens. We want to go early and come back early; they have to travel the next day."

William waited to be asked to join them.

"Goodbye," they said, outside his hotel, "it was nice meeting you. Give our love to Montreal."

"I'll ask around about rides for you," Johnny said. "If anything turns up I'll leave a message at the hotel. Sweet dreams."

"Thank you for the evening."

"My pleasure."

Was he going back to that woman at the bar? Was that why he was in such a hurry? And I wouldn't have minded a day at a village up here. Why didn't he invite me along as well?

He hadn't realized he'd spoken aloud until the watchman stirred on his bench. His truncheon lay on the ground beside him.

"Ho?"

"Sorry," William said, "it's all right; it's only me."

He stumbled through the courtyard with its smell of bad drains and wet cement, moved past the locked kitchen and around the inside watchman who slept outside his door. From a room at the end of the corridor came the sounds of a man and a woman making love ("having sex," he thinks). Johnny said "chop" meant both "food" and "sex." Eat me.

It was weird standing there in the dark, just hearing the sounds, like someone pushing a large stone uphill, grunts and gasps and groans from the man and the woman uh—uh—uh rising aah—aah—aah—then down again uh—uh—uh then up. Waves of sound.

He carefully unlocked his door but even inside the sound carried along the corridor and through the wooden louvres. He stood just inside, with an enormous erection, listening, touching himself, then trousers off, underpants, pulling at himself until his knees buckle. The man yells Christ Jesus and William wants to yell, A-men. But the watchman on the bench does it for him.

"A-men. Praise the Lord." And goes back to sleep.

On top of the embroidered coverlet with its delicate pink-and-blue bird of paradise design (H. St. V., Made in China) William lay sweating, shaking and afraid. He had vomited so much and shit so much that his asshole burned and his ribs ached. He'd been kicked in the stomach by one demon while another shoved red pepper up his ass. It was just coming light and the first rooster had crowed. Worse still, a baby goat was crying for its mother. Maaaaah, then a wait and the mother's reply MAAAAAH. Then again the baby—the mother—the baby. The mother sounded far away, and although she always replied to her frantic baby she didn't come any closer. Maaaaah—two three four—MAAAH. Was she tethered, the mother? Was she on the menu for tonight? His head ached from fever and being sick and the animals didn't care: Cock-a-doodle-doo, Maaaah. Bicycle bells and honking lorries out on the road, men calling to each other in the courtyard, someone sweeping. What, William thought, no music? That would come soon. One of the workers' boom boxes: World Beat Beat Beat Beat, the girls who worked in the bar dancing as they polished glasses and arranged bottles.

He had had a terrible dream last night and now he knew he was never going home. He was in Calgary for some reason—it was clear in the dream, but now he couldn't remember—and he had been taken to the bus depot so that he could get a bus to Vancouver. He'd fallen asleep, knowing he had plenty of time, hours, before the bus left, but woke up with a start to see people lined up outside, tickets in their hands.

He went quickly to the ticket desk—it was a desk, not a window—and asked if that was the bus for Vancouver. The teenaged girl said no. "Will the bus for Vancouver leave at 8:30? I'd like a one-way ticket."

"There is no bus to Vancouver."

"What d'you mean, no bus to Vancouver? Of course there's a bus to Vancouver!"

She shrugged her shoulders, pulled her gum out of her mouth in a long pink string, put it back in again. "Ask your politicians," she said.

He noticed she was wearing a flat, conical hat, like a Hausa hat in shape, but white on the inside, with all the bus routes marked out with various coloured lines. To his relief he saw a red line connecting Calgary and Victoria.

"But there is a bus to Victoria?"

"Of course."

"I'd like a one-way ticket to Victoria."

"That bus is reserved."

"Well then give me a reserved ticket."

"It's reserved for natives. You will have to wait." She snapped her gum. Then he woke up sick.

The cramps seized him again and he stumbled into the small bathroom, which stank of diarrhoea and vomit. The toilet would no longer flush. No water. No water in the bucket either. No water period. And all his emergency roll of toilet paper gone. He wiped himself with the towel and saw blood. He was bleeding; he was really sick; he needed to see a doctor.

Pride kept him from leaving his room to find one of the workers at the hotel. He could hear them talking loudly to one another now. Everything boomed inside his head, which seemed to have filled up with water. When the bucket boy came he'd tell him to go for a doctor; he'd wait until then.

He lay staring at the calendar on the wall. Oxford's Dreaming Spires. May, 1982.

He'd been poisoned. Someone had poisoned him yesterday or last night. Or he'd touched something. Or the madman had cursed him. Don't laugh, he said to himself; you've heard of such things. I'm not laughing, can't you see I'm not laughing.

("William," his mother said, stripping the wet sheets from his bed, "what are we going to do with you?" She said it nicely. It was a game but not a game. He'd wet the bed again. "Throw me in the garbage?" he said.)

But he didn't come here to die. He wouldn't take this lying down. Laughing weakly at his pun. He got up, dizzy, hung onto the wardrobe—clean shorts, clean underpants (he wadded up a facecloth and stuck it in his underpants just in case), clean tee shirt: "Montréal, rue Prince Arthur."

When he bent over to fasten his sandals he nearly fainted.

So thirsty. He needed to drink something, something sweet, something to replace all those electrolytes.

He made his feet walk out of the room, down the corridor (the watchman outside his door was off duty, had gone home, ha ha, to sleep), through the courtyard, good morning, fine morning, past the sweepers, the old man at the entrance.

He swam through the early morning traffic. There was a soft mist rising, making things seem more dreamlike than they already were. A man went by on a bicycle, holding a goat by its hind legs as it lay across his front wheel, steering with the other hand. Was the kid now bleating to emptiness and silence?

He stopped to retch into some bushes.

Someone jostled him and he nearly fell over. He should flag down a taxi and go straight to a hospital but he wanted to see Johnny first, ask Johnny for advice.

Cramps again; something trickled out into the facecloth. Blood? Was this how women felt?

At the Wayfarers' Inn early customers were already eating their eggs and bread. Johnny hadn't arrived yet, the woman said. The smell of fat and the sight of food made him so nauseated he decided to wait outside. The woman gave him a mug of tea; he put spoon after spoon of sugar in it. Then took three steps out the door and fell, the mug flying out of his hand and down into the dusty red road.

"Which is where we found you a few minutes later," Johnny said, "surrounded by a lively bunch who had done nothing at all to help you because they were so busy debating among themselves about who to send for, were you alive or dead etcetera. Typical. I expect they were already looking forward to the funeral."

William had forced himself awake because a giant mosquito—one of the kind that didn't hum—was biting him in the arm. If he didn't slap it away it would suck out all his blood. He needed his blood, all of it, now that blood was coming out his ass. It didn't just tingle, it hurt. A mosquito to go in the *Guinness Book of Records*, along with the giant cockroach.

Must slap. Must *SLAP*.

"Don't do that son, I haven't a clue how to put the damn thing back in." Someone was trying to kill him. The poison hadn't worked so they'd brought in a killer mosquito. MUST SLAP. And someone being tortured in another room, a woman, screaming.

"Don't kill me," William begged. "Please."

"It's all right, lad; you'll be all right. Open your eyes."

A gentle hand on his forehead, a cool cloth.

But they did that, didn't they? Nice to you one minute and torture you the next. Now the woman was groaning and moaning. They were beating her, or worse. He had to get help. He rolled away from the voice by his side, onto the floor.

A crash in the darkness. More pain. And a voice, shouting, Nurse! Nurse! Hurry up. He's pulled the bloody thing out!

"And so there I am, finger pressed over the vein like the Little Dutch Boy and you all tangled up in the IV stand and tubes and so on. Dr. Odonkoor had just come back to deliver that baby, thank the good Lord, or I might have had to sit there all night and missed my beer. That was the second scare you gave me yesterday. I'm getting a little long in the tooth for such carryings-on."

William smiled. "My grandfather says that—'long in the tooth.'" He lay in a narrow, white-painted iron bed, under a sheet so new the creases were still in. One arm was held to a board with gauze bandages. A long needle connected to a tube dripped fluid into him drop by drop. In the far corner was a small iron crib.

"Where am I?"

"Well you're not in prison, which is what you seemed to think last night. You're in Dr. Odonkoor's clinic and you've got a regular army of expensive medicines with fancy names dripping into that arm over there. *And* you're to try and swallow a few pills now that you're *compos mentis*."

Johnny held up a handful of coloured pills and a cup of water. He held William's head up so he could swallow.

"Now try to keep those down, will you? We want you on your feet as soon as possible."

William lay back against the pillows.

"Where are the girls?"

"Gone. I took them to the lorry park this morning and they sent their love. I think the dark-haired one fancied you."

"I think they both fancied *you*."

Johnny smiled. "Yes. Well."

"There was a woman screaming—or was that a dream?"

"There was a woman having a baby, that's all. A fine boy, 8 lb. 6 oz."

"I thought she was being tortured."

"Sometimes women scream when they're having babies, mate; it hurts."

"It sounded terrible." He'd seen a few movies, of course, but it wasn't the same as really hearing it. How could they stand it?

"Didn't they give her anything?"

"This isn't the metropolis, you know. Of course the doctor has stuff he can give if necessary but this was just a normal birth. My mother had *me* on the kitchen table."

"Really? Do you have any brothers or sisters?"

"I have a sister, Hazel."

"I thought you said your father took one look at you and buggered off."

"Yes. Well he must have buggered back in again once or twice. Unless it was the dustman."

A normal birth. *Normal.* William thought of the screaming and moaning. He thought of Chantal's body, Chantal who almost looked like a boy from behind, her vagina which she liked him to explore with his fingers and tongue. It seemed such a small place for a baby's head to come through without ripping her to pieces. And she wanted children.

"My wife said they forget about it very quickly. They must do, mustn't they? Or once birth control was discovered—and it's been around for a long long time in one form or another—there'd be nothing but only children."

I'm an only child, William thought. Maybe my mother couldn't forget. Maybe it's as simple as that. They might not all forget. But she had been in Montreal—they would have had all kinds of things to give her for the pain.

"Cheer up," Johnny said. "Just be glad you're not a woman. I have to go off now that you're awake and sure to live. I'll come by later. I don't suppose there's anything you fancy eating? There's water right there on the night table and a bell. Just ring it and one of the nurses will come running. Dr. Odonkoor will be back at five to change the drip. The nurse may call it 'water' but it isn't water, believe me. The best thing you could do for yourself is sleep the rest of the day away."

"What have I got?"

"We're not sure; there's no lab. But you have a lot of the symptoms of typhoid. Who knows? There's a lot of things here don't even have names. Look sideways and you can get sick. Don't worry, Dr. Odonkoor is a good man—he'll get you better fast."

Wasn't typhoid catching? And he'd had his shot—his arm had been hot and sore all that weekend. He thought of his room at the H. St. V. The toilet, the basin, the bedclothes. If it was typhoid shouldn't they be warned so they could boil everything, take precautions?

Johnny would have seen to all that, wouldn't he? Johnny would see to everything, the Crocodile Dundee of the Upper Eastern Region. William, in his clean bed, his quiet room, the drip running into his arm, tried not to think about where he'd be if it weren't for Johnny. How did you get like that, brave and kind, practical and yet romantic (the chic jumpsuit, the stories, the very fact of his being here). William tried to imagine Johnny in another setting, in coveralls, in a garage. "There you go, mate. That'll be twenty pounds." Although he'd lived in Canada for years, William imagined him in England, manager of the World's End Garage. Or head groom, training horses. Or in paratrooper boots, jumping from an airplane. But never in a shirt and tie.

And what would anyone guess about me, he thought. Scout leader? Australian? Someone dreamy and shy, possibly good with children, young boys. Baden-Powell. The Scout handshake had something to do with Africa. Only the right hand clean in thought, word and deed.

"You look Australian," Chantal said. "One of those rangy ones—*un grand slaque*. Not the ones who wear the bathing caps."

Johnny's hand on his forehead: "It's all right son, it's all right."

He fell asleep.

William stayed at the clinic for five days. Dr. Odonkoor changed the IVs, Johnny brought him the papers, bottles of water, dry biscuits, news of the world outside his room. The staff nurse, Esther, was friendly but brisk; the practical nurse, Comfort, wanted to talk. Her preferred position seemed to be horizontal, stretched across the bottom of his bed after shoving his long legs to one side. Once he woke up to find the sheet pulled down and Comfort staring in fascination at his body.

"Stop that!"

She pulled up the sheet and smiled, not at all embarrassed. She propped herself on one arm and asked him questions. Were there really black nurses in Canada? Was it nice in Canada? Would he make arrangements for her to go there?

The Fanta lady had asked after him, Johnny said, and held up three bottles of Fanta. The people at the Wayfarers' Inn sent greetings. How fortunate he was to have fallen ill among so many good Samaritans.

After William was a little better, Johnny brought in the newspapers every night. They were a day or two late by the time they got to Bolga, but who cared.

"Did you tell me you were born in December?" he said one evening.

"Yes. December 15th."

"Here's your horoscope then: 'Sagittarius: Careless driving can prove hazardous. Don't rush out excitedly on hearing a piece of bad news. A medical checkup will prove useful.'"

They had a good laugh over that.

And one evening, the only mention of Canada in all the time he'd been in this country: at a medical conference in Montreal a doctor reported that a female patient of his, now dead of AIDS, had said she'd slept with fifty members of the NHL.

"Silly buggers," Johnny said. "*That* must have caused some interesting conversations in the changing room."

One afternoon a small delegation from the hotel appeared at his door: the old Muslim man who guarded the entranceway, the man who slept outside his door, one of the workers. The manager had sent them.

"Please, how is your body?"

He still had fever, which is why the doctor wouldn't let him go. In his dreams he went in and out of houses, up and down narrow streets, always looking for a particular place but never finding it. Sometimes he was alone and sometimes he had a companion, but when he awoke he could never remember whether s/he was female or male. Once, a signpost, black letters on fingerboards

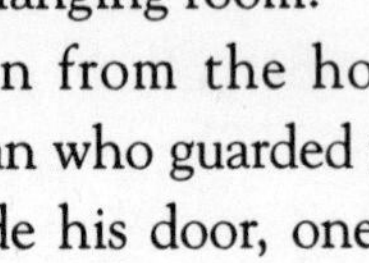

Always he woke up too soon.

The frightening thing about the dreams was that everything was red—streets, houses, clothes, skin. The only thing white he remembered were the signposts.

"Do you like it here?" Comfort said.

"Do you mean here at the clinic or here in Ghana?"

"I mean here in this country."

"Yes. Sometimes it's all a bit too strange and I don't like being sick, but yes, I like it here."

"I don't like it here. I want to go to Canada." She said most of the girls she knew were becoming Christians because Christian men only had one wife. As for Muslim men...!

The women Chantal knew, her *copines*, read Alice Walker and shuddered at the thought of genital mutilation, which still went on. Girls, children really, cut up, sewn up, torn, some in an operation whose name he couldn't remember, sewn up so tight only a thin reed was inserted, while they healed, just enough of an opening for pee and menstrual blood. In the African Muslim world, they read, the honeymoon centres were built away from the towns so the screams could not be heard.

Women did this—with rusty knives and incantations; they declared the girls were now women. What mind thought that up, hundreds of years ago. A male mind, cried Chantal and her friends, the whole purpose of such rites being, *au fond*, to make sure the women would not enjoy sexual pleasure.

"How do you know?" William asked. "Aren't you judging from your own culture?"

"I'm judging from my own *anatomy*. Some man, some king or chief, some big guy, noticed his wife or mistress was really enjoying herself so he began to worry about that—I mean, she might enjoy herself with someone else, right? So he decreed that from now on a girl's coming-of-age would be 'celebrated' in a very special way. Lucky lucky girls to be so honoured!"

"Aren't boys initiated—circumcised—in Africa?"

She didn't know; she was all worked up and didn't want to talk about boys. Anyway, male circumcision wasn't mutilation, was it?

It might be, said William, if you were twelve years old and it was done without anaesthetic, with a rusty knife.

Then a West African writer, a woman, came to read and speak at a festival. One of Chantal's gang, a journalist, asked her point-blank about female circumcision. The woman, who had been jolly and very friendly up to that point, became angry.

"You don't know what you are talking about. We who have been through this thing together, we are sisters, part of a group. Alice Walker go home; don't mess with our traditions!"

"But," said Chantal's friend, the journalist, "but...."

Here was Comfort, lying across the bottom of his bed, propped on one arm. He could ask her if it still went on up here, in Muslim country. Or he could ask Dr. Odonkoor. Why not? Chantal would have asked (but Chantal was a woman). He'd found the Koran in a drawer at the H. St. V. and had flipped through it once again, looking for any mention of such practices. Nothing.

After the wedding night was there some relief? After the screams, which must be heard by the bridegroom but not by villagers.

And women did it to other women, the old to the

young. Tribal marks he could understand, but this?

In the end he didn't ask; he couldn't think how to bring the subject up.

"Excuse me, have you had a clitoridectomy?"

On the fourth day, the day Dr. Odonkoor removed the drip, William was allowed to get up to go to the toilet. The world swam and the floor was soft and spongy under his bare feet. He had no dressing gown and he'd forgotten to ask Johnny to bring him a piece of cloth from his pack so he wrapped the top sheet around himself in case Comfort came in. He was sweating by the time he had crossed the floor to the bathroom. He couldn't stand and had to sit down to pee. (A sudden memory of his father's hand, showing him how to aim into the toilet bowl.)

There was a shower. He'd had bed baths but he longed for a shower. Folded the sheet, hung onto the wall, stepped in and turned on the tap. It came off in his hand; nothing was connected up. He nearly cried with disappointment and rang the bell for Comfort to bring a basin and cloth as soon as he was back in bed. His arm was sore.

"The shower doesn't work."

"Tsk."

"The child is not comin'."

William had awakened to running feet, screams, Auntie! Auntie!, the squeal of tires on gravel, the doctor's voice. Questions and answers but he couldn't hear what they were saying. This was far worse than the other time.

He covered his ears. (Once, on a school trip to a lumber mill, the huge scream of the saws as they sliced into the logs.) He couldn't stand it. *He* couldn't stand it? He wrapped the sheet around him and went to the door. The night nurse saw him.

"Go back to bed!"

"What's happening?"

"The child is not comin'. He is stuck."

Then the screams turned to whimpers. The doctor shouted out a command. William lay in the darkness. Was she dead? No, faint whimpering, murmurs from the nurse. And finally, headlights and more noise, men in the hall, the woman, sobbing, Auntie, Auntie. An engine starting up.

William was surprised when the doctor knocked on his door and came in, turned on the light.

"I saw you at the door. Don't worry, she'll probably be all right."

"Where has she gone?"

"To the hospital; she needs a caesarean. Only the child's hand is showing; we can't turn him, he's stuck. What makes me so angry is that I could have performed the operation, right here. I have a fully equipped theatre right next door to this room."

"Then why didn't you?" There were bloodstains all down the front of the doctor's coat; he didn't seem to notice.

"She's only eighteen, a Muslim girl. She's had three miscarriages before this and I needed parental permission. She was dropped off with an old woman, her aunt, who speaks no English and is half gaga. I couldn't—none of us could—make her understand."

"Won't the hospital have the same problem?"

"They've sent a fellow to find the father and the husband. The old lady seemed to think they had travelled. I can't cut her open without permission; the hospital can." He stood up.

"Go back to sleep; she'll be all right. I hope so. I just thought you should know what's gone on." He paused by the door. And came back.

"But it makes me so angry just the same. It shouldn't happen."

"How do they bear it?" William whispered.

"Oh the ladies are the strong ones, make no mistake!"

He lay awake the rest of the night, trying to write a letter to his grandfather but it was no good. Once, his mother said, when he was very very small, he was angry about something, brought in a sheet of white paper and drew black scribbles all over it, walked out. "A picture being worth a thousand words," she said, "I understood."

What colour would describe terror, the terror of that girl, alone on a stretcher except for the old aunt, the child's small fist sticking out of her, racing through the hot night to the hospital? Where *was* the hospital? How far away? Baby, don't die; don't die, Baby.

Red streamers for the screaming, and orange and yellow—and black for anger and despair. Then tear the paper into jagged pieces.

Comfort had told him the doctor did not believe in abortion and would not do it, but he was the best and kindest doctor in the district. There were certain herbs you could get in the market, and a certain root you could push up inside yourself. When it didn't work, when the women were infected, then they came to him; then he had to help them.

Chantal had had an abortion when she was nineteen; she spoke of it only once.

"Why do you look so shocked, William? These things happen. It wasn't an easy decision and it wasn't a pleasant experience I assure you. Anybody who thinks it's just stick your legs in the air my dear and phfft, phfft, thank you you can go now is very much mistaken."

"Who was the father?" He hadn't meant to say it out loud.

"There was no *father*; there was no *baby*. There was sperm and an egg and an eight-week foetus. It was not a good time in my life and I should never have mentioned it."

"But you did."

(They had been talking about Chantal Daigle who had run away because her boyfriend decided he wanted her to have the baby.)

All the next week she didn't phone him or throw pebbles up at his window—Come down, come down—and he thought he had lost her. He left messages on her machine, Chantal I am sorry I will never mention it again. Chantal there is a film at the Faubourg you might like to see. Chantal I am going skating would you like to meet me.

And then, one day, there she was, taking his arm as he crossed the street.

"Let me tell you a joke," she said as they waited for the light. "A Québecoise has a friend come up from New York, a friend who has never been in Montreal before. She picks him up at the railway station and outside they stand on a street corner waiting for the Walk signal. Finally it changes to green, 'Allez.' As her friend steps off the curb she pulls him back. 'No, no,' she says, 'that's only for the French people.'"

William looked at her, puzzled. What did that joke have to do with anything?

"Well maybe there should be some sort of signals for men and women, William, 'Allez,' 'Arrêtez.' When we talk, when we are in a painful discussion."

She began to cry and shy William no longer cared that he was in public, on a crowded street. He kissed her and kissed her and spoke into her hair—"It's all right, it's all right, I love you."

The next day at noon Johnny came to get him in the Range-Rover. The doctor had stuck his head around the door at breakfast time—"All well. Mother and son resting comfortably and you are all well also. You can go home at noon."

"You're coming to my place for a few days," Johnny said. "You're too weak to be on your own."

"Are my things all right at the hotel? I owe them money."

"Yes, yes. It's all arranged, hop in."

There were two new visitors in the guest room, two Englishmen working on a radio project about hygiene and water. William was to have Johnny's bed; he was quite happy on the sofa. It won't be the first time, he said. Put your feet up and we'll talk about Wa tomorrow.

At suppertime Johnny made a curry—"not for you, me lad, you're having soft-boiled egg and toast"—and the four of them sat at a rickety table. Something was wrong with one of the tape recorders; they needed Johnny to look at it.

"I should have known this wasn't a social call," Johnny said and winked at William. William began to think that Johnny's kindness wasn't really "personal"; if he was presented with a problem, whether the problem was a broken tape recorder or what to have for dinner, a bellows that took two men to operate it when one would do, a sick friend, someone needing a place to stay, he wanted to solve the thing and get on with life. He really was what he claimed to be, a "practical man."

William could hear the three men laughing and talking far into the night. He couldn't decide if he felt left out or comforted by the sound of their voices in the other room. He was glad no women were staying at Johnny's just now. He didn't want to think about women, what they went through. What was Nature thinking of, to make them suffer like that? They knew about it—what it would be like—from their mothers, sisters, friends, and still they wanted it. "They forget," Johnny's wife had told him. Surely there must have been a better way? Hens, turtles, fish—look at them. Only mammals suffered so, and women most of all. The Bible explained it with a curse but the Bible—the Bible was written by men.

The next day Johnny told him he couldn't go on, on his own; he was too weak. William was relieved. Johnny was going to take time off and go with him. But no. He would find him a ride with someone going that way. Meanwhile he was free to stay as long as he liked, get his strength back. Just say the word when he was ready.

The Chairman (Provisional) of the PNDP, Jerry John Rawlings, was coming to visit the north. Strictly P.R., Johnny said. William remembered seeing Rawlings on the TV in a soft blue suit, talking about the future of the country, pointing out at his unseen audience, "I need You and You and You and You." Johnny said no doubt there would be a big reception and some of the chiefs would come in on horseback, which was always quite a sight. It might be worth hanging around to see.

"I've seen him—Rawlings," William said and tells Johnny about Mandela.

"God. Yes. Twenty-seven years. I'd go mad. Wonder what he thinks of this sad place."

"He made a strange remark during some banquet he was at. Said the best thing Rawlings has done is keep the memory of Nkrumah alive. That's a bit of a put-down, isn't it?"

"I suppose he means that Nkrumah was the first one to think of Africa as a whole, a sort of United States of Africa. Fat chance. In some ways things in Africa are probably worse now than when he was locked up. Most of the leaders now are savages or wankers."

"Rawlings too?"

"No. Not him. He's all right but there's a lot of people hate his guts. We'll see."

In the end, William decided not to stay. Not even to see the chiefs and the decorated horses. Now that he had been ill he felt more useless than ever. Purged of something yes, but insubstantial, a ghost. Johnny called in a favour and arranged for a ride to Wa. A few mornings later they stood together outside his house, waiting for the friend of a friend of a friend.

"Here he comes now," Johnny said. "Are you sure you've got enough water?" He hummed a few bars of "The Long and Winding Road."

"I owe you a great deal."

"Nonsense. I've enjoyed it. Your time will come. Who knows, if they won't renew my contract I might end up on *your* doorstep."

"Any time."

"Drop me a line and let me know how you get on. And if you hear of anyone coming this way, tell them to bring some tonic, lots of it, as much as they can carry and I'll pay them back. The whole bloody town appears to be out of tonic water."

"I'll think of you jumping up and down at the New Year's Gala."

"Wouldn't miss it for the world."

"Goodbye."

"Safe journey." He was still standing there when William looked back.

William, bumping over potholes in the dusty road to Wa, imagines the witty letters he will send to Johnny (and Camel Lights and cases of tonic). Imagines Johnny showing up on his doorstep. His parents' faces.

Only he didn't live at home any more; he was only a visitor. Chantal would like Johnny. She'd probably fall for him.

Why was he going to Wa (Wa-Wa)? Why not find an excuse to stay in Bolgatanga.

He thought about his watercolour block, the splashes of colour, the notes underneath. The grey and white of the guinea fowl held up by a boy in the market. The orange glow, at dawn, of bread baking in clay ovens. The slash fires. The black-and-white cattle as thin as in Joseph's dream.

Several splashes of various browns and yellow-browns, unlabelled. The colour of his sick shit, his vomit.

Fever dreams as red and hot as pepper.

Termite hills
Soldier ants
Rags
Market cloth

The pale purple skin of onions, the deep black-purple of the eggplants they called Black Beauties.

He felt boneless, weightless. Beauty had passed through him as well as foulness and disease. Remember that. He slept.

The education director was a woman in a stylish dress, long skirt and peplum blouse. He knew it was stylish from Chantal, from Abidjan, from the signboards he'd seen in front of the dressmakers' shops. Peplums were "in." She wore dangling earrings and smiled broadly at him as he came into the office. Mrs. Ibrahim. "Please call me Mary." William had given up trying to guess ages. It worried him that he was going to tell her lies.

A man in khaki shorts and a torn singlet was just leaving, a sheaf of papers in his hand.

She smiled again. "Always delegate if the affair is trivial; come in. Welcome."

A large blackboard covered one wall; enrollment figures for each school in the Upper Western Region.

He sat at a desk across from her and said he was a graduate student (true) in Education (untrue) and was doing research into rural schools, important schools right away from the big urban centres, especially but not exclusively girls' schools. The Department of Women's Studies at his university was helping in a small way to fund his trip.

"Wa is hardly an urban centre," she said, "we've just got our second taxi; but it is a very interesting place nevertheless. You must see the Wa Naa's Palace and perhaps visit a Muslim school. Let me think."

"I've heard of a place called St. Clare's," he offered.

"A good place to start! The very thing! I went to St. Clare's for a while, before I was sent abroad, and my mother was in one of the very first classes. I loved St. Clare's."

"Would you tell me a little bit about your life there?"

"It was a long time ago. Things have changed."

"I'd be interested just the same—as background."

They moved to more comfortable chairs and coffee was ordered.

"Did you know St. Clare's was started by Canadian priests? Oh yes, and one of the fathers is still alive; he lives outside Montreal.

"If it hadn't been for him I might not be here today! But I think I should begin with the story of my mother. My mother is also very much alive, very old but still taking a lively interest in everybody's affairs. Well, when she was a young girl, twelve or thirteen, her parents married her off to one of the most powerful chiefs in the district, a very big chief with lots of horses and cattle, lots of subchiefs under him, a man, as you might imagine, who was used to being obeyed.

"My mother was already connected to the mission at Jirapa—she was a catechumen. Do you know what that is?"

"I'm afraid I don't."

"Well, let us just say she was taking instruction to become baptized into the Catholic Church. Now this chief was not only seventy years old—and she was a young girl, a young girl with a mind of her own—but he also had several wives, which was against the teachings of the Church. The mission had let it be known that a woman who was being forced to marry against her will could take shelter there until things were sorted out.

"So there, one September morning, just before dawn, we see my mother running along a forest path and towards the mission. She has spent all night in the bush and now is out of breath, running as though her life depended upon it. She saw the priests as they were setting out for church, called to them and collapsed at their feet.

"The priests took her in and she joined several others who had fled from similar situations.

"Needless to say this old man came galloping up very shortly, with all his retinue, and demanded that his prize be given back. The priests said no—there must be a hearing. They contacted an even bigger chief and at the hearing my mother pleaded her own case. She wanted to be baptized into the Christian Church. Christians could only have one wife. Finish! One time! My mother was no shrinking violet.

"But the big chief stuck by the other chief. Women did not have the right to decide how they should live their lives. They were property. My mother declared that she was not a cow or goat to be traded and she would not go with this old man.

"They tried to drag her away but the wonderful father stepped in front of her and they backed down. Temporarily."

She stopped talking and sipped at her coffee.

"Go on," William said, "don't stop there."

"Well, the priest went to the D.C., but he didn't want any trouble so he sided with the chiefs. Went on about moving too quickly; why, English women had only recently got the vote and so on and so forth.

"The priest became very angry and said, 'Very well, you can take the girl—truss her up, for she won't go any other way, and deliver her to this man.' Of course the District Commissioner wouldn't do that and so my mother was saved. Later on she married a Christian and had children; I'm one of them.

"In those days the men believed that women were stupid creatures. When the Franciscans opened their primary school for girls in 1940 people came just to see them read and write, things they thought only males were capable of doing! Times have changed quite a bit since then."

"When was St. Clare's opened?"

"In 1959. This was always a secondary school, by the way. And of course more battles had to be fought. Only twelve students the first year—like the Apostles! But gradually people came round and now it is the most famous girls' school in the country. Girls come from all over—other countries even. We are very proud of St. Clare's."

William tried not to sound too eager. Took up his coffee cup and set it down.

"You'd like some more coffee?"

"No, thanks, that was lovely. I've been quite ill with some bug so the caffeine really hits me." A pause. "When were you at St. Clare's?"

"As soon as I was old enough my mother sent me off. I loved it. You know, another thing the men of those times believed was that only men were intelligent enough to do tailoring. And those blessed nuns came along and taught us how to knit! I became addicted to knitting, we all did. We knit in the dark—we must have sounded like a lot of small beetles clicking away. We knit as we walked along and talked. One night I fell into a drain because I was knitting and not looking where I was going. I nearly broke my leg."

"Where did the wool come from?"

"The sisters got piles of old sweaters from somewhere, which they unpicked, and people sent us balls of wool from abroad. Those sisters were very good at getting what they needed. Then they took our knitted things and sold them somewhere; we knit scarves and tea cosies at first but then we graduated to matinée coats and caps for babies. I became a champion knitter. It got me a lot of boyfriends when I was in Boston. I even learned to knit socks."

"You were in Boston?"

"Oh yes. I went to Winneba Teacher Training College on the coast and then I went to Boston on a scholarship. I have an MBA *and* I know how to ice-skate."

William was astonished, but why? Her mother's daughter.

"Yet you came back here."

She smiled. "I was always cold in Boston. And—well, I owed something to my mother. And to education here. You know, we were so eager to learn. It was like flying! We were so eager to study we tried to read by the light of the moon. We finally got a generator, which was on for just two hours a day, one hour in the morning, one hour at night. We got up in the dark, dressed in the dark and were in the classroom, books open, sitting in the dark, waiting for the sound of the generator. We didn't want to waste a moment of that precious light."

It was his recent illness that made William blink back tears.

"Were there any foreign teachers at your school?"

"Some of the nuns. One was Filipino, Sister Navidad—she is still alive—and one was French Canadian, with a man's name, I can't remember. She went back to Quebec, I think, a long time ago. But if you mean all the young people who came out later, with the Peace Corps and VSO and COW, no. There was one at Winneba, later on, I remember. Dave something. He played the trumpet." She went back to the desk and scribbled something on a piece of paper. "This is a note to the headmistress; she was in my year. I'm sure she can help you.

"It's best to go out there early and go by taxi. You'd better book today as there's only two. I'd give you my car and driver but tomorrow I'm off to a meeting in Tamale."

She shook his hand. "One of our forest spirits has red hair. Mothers use him as a bogeyman sometimes. He sits on a branch and each of his feet has a long spike on the end so he can skewer his victims as they pass beneath the tree. Worse still, his feet are on backwards, so you can't tell if he's coming or going. If a child cries when he sees you don't be alarmed; he may think you are Sasabonsan."

"Babies do cry sometimes—when they see me. I thought it was because I was white."

"That too."

They stood smiling at one another.

"Look," William said, "would you have dinner with me tonight—if you're free?"

"Ah, but I'm not free. I have two daughters to go home

and see to, and my old mother. I will be away four days and I must prepare for that as well. But thank you."

"How old are your daughters?"

"Ten and eight. My son, who is away at Legon, calls them 'the rats.' When he writes a letter he says, give my regards to the rats. I tell him God has been very good to me, to give me only one son."

Before he left Bolgatanga William had discovered three more pencils and a maple-leaf peel-off decal in the bottom of his pack, wrapped up in the Ace bandage. Was she too sophisticated to be offered any of this, even for her children? He hesitated, then took out two pencils and the decal. "Do you think your children would like these? I wish I had something for you."

"They would love them. Peter can put the decal on his motorbike. Thank you."

"Is there anything I can send you?"

"Well, let me think. Yes. Some maple sugar. Ghanaians like sweet things, as no doubt you have found out already. I became quite passionate about maple sugar."

A couple in their best clothes, with an uneasy teenager between them, stood up as she came out of her office. ("My driver can at least take you back to the hotel.") She smiled at them, held the door open wide, "Please come in, I'm sorry to keep you waiting."

Police checkpoints on the road to Jirapa. Corrals (kraals? he thought, same word?), circular, like crowns of thorns, the cattle variations on a theme of black and white. The taxi-man, whose name was Francis, came to a halt about fifteen minutes into the trip; the muffler had come loose. Johnny said, "to say a taxi is roadworthy simply means that it moves." William could see the red road through the missing floorboards.

White storks. White lilies on lily pads. A long line of women and children with buckets on their heads, heading for the river. Vultures circling in the bleached blue sky. Now that the dry season had begun it was cooler in the evenings and the mornings; he thought of Indian summer back home: "Season of mists and mellow fruitfulness."

Francis raised the car with a jack as rusty as the road, tied the muffler back on with a piece of red string. William's offers to help were waved away with a grin. It was very noisy after that, but it was noisy anyway; loose stones hitting the bottom of the car sounded like broken glass. This time, William had a seat belt but nothing to fasten it to. He'd asked Francis would he mind turning off the tape. Francis didn't mind but was obviously surprised. Who wouldn't want to listen to King Sunny Adé at full blast?

"You don't like African music?"

"I like it very much, but I'd just like quiet for a while."

Solitary trees sticking up out of the savannah. In Kumasi everything was lush and green: "The garden city of West Africa." What a different landscape it was up here, closer to the desert. William, being a Canadian, had always thought of "north" as "cold." He smiled to himself. How our geography shapes us.

Mounds for yam plantings and maize, little cones of red earth. Huge termite hills, taller than a man.

A group of women with white enamel pans, bending over from the waist, legs straight as long-legged birds, washing clothes and gossiping.

Round houses with thatched roofs, familiar from the *National Geographic*, from that long-ago Sunday School class (special envelopes for missionary work). Bare-breasted women as well, also like the *National Geographic*. Never any bare-breasted white women shown. White women bared their breasts only for their doctors and lawfully wedded husbands.

Naked children.

"Francis, do you think you could slow down?"

The taxi honked whenever it passed anything with ears to hear. They all did it, rather like dogs barking or geese honking. Watch out! Look at me.

(Mrs. Ibrahim's driver had taken William to Francis's house.

"How much will you charge to take me to St. Clare's Secondary School, near Jirapa?"

"How much will you offer me?")

Men sitting under a tree.

The night before William sat and wrote letters in a large, thatched-roof gazebo until he couldn't see the words. There was a bar at one end but he didn't trust himself to drink anything alcoholic just yet and he couldn't face Fanta. In the restaurant he ordered yam chips and rice and chicken. Please, no pepper. Bland, restorative food. A group of men in white shirts sat together at a round table, eating plates of stew. Lots of loud laughter and beer.

Finished with his meal, William wandered next door to a building that said VIDEO CLUB! What would it be this time? *Terminator? Escape from P.O.W. Camp?* If he didn't like it he'd just go to bed, lie awake and think about the morning.

He opened the door and went in; he'd seen a man on the roof adjusting an antenna, calling down to someone inside. The man inside was fiddling with the dials of a brand-new television set and VCR.

"Not operational!" the man said. "Not exactly shipshape tonight."

"Can I help?"

He tried, the men tried. The problem was the antenna; it wasn't quite right. All that they got was snow and once, just for an instant, a woman's face appeared, said something (but there was no sound), like something out of a seance.

"I think we've got it—almost," William said, but he was wrong.

The men from the restaurant came in and sat down.

"Tomorrow night," said the inside man, who turned out to be the assistant manager. "Fully operational." The travellers were in an argumentative mood. William admired the brave smile of the assistant manager, who wanted so desperately to bring the mysterious lady back again.

The men said something in dialect, then got up and left.

"I'm sorry," William said. "I guess I don't know much more than how to turn them on."

The other man came down from the roof.

"Do you have much TV in Canada?"

"Oh yes. Much."

The assistant manager looked wistful.

"Excellent reception?"

"No. Not everywhere." William tried to explain a satellite dish. Johnny, where are you now that we need you?

He went to his room and got ready for bed. Lots of water, at least. The soap said UX. Realized he hadn't really been alone in days. Picked up a book Johnny had traded with him, a murder mystery one of his guests had left behind: Ruth Rendell. Not his favourite—her obsession with obsession made him uneasy. Whose side was she on?

Francis parked his taxi in the shade and told William to honk three times when he was ready to leave. They had come tearing up the broad drive and arrived in a great cloud of dust. William was glad he had the note from Mary Ibrahim in his pocket. There were girls everywhere, girls sitting on benches under the shade trees, girls walking towards various rooms in the long, low building that must be the classroom block. Presumably the headmistress had her office there.

Some of the girls watched him walk across the compound; some ignored him completely. Perhaps they thought he was a priest without his robes. He knocked on the door that said "Mrs. Johnson." A teacher stuck her head out. "Yes. What do you want?"

"I'd like to see Mrs. Johnson if she's not busy."

"She's very busy."

"Tell her I've come all the way from Canada. Tell her I have a note from Mrs. Ibrahim with me and I'd very much like to see her."

The door was shut in his face and voices were raised inside. Or one voice, answered by a deep, bubbling laugh.

The teacher opened the door and pushed past him. "She says to go in."

William was embarrassed. Obviously something was going on. But a kind-looking woman (she looked much older than Mary Ibrahim; were they really at school together?) stood up, smiling. "Come, Come, Come."

"I'm terribly sorry if I've interrupted something."

"Not at all. Veronica was in the midst of telling me all her troubles, but she should be teaching now anyway. You have a note from my friend?"

William handed it over. He was so nervous he could hardly speak. And to tell more lies. He was not religious, not at all, but this was a Catholic school. Some residual fear made him hesitate.

"I'm a graduate student at a university in Canada," he said, "and I've begun a study of famous schools in anglophone West Africa. Most of them seem to have been started by the missionaries...." (Who else would start them, you fool?) The palms of his hands were sweating. The round-faced Pope looked down on him from one wall—hadn't he been an actor at one point himself?—a man who must obviously be the founding Father from the other.

Bless me Father for I have sinned. Isn't that what they said?

Half an hour later he saw his parents in the Anniversary Album. Just at the corner of a black and white snapshot, smiling directly at him. The nuns in their white habits lined up behind what must be the graduating class.

"You have male teachers here?"

"From time to time. Mr. Odai is teaching English literature for us at the moment. He is excellent. Perhaps you would like to sit in on his class this afternoon? They are reading *Titus Andronicus*. Not what I would have chosen, but.... But it's not like the old days, when everything we read was from Europe or elsewhere. Now Chinua Achebe is on the curriculum, Wole Soyinka, Ama Ata Aidoo. And the history books begin to tell our story. We have truly come a long way."

"Do you ever get any of the young volunteers—VSO, Peace Corps, COW?"

"Not for a long time. Not since I have been here." She paused. "We did, once upon a time. Perhaps it was not a success. Besides, we have our own trained teachers now, as well as national service—one year if you complete elementary education, two if you pass your 'O' levels. I'm not sure it's a good idea—teaching as national service I mean, not national service itself. Teaching is hard work, just as hard as working in the fields. Just as many stones. Just as much dry earth. Young people choose it as their national service because they think it will be a—what would you say?—a *cushy* job. They are bad, lazy teachers, just putting in time. Why? Would you like to teach here?"

"I'm going into educational theory actually. And I'll probably be teaching teachers at some point, not teaching in a school." (More lies. Did the Polish Pope frown, just for a second?)

He was shown around the grounds and then he took her picture underneath a baobab tree. Promised to send it to her. She was so nice. Why hadn't he told her the truth? Speak now or forever....

"Mrs. Johnson, did you ever hear of a Canadian couple who taught at this school, in the late sixties? There was some trouble, I think. When I was in Tamale someone mentioned it—because I was Canadian, I guess." His voice trailed off as she changed, right before his eyes, into one of the masks along the hall between his bedroom and the toilet.

"That is something," she said, "that I know nothing about." She turned away.

"Safe journey."

He wanted to run after her. Please, oh please, but knew he had been dismissed finally and forever. He'd come all this way for nothing. He had been conceived here (maybe), almost born here, lived here until he was five months old. Then something happened and now he would never know what.

Because he was a liar, liar, liar.

They had passed an enormous statue of St. Clare, holding out her hands, as they drove in. He'd go along with his camera and take a picture of it while he thought what to do next. There were only two pictures left on this roll. He'd take one of the compound—as much as he could fit in—and one of the saint. Maybe if he showed them the photos when he went home he could trick them into confession.

No. Enough tricks, William. Tricks get you nowhere. Just take your pictures and go away.

The rains had not been kind to St. Clare. The paint on her brown robe had flaked off in places, making her look ragged, more like Cinderella than St. Clare. But her arms remained outstretched in blessing and her smile was kind. She was Francis's friend, he knew that, "Sister Moon," but what had she done to deserve sainthood?

He stepped back, took out his light meter and began to adjust his lens. All the girls seemed to be back in their classrooms—there was a low hum from that direction. Otherwise the place was completely still. No wind, no birds, not even a distant taxi horn. "A still moment, before God." Where had he heard that? Some story he'd read in English 100, sitting in a classroom, legs stretched out into the aisle. Something to do with a story about John James Audubon?

They were also called the Poor Clares, he knew that too. But why? There was a painting by El Greco he had seen but he couldn't call it up. Not of St. Clare, though, of St. Francis.

"Go away."

He was so startled he nearly dropped the camera. The woman who had been in the headmistress's office, the cross woman, had come up behind him.

"I beg your pardon?"

"Just go. We don't want you here."

"Why? I've done nothing to you; I just came to see the school and I'm leaving as soon as I take this picture. I'm sorry if I interrupted your conference with Mrs. Johnson, but she did invite me in." He tried to keep his voice reasonable, calm. She was so angry she was trembling, probably on the verge of a nervous breakdown. It would be hard work, teaching; he doubted if these girls were as eager to learn as they had been in Mary Ibrahim's time. He put the camera strap back around his neck in case she tried to knock it out of his hand.

"Mrs. Johnson said I could take a few pictures; I did ask permission."

Her head was shaved; she was in mourning.

And then he knew. He reached out and grabbed her arm; it trembled violently.

"I think you knew my parents. Sandy MacKenzie. Patricia."

"Let me go, I know nothing."

"I saw the way you looked at me. Sandy MacKenzie. I think you knew him."

"I know no one of that name." She struggled to free herself.

"Listen to me, please listen. Something happened here, didn't it? You were here—or you know something. Something to do with Sandy MacKenzie. Patricia. Canadians. They had a baby."

"Let go of my arm. I know of no such people." She spat at the ground.

"I was just a baby here but somehow I remember this statue, something, way back, to do with this statue."

He was down on all fours, had released her arm. The coarse grass. Laughter. Something to do with pain?

He looked up. She was walking away from him. Almost running.

"Please talk to me!"

She stopped and looked at him over her shoulder.

"Talk to the grass," she said.

He sat back. A circle of thin brown legs, laughter. He was too far gone to care.

"Yes. Could I have been crawling so early? I must have been. Or somebody set me down. I bumped my head, my nose on that enormous foot. Somebody picked me up. Mother? A nurse-girl? No. I can't remember."

He jumped up and ran after Veronica.

"Listen, if you won't tell me anything there must be somebody who will. Give me a name, a place to go."

Her hand was on the door.

"If you are the son of those people, then I am sorry for you."

"You know I'm the son. *Please.*"

She shook her head. "Go to the hospital. There is an old nun, Sister Navidad, very sick, sick too much."

He grabbed her hands.

"Thank you. Thank you so much!"

"You won't thank me—later on."

He ran towards the taxi, camera banging against his chest, found Francis asleep in the back seat, all four doors open in the vain hope of catching a breeze. Shook him awake.

"Yes boss, yes boss."

"I want to go into Jirapa itself. How far is it?"

"Three, four miles. Not far."

"I want to go to the hospital there, quickly."

"You are sick?"

"No. Just take me there, okay?"

"No problem."

"She's dying," the staff nurse said. "She really shouldn't be disturbed." But he knew there was an advantage, here, to being a Canadian. The Canadian priests were behind the building of the hospital and the church as well as St. Clare's.

"I've come from Canada," he said. "I didn't come expressly to see her, but she knew my parents a long time ago, at St. Clare's. The teachers there told me she was ill."

The nurse hesitated.

"She may not remember them, her mind wanders."

"I'd really like to see her just the same. Just for a few moments. So I can go home and tell my parents."

The nurse glanced down at the watch pinned to her bib.

"Very well. Five minutes at the outside."

"Could you leave us alone?" She nodded.

They walked down the corridor to a room at the far end. William tried to brush the grass stains from his trousers. The nurse smiled.

"She won't notice what you are wearing."

The small room was nearly dark, the louvred shutters

closed against the heat. A nun was sitting by the side of the bed and the staff nurse beckoned to her. They went out.

The old woman was just a shape under the white coverlet. A small candle in a red glass burned by her bed, the sort of candle that burned by the hundreds at St. Joseph's Oratory in Montreal. Chantal had taken him there to see the crutches and the candles and Brother André's heart. The only thing he had liked was the smell of the burning wax.

The nun had her eyes closed but her lips were moving silently. She smelled. The whole room smelled sweet, waxy, nauseating. He thought of the "odour of sanctity"; this woman had probably led a long and faithful life. Why did she have to smell of old age and incontinence and death?

He stood quietly, looking down at her. What was it like to have faith?

He shouldn't be doing this. He should just go away and leave her in peace.

"Sister," he said softly, "Sister Navidad."

She opened her eyes and saw him. He couldn't believe the voice that came from that shrunken, caved-in mouth.

"*Asesino!* Murderer! Get away from me! Get away!"

Running feet and then he was yanked out of the room while the old nun's curses followed him down the corridor.

"What did you say to her!" The staff nurse was furious.

"I didn't say anything. She thought I was...someone else. Oh God."

So that was it. But who? (The long-legged schoolgirls in their uniforms more suitable for younger girls, dresses unzipped partway down their backs. He'd seen that everywhere. But his mother was there, and later he was there. And who was now dead? A crazy old woman's exaggeration or the truth? The murder of innocence or something worse?)

Slumped on a bench in the hospital corridor, abandoned by the staff nurse, he thought about the teacher, Veronica: "You won't thank me—later."

By the time he got back to St. Clare's a security guard had been posted at the gate. The taxi was turned away.

"Where to now, boss?"

There was a decal on the glove compartment: it said Don't Get Hooked on Anything but Jesus.

The next day, before dawn, he had Francis drop him at the bus depot. The ticket-seller was the taxi-driver's "brother," so he was promised a good seat. Now he looked at his ticket. 5E. E for Empty. At St. Clare's Mrs. Johnson had taken him to the bookroom where he looked at old textbooks covered in dust. One of them had, in the back, Africanized versions of English nursery rhymes.

> Elephant Elephant
> Where have you been?
> I've been to the river to wash
>   myself clean
> Elephant Elephant what did
>   you see...?

When his turn came he mounted the steps of the bus. He felt so sick he wondered if he were falling ill again. He was glad he was sitting by the window.

He would never come back to this place, never. Let his parents keep their dirty secret, whatever horrible thing it was they'd done.

Yesterday, wandering around the town, he'd been tempted to send them a postcard; he had one of the Wa Naa's Palace that he'd stumbled across by mistake. Just two words would be enough:

I KNOW

Then never go home again. Marry Chantal and raise chickens in the country. Be a better grandson to his grandfather as he grew old. Perhaps he could come and live with them. No mention of Africa, ever again. No stories told to their children; maybe no children.

Once upon a time / *Il était une fois*.

A different thesis topic, even.

An enormously fat woman sat down to his left.

"*Desbe*." Good morning.

"*Naaa*."

She had too many parcels to fit under her feet so she directed William to share his space with her.

Everybody was in. The ticket-seller slapped the side of the bus twice, as though it were a horse, and the bus began to move. The land was covered in mist and the mist rose all around them. On one side the moon was setting; on the other the sun began its long, slow, pointless climb to the roof of the world and down again. Through the half-opened window came the sound of the first cock crowing.

Late in the afternoon they stopped at a market day outside Techiman. William stayed on the bus, but he bought some oranges out the window. The bus had gone on for perhaps five miles before he realized that the two-hundred-cedi note he'd handed down to the orange-seller had really been the one-hundred-dollar Canadian bill he'd been keeping for emergencies. Two hundred cedis, and she had given him change, one hundred fifty cedis change. He stared in disbelief. He had paid ninety-nine dollars, plus a few cents, for six oranges.

"Stop the bus," he yelled. "Please, you've got to stop the bus!"

William was in the window seat on the right-hand side, fifth row back. Next to him was the enormously fat woman who had been buying things out the window all the way along, or getting others to do it because she couldn't reach. At the moment the curved stalk of a large hand of plantain rested across William's left knee like the muzzle of a dog. Other produce left little room for his legs. In the jump seat next to the fat woman a man was sleeping with his head and arms against the back of the jump seat in front of him. The bus was full. William couldn't move; all he could do was yell.

"Please stop the bus, please!"

"Somebody want to vomit," said a voice from the back.

"Somebody wants to free himself," said another.

Without turning round, the driver called something in

a language—one of the many languages—William didn't understand. His voice was angry and dismissive. The driver's mate spoke some English, a little bit, "small-small," so William poked the woman in front and motioned her to poke the man in front of her and made signs that he was to poke the mate, who was also asleep. He came to with a start and said something in the vernacular; he too was cross. It was a long way down from Wa and they had already been travelling for hours.

The people in the first three rows began to chatter. William caught the word "'Bronie" and the driver's mate stood up from his seat and looked back sourly. He was a small man, very dark, with two tribal scars on his right cheek and a shirt that had been white when they started out. Now it was covered in streaks of red dust. Everything was covered in red dust, every thing and every one. The women wore scarves and headdresses but the men were beginning to look as though they all suffered from *kwashiorkor*, that disease that turned their hair rust-red and their skin blotchy.

"Yes?" he said. "What is the problem?"

"Back there," William said, "at the market. I gave the orange-seller a large sum of money, Canadian money—a *very* large sum—instead of a two-hundred-cedi note. They look alike. We have to go back."

The man stared at him.

"Do you understand?" William said loudly, desperate. "It was a very large sum of money. I need it. We have to go back. It was"—he did a rapid calculation—"it was like giving someone thirty-four thousand cedis for six oranges!"

The man stared at him for another few seconds and then began explaining to the driver, in a loud voice, what had happened. The passengers who could hear clicked their tongues against the roof of their mouths. Tsk, tsk. A few laughed. They began to discuss the matter amongst themselves, passing the information back to those who hadn't heard. The driver shouted out a few sentences but he didn't slow down.

"We can't go back," said the driver's mate. "Because of the flat tire we are already late. It is impossible that we go back."

"*Please*," William cried, "I'll explain to his boss. I'll pay the extra gas. I need that money."

Once again, a rapid exchange of words. Once again the passengers on the bus discussed the matter. Voices grew louder. Obviously some were for but many more were against.

"He can't go back," the mate said. "He is not allowed."

"He is not allowed to take on more passengers than he has seats for, is he?" William shouted. "He's not allowed to do that and yet he does it, you do it. I could report you for that you know."

The mate didn't bother to translate.

"He can't go back," he said.

"Then stop the bus immediately, let me off!" He stood up and banged his head.

"You want to get off?"

"I *have* to. I have to go back and get the money. It's a lot of money. I can't just let it go. STOP THE BUS!!"

The mate said something to the driver and as soon as

they rounded the next curve the driver brought the bus slowly to a stop.

Before William could get out all the people ahead of him on the right-hand side had also to get out. The two old Muslims who had been sleeping in the stairwell were woken up and told to step down. The jump seats had to be folded away so the aisle could be more or less cleared. More or less because the aisle was also crammed with sacks of yams and bags of oranges, sleeping mats, some tins of oil. The driver's mate, who also took tickets and assessed baggage fees, had had shouting matches with two women at the back; each had shoved on enormous sacks that must have weighed a hundred pounds or more. William had seen one of the relatives stagger under the weight as he lifted a sack up off his head and through a back window.

William stood by the bus door.

"I need my pack," he said.

"You want me to open the luggage container?"

"I know exactly where it is. Please."

He gave the man a hundred cedis and the man shrugged. Why not? Everyone in the front section of the bus had already piled off as they usually did, whenever the bus stopped for any reason at all. A man held a small child up to pee. Several people disappeared into the bushes. The driver remained behind his wheel, shouting and cursing. He honked the horn angrily, three times. If they wouldn't come he would leave without them.

As William walked away, his pack on his back, the mid-afternoon sun beating down on his neck, several people called after him but he didn't turn around. He knew he was being stupid and sulky; he knew they were discussing him right now, as the bus moved on towards Accra; foolish 'Bronie, silly white boy. Even if he found his money it could cost him plenty—*plenty*—to get a taxi to Kumasi where he could pick up another bus to the capital. He must be a rich boy. Or maybe no. Maybe he was rich back home but not rich here, one of the hundreds of 'Bronie students who came for a couple of years, sent by their governments. The women had dresses made of the market cloth and liked to dance at festivals; the men wore shirts of the same cloth and had hairy legs. They stayed a while and then they left. They were not important; they were all one face. They were a source of great amusement. They saw the decal Chantal had sewn on William's pack.

"Canada," they said. "Oh. Fine. Fine country."

The young ones wanted his name and address so they could write to him, be his friend. "I want to go to Canada."

The village was farther back than he had thought. By the time he reached it, he was hot and cross and tro-tros crowded the highway, everyone honking. A man walked by holding a goat by its hind legs, pushing it along like a wheelbarrow. Women with headloads were everywhere; women selling oranges were everywhere.

"ANKA! ANKA!" they called in their flat nasal voices. He looked for his orange-seller. How far along had they been? It was only as the bus was ready to pull away that he thought about buying a half-dozen oranges for later on. She had been very pretty, his orange-seller; that's why he wasn't paying enough attention to what he was doing. That and the fact that the bus was about to leave. He had been watching his own long freckled arm reach down to take the oranges from her and then reach down to hand her what he thought was a two-hundred-cedi note. Watching his long freckled arm reach out and down again, watching her young breasts under the faded green jersey, how they rose as her arm rose to meet his, and then once again as she handed up his change. He had seen her breasts rise, and her brilliant smile and had been thinking about his father, all those years ago, as well as the contrast between her life and his. That's what he had been thinking about as the bus pulled away. It was something else, some intuition, that made him unzip his money pouch and feel for the hundred-dollar bill. Had he not been, suddenly, thinking about his father all those years ago; had he not been tired and confused and burdened now with knowledge he wished he didn't have...

He couldn't find the girl. He asked everywhere. He found a schoolboy who spoke English and he went round with the boy, describing the orange-seller—young, maybe seventeen or eighteen, in a green jersey and a cloth with... what on it? William closed his eyes—of course, it was Anansi.

No one had seen her; no one knew anything about her.

"They're lying," William told the boy. "Somehow she's realized that bill was a lot of money and she's hiding. Tell them I'll offer a reward."

They went back up and down the street of stalls, of people selling yams and charcoal and chickens and goats; they asked the women selling fried chicken, selling kenkey and kelewele. They offered the reward. Nobody knew her;

nobody had seen her. The band of little children that William had thought so charming earlier in the day, the little troupe that had followed him, as children always did, laughing and pointing, 'Bronie, 'Bronie, 'Bronie, now infuriated him. They probably knew where she was as well. There would be a big feast tonight—a sheep slaughtered, palm wine drunk, everybody laughing at the stupid 'Bronie who had given the girl all that money for a few oranges. Basa basa. Crazy.

He wanted to stop and get something to drink but he was damned if he'd put one more cent, one more *pesewa*, into this village's coffers.

A taxi-driver honked and leaned out his window.

"Chief! Where is it you want to go?"

William waved him away. "Later," he said, "maybe later."

He and the schoolboy went up and down three times. They told a policeman who also went up and down. The girl had vanished. She was probably from another village, the boy said, coming for market day. Yes, said the policeman, that was probably what happened.

William gave up. He left his name and the address of the High Commission. He said to the schoolboy to write out a notice and pin it in a public place. Five hundred cedis reward. No questions asked. He would leave five hundred cedis with—with whom? Could he trust the boy, the policeman? He would leave five hundred cedis with the High Commission in Accra.

The market was crowded, overflowing with buyers and sellers, but the area of the market was not large. All of this palaver had taken less than half an hour. William was tired and hot and discouraged. Had he not just written to Chantal that these people were the most honest people he had ever seen? Ha. Double Ha.

The children followed him as he headed back towards the main road south.

'Bronie / How are you?

I'm fine / thank you.

They pointed and laughed, pointed and laughed. The sun beat hard on the back of his neck. Suddenly he bent down and his pack nearly toppled him. But he found what he was looking for, some stones. He began shouting and throwing stones.

"Do you know what would happen to kids in my country if they behaved like you? If they pointed at a foreigner and laughed and made up stupid rhymes about him?" (He threw another stone and another.) "They'd have their bottoms smacked, that's what would happen." (Another stone, another.) "They'd have their mouths washed out with soap!" (Stones. He needed to find more stones.) "Their parents might be hauled up in court as racists." (stones) "Yet I'm supposed to think you're cute." (stones, stones)

"I'm supposed to give you candy and *pesewas* and not mind being laughed at by you little brats."

The children danced out of range of the stones. Eventually, tired of the game, they turned back to the village and William went on alone. Taxis honked, offering him rides, tro-tros went by. "God's time is best," "Except God," "Psalm 100."

He shouldn't be out in the sun any longer, hatless, thirsty. But he couldn't take a ride, not yet. For to his horror and shame he was crying, bawling like a child of six or seven, the tears making white tracks in the red dust covering his face. He had thrown stones at little children. He had cursed them. How could he? Over money! All worked up over money! And his mistake, not hers.

William, walking down the highway sobbing. What was to become of him now?

Cabs honked, people called out, villagers stared. A white man, hatless, walking by himself down the highway. Will they talk about this later, speculate, make up stories? He was so thirsty he could barely swallow; his head ached; he thought of abandoning his pack as it became heavier and heavier, as though someone invisible were filling it with stones.

At the next village he would stop and ask for water. His water-bottle was still on the bloody bus. He'd like to step off the road and sit down for a while, but he had seen too many tire-flattened snakes to want to risk the tall grass.

Honk Honk Honk Honk Honk.

"Yes, I know," he muttered to the ground, "you think I'm funny."

Honk Honk Honk Honk Honk.

A large State Transport bus, coming to a stop on the other side of the road. Shouts. Cheers.

"Hey! Canada!"

They had forced the driver to come back. The driver's mate was furious.

"Get in," he said. "You have caused big trouble. Bring your pack."

One of the old Muslims had taken his empty seat; he would have to go the rest of the way to Kumasi sitting in the stairwell.

The passengers in the front row had left the bus and were spread out across the road, blocking traffic so the big bus could turn around. Then they were off again, heading south.

"Bye-bye," they called to him when the bus pulled in to the depot at Kumasi. He was tired and hungry and knew it would be better for his health if he stopped here and rested, went to Mrs. O-B's or Violet's Rest House, but he couldn't face anyone who knew him even slightly. His ticket home was from Abidjan in five days' time and he was booked through to Cape Coast on this bus, almost as far away as he could get from Wa.

And so he kept going. Not so many people on the bus now, even with the ones who got on. He got his old seat back and the mate, having forgiven him, put his pack underneath. The sun was nearly down, cooler now. There was already the smell of charcoal fires and soon the yellow glow of lanterns. He'd been travelling for over twelve hours and more hours would pass before they reached the coast. He hoped there was a bank—there must be a bank—and he hoped a hotel would trust him for the night. He was down to his last few traveller's cheques and had only enough cash for a taxi ride and maybe a brochette.

William wondered what Johnny was doing just now. Having a wash, putting on clean clothes, heading out for supper or dining in? He wanted to talk to Johnny, ask his advice. What do I do now?

(And Johnny would probably say, "So you've found out the dreadful secret. Does it make you feel better? So your father's a bastard, so what?"

"A murderer."

"I suspect she meant that—what do you call it?—metaphorically. He took advantage of one of her girls. Those old nuns were fierce. Even back home. Trying to get into the knickers of a Catholic girl was almost impossible.") It would be like Johnny to stick in that "almost." ("How does that affect *your* life? What's it got to do with *you*?")

They came back early; they didn't finish their tour. Somebody must have got him off, got him out of the country. COW must have known—and some of the other volunteers. There must have been rumours at least. A violator and a coward.

And his wife and baby went with him. My mother—who sang like an angel. Up to that point. And after that she sang no more.

The night before he lay on his bed, shaking. Perhaps the family of the murdered girl (last night he was convinced she really had been murdered—and it had to have been a girl, one of the students) would come for *him*, would have been told by now, "His son is here; take him." Dragged out of bed and into the bush, stripped naked and tied to a tree. A few cuts made in the flesh—to attract the ants. Never found.

Enquiries made: "Please, he has travelled." Would Johnny come looking for him? Would his parents come back—would they dare? Telling himself not to be ridiculous he shoved a table against the door, slept in a chair with his flashlight on his lap. Or tried to sleep.

The drumming began. Each noise from outside made his heart jump, the tips of his fingers tingle. The night whispered to him, William, they are coming, they are coming for you. The sins of the fathers. He encountered the masks in his dreams.

Too many brutal action films. Don't be stupid—it was all a long time ago.

The old nun had thought he was his father, but his father was already going bald then, wasn't he? And it was his mother who had the red hair. The teacher had recognized him too—or the family likeness. Magic. Ju-ju. Maybe not tie him to a tree, put "medicine" in his soup and make him drink it.

Had she threatened to tell? *Did* she tell? How had he killed her? With a pillow? A stone? Which girl was she, in that fuzzy old photograph; he hadn't paid much attention to the girls in the picture, too busy looking at his young mother and father grinning at the camera. Here we are in darkest Africa. Having a wonderful time.

The taxi-driver at Cape Coast had a brother who worked at a hotel near Elmina. "Very high class. You will like it." Already speeding away into the dark.

"Look, I don't have much money and I'm beat. Just take me to a hotel here in town."

"No good hotels here in town. At all."

"Really? I can't believe that." But too tired to argue he allowed himself to be driven away from Cape Coast and farther along the road.

"Please. Where you from?"

"Canada."

"China?" the driver said, but William was again asleep.

The next morning he woke up very late, took a long shower and stepped outside. He had heard the ocean last night but hadn't realized it was right in front of him, just a few yards away. The surf was incredible, huge rolls of blue-green that crashed against the sand and then were sucked back out again with a hissing sound. He could see dugout canoes way out—they must be fishing. He'd have a swim after he found something to eat.

The room he was in was really a little cottage, with a small verandah facing the sea. When he walked over to the restaurant he saw that his cottage was attached to another and that there was a whole series of these duplexes along the sea front, all painted a shocking pink, somewhere between "carnation pink" and "thistle" in his old Crayola set. The colour of coconut ice. There were coconut palms as well, twenty, twenty-five feet tall, like enormous feather dusters or exotic one-legged birds. ("William, those are palm trees, not parrots or cockatoos—palm trees are green green green.") The paths were swept and tidy and a cleaner saluted him as he went by. Not the sort of place where you'd be likely to meet the locals but not the Hilton either or Club Med. The cottages were old and rather shabby on the inside, in spite of their colourful exteriors. The water ran from the shower in a thin, grudging stream.

The dining area was large, with a two-level verandah

off a small bar and a kitchen. No one was around but a woman appeared when he knocked on the kitchen door.

"I know it's too late for breakfast but do you think I could get some toast and an egg, I'm in number 5."

She stared. Maybe she didn't speak English. But then nodded, taking out a little yellow pad, just like a waitress back home.

"Fried egg?"

"No. Boiled, if possible. And coffee if it's not too much trouble."

She shut the door.

He sat down at the edge of the verandah, on the lower level, where he could watch the sea below. Far to his right, maybe two miles away, Elmina Castle shone whitely in the sun. Johnny had said he ought to see the castles and had lent him a book, *The Castles and Forts of Ghana*, while he was recuperating in Bolga.

"Do you get down to the coast often?"

"Not very often. At Christmas time or when I feel I'm really getting bushed and can think up a reason to collect some piece of machinery from Accra. A little rest and recuperation—just to prove I've still got something down there between my legs."

Man of the world William: "Aren't you afraid of getting AIDS?"

"Of course I'm afraid of getting AIDS. I'm very careful." Then he added, "Have you ever been with a prostitute, William?"

"Never."

"I guess I should say lucky you, but it's different out

here, mate. They don't see it as morally wrong; they're not all hung up about it, about 'love,' whatever that means. They don't feel about romantic love the way we do: 'If you love me, bring money.' A very practical attitude towards such things. The sad thing isn't the prostitution—or I don't think so—but the distrust of condoms by the men. Goes against everything in their tradition. And with the economy so bad a lot of young women go to the Ivory Coast where AIDS is a *big* problem, then come back here to infect others. I don't know what the answer is—the 'white man's grave' is everybody's grave these days."

"So why don't you go home?"

"Clean water, clean girls, plenty of tonic? I should do, shouldn't I? If I don't go soon I'll be unemployable. But not yet, not just yet. Unless they kick me out."

The woman brought him a thermos of boiling water, a tin of Nescafé, some bread and butter or marge and a plate with three boiled eggs in plastic egg cups.

"Oh," William said, "I asked for one egg. And toast. Toast and one egg. Not three. You can take two of these back to the kitchen."

"The kitchen is closed."

Well, maybe he was hungry enough to eat three boiled eggs. But they were hard-boiled, too dry, so he ate one and pocketed the other two for later. He'd get some fruit in Cape Coast and more water, more nuts. He decided on Cape Coast as more likely to have a bank that would cash traveller's cheques. The office would cash them here, of course, but at who knows what rate.

Before he left for town he washed out yesterday's

clothes (pink bar of soap, "LU," but not so pink as the outside of the chalets) and draped them over the verandah wall. A strong breeze blew from the sea so he found fallen coconuts and stones, which he washed, to weigh the clothes down.

When he came back, two hours later, a young boy was sitting in the chair on the verandah.

"Mister," he said, "you not leave your things outside. Plenty thief-man. *Plenty*."

"Well, thank you for telling me."

"I been watching your things. One hour. More."

"And you'd like a dash?"

The boy nodded.

William sat down in the other chair.

"I'll get you some money in a moment. What's your name?"

"Kwame."

"That's my name, too. *I'm* Kwame. William Kwame."

"You a white man."

"I know. I'm very conscious of that fact. But I lived here once, up north, and my parents named me Kwame."

"Up north?"

"Yes. Near Wa."

He could see the boy rolling this information over in his mind. What he couldn't see, or didn't register, until the boy stood up, was that the child had only one hand.

The boy watched him.

"Somebody chop it off," he said calmly.

"Oh Kwame, I'm so sorry."

William got some money from his newly bulging daypack and came back outside.

"Thank you for minding my things."

The boy accepted the money without looking at it, shoved it in the pocket of his shorts.

"Do you have any pens?"

"Pens? Only Bic pens left, nothing fancy. Will a Bic pen do?"

"And one for my brother."

"I'm getting low on everything, Kwame, but I'll see what I can do." He found two pens—that left five—and brought them out.

"Where is your wife?" the boy said.

"I don't have a wife."

"Your girlfren'."

"I don't have a girlfriend. Not here. Back home."

"In Wa."

"Not in Wa, in Canada."

"Will you take me to Canada?"

"I can't do that."

The boy went back down to the beach, walking slowly. Soon he was joined by two other boys about his age. They broke into a run and disappeared in the direction of Elmina. William went inside and fell asleep. Everything was slightly damp to the touch. And musty smelling. But he liked the sound of the sea, the sight of the sea. That was the Atlantic Ocean out there—more or less—*his* ocean, or one of them. Soon he'd be on the other side; he'd had enough of Africa, he shouldn't have come. Beware, beware, the Bight of Benin. It was all too excessive, too confusing. What had really happened to the boy's hand? Were he and his friends planning to rob him now they knew he was alone? Chantal had a friend in New York City who was robbed five times before she gave up and moved outside, to Chappaqua. She'd had grilles put on her windows and still they got in. The police told her they figured the thieves were using small children, maybe some as young as four.

It was his left hand that was chopped off—a small mercy. William had seen the men making machetes in Kumasi market, sparks and the smell of metal as they ground them to a razor edge. He'd seen women by the roadside chop off a bunch of plantain or divide a big yam with one swift thwack. But children exaggerate, don't they? Like to tell stories? He might have been born that way. Would women shun him, later? He had a beautiful face, vaguely Spanish or Portuguese. It wouldn't be surprising if he had a great great great, many greats, grandfather who came to this coast even before Columbus discovered America. The Portuguese built Elmina; the book said the name was probably Portuguese, Costa da Mina; the coast of the goldmines.

He couldn't sleep; he'd get up and write his last letters before heading home. Would he get there before them?

He really should get up.

He slept.

William was out on the verandah trying to write a letter when Kwame came back with his friends. The boy had a bright blue flower tucked into his hair and was carrying a plastic bucket.

"Mister, you want to buy some fish?"

"No thanks, I have no place to cook them."

"Give them to the cook; he cook them."

"Do people staying here do that? Buy fish from you and give it to the cook?"

The boys nodded. The tallest one looked at William.

"He say your name is Kwame."

"That's right—one of my names. William Kwame MacKenzie."

The boys laughed. They said their names were Shadrach and Peter.

"Are these your brothers?" he asked Kwame, who had set down the bucket and was waiting patiently while all this palaver was going on. He nodded.

"Is your father a fisherman?"

"No. *His* father fishman," pointing to the tallest boy.

"But I thought you said this boy was your brother."

They all laughed.

William bought some of the small silvery fish in the bucket—they looked like sardines—then the boys went with him to the kitchen where he negotiated with the cook, who seemed to be used to such requests.

"And yam chips please, can you do that? for about half-past seven?"

He bought them each a Fanta and himself a Club beer and went back to his verandah. A car was parked in front, a black sedan covered in dust.

"Somebody come."

"It's probably for the other side." The weekend was starting and there were several cars parked outside the other chalets.

"Hello William. I've been looking for you. Nearly got in a terrible accident—when did they switch to the right-hand side of the road?"

"What are you doing here!"

"I came to see you."

"Well I don't want to see you; I have nothing to say to you, nothing." He was backing away from his mother as he spoke, shouted. Wanted to turn his back on her, run inside and slam the door.

"Well I have a few things I need to say to you."

"Need!" he shouted, "*need??* I don't give a shit about your 'needs.' Just go away."

"What did you find out up in Jirapa?"

"Enough. I saw Sister Navidad. She's in the hospital, dying. She thought I was my father. She sat up in bed and screamed at me. She called me a murderer." He turned on her, desperate: "Why didn't you stop me from coming here!"

"Oh William, listen to yourself. Nobody could stop you. You wanted to come—you wanted to find out something you could damn us with. That's what you came for, isn't it?"

William ignored this, listened to the crashing of the sea instead, refused to look her in the face. The sea was a heap of broken mirrors; it hurt his eyes.

"I'm surprised you had the nerve to come back here," he said, still squinting his eyes and looking out to sea.

"I wouldn't have," she said quietly, "except for you."

The three boys were sucking on their Fantas and watching with great interest. His mother suddenly noticed them, fished in her purse.

"Would you boys go over to the bar and bring me a gin-tonic? No ice. We'll be on the verandah of number 5. You can leave those fish here and we'll mind them."

As the boys ran off she called after them, "Wait!"

"Have you bought any of these?" she asked her son.

"Enough for one."

She called the boys back. "Take the bucket as well. Tell the cook we want another portion of the fish, a large portion, for whatever time he's cooking the first batch. I'll give you more money when you come back."

"Yes, Madame!"

"I really don't want to eat with you, Mother. I'm going to eat alone and go to bed early. I can't stop you staying here but I plan to go to Abidjan tomorrow." His toenails needed cutting; he'd do that once he got to Abidjan. Would his feet ever be really clean again?

"Look at me, William."

He raised his head. When had her hair become so streaked with grey? He felt as though he was looking at a stranger or a distant relative perhaps—the family resemblance could not be denied. He felt no warmth towards her, this middle-aged woman in a blue sundress. Just anger and a terrible desire to get rid of her, never to see her again.

"Will you listen to me for just a little while before you write me off?"

"Why should I?"

"Why shouldn't you? Couldn't we have dinner together and then, after dinner, sit on the verandah while I try and explain some things to you. Maybe I should have done it long ago. I've booked number 6 so I'll go and shower and join you in a few minutes. Here's some more money for the fish and a dash. The small one is beautiful, isn't he? I wonder how he lost his hand."

"He said a man chopped it off."

"It's possible."

He blocked her way.

"Just tell me one thing. *Is* he a murderer?"

"No. No he isn't. If anyone's a murderer, I am."

She walked across the grass and around to her door. Turned.

"Please don't go away. For my sake. Wait for me?"

"I'll wait."

The sun was completely down now, just a greenish glow in the west and the lights from the town of Elmina.

"I'd forgotten there was no twilight," she said. "Day just there and not there." She paused. "I think we should go and have dinner now and then come back. I'll talk if you want me to. Those fish won't take long."

He went to his room to put on long trousers and get a flashlight; she went to hers. He wasn't sorry they were eating first. He sensed she welcomed the darkness in order to tell him her story.

Over dinner he said to her, "How did you find me?" Then, "How can we *eat*?"

"Hunger, I guess." She ate the last of her little fish and sucked her fingers. "Johnny was pretty sure you'd turn up here."

"*Johnny*? How do you know Johnny?"

"I don't; I've only heard his voice; he called me. It was fortunate your father had gone kayaking. I was getting ready to go to Kuala Lumpur."

"Johnny called you up? I don't understand."

"He was very funny. His opening sentence was something about there being over a hundred MacKenzies, 'Mc and Mac' in the Victoria directory but at least there were only twenty Williams. He'd just started down the list and we were the fifth."

"But *why* did he call?"

"He was worried about you. Said you'd been very ill—you have been, haven't you? I can see it in your face and you've lost weight. You should get out of here; it's not a good place to recuperate. From anything. Anyway, he said he didn't want to be a nosy parker but you had gone to Wa and if you were going to find out something awful up there—I guess he said 'over there'—then maybe one of us should be here to pick up the pieces."

"He said that?"

"Yes he did. I told him I couldn't go to Wa, just couldn't. He said maybe I wouldn't have to, but for me to fly to Accra—he gave me the name of a hotel—and he'd phone me there on the thirtieth, yesterday. He had to phone from the Bolgatanga post office so it was no good me phoning him. I came in yesterday, he phoned last night, I rented a car and here I am. Barclay's Bank knew you were staying here. Johnny only traced you to the Wa–Cape Coast bus. Who is he, by the way? He sounds nice, and very concerned about you."

"He is nice; he's more than nice, he's amazing. Works for COW as well as another organization. He's a mechanical engineer." (And he did care, William thought; I wasn't just a problem to be solved.)

"How old is he?"

"Old enough to be my father."

She looked at him and shook her head.

"Shall we go back now? I'd like to take another drink with me, do you want something?"

"Just water."

He lit a mosquito coil and placed it on a small table between them. She wanted to continue sitting out.

"It all started with a mistake on a telegram."

"'Lillian' for 'William'; I know that."

"How? How do you know that?"

"It was one of your dinner-party stories. Over the years I heard bits and pieces. How you saw each other naked before you'd even said hello."

"Yes. Amazing how cruel one can be for the sake of a good story. Well, that's where *our* story started, Sandy's and mine, but of course that wasn't the beginning. I'd already been in Africa five months when that happened. We came to Africa separately; we left together, with you. Or at least we left on the same plane.

"Cheers," she said. William did not reply.

"We have this dream," his mother said, "when we are young. Of how we will be *vis-à-vis* the world. I think, for my generation at least, this was the first time that dream included as many young women as men. I suppose it's not only romantic but necessary—the eternal me me me, how am *I* going to be—and sometimes it gets things done. The Peace Corps, VSO, COW, all tapped into that dream and hundreds, thousands maybe of young people our age, Sandy's and mine, rushed to prove ourselves in the Third World. We had Kennedy; we had King; we had our own romantic image of ourselves. We had the Beatles: *Help Somebody*. We had the Golden Rule. If you don't live up to that vision, for *whatever* reason, what do you do with the rest of your life? And in my case, having been adopted by fine and caring people, perhaps I felt it more than most. I was swept up out of a social worker's arms and into the middle class. It could easily have been otherwise."

(William wants to interrupt, to say, oh Mother, Mother, I stoned some little children. *That* will stay with me for the rest of my life. But he keeps quiet; she is not the one to grant him absolution.)

She paused. The insects carried on with their wire-thin complaint; the sea rolled in with regular crashes. "Breakers," she said. "I wonder who first named them that? My mother had an ancient aunt, quite senile, in a nursing home in Kingston. She'd lived by the sea as a child and she always sang just one line of a song her mother must have taught her: 'Every little whitecap has a nightcap of its own'—the sort of song you'd sing to put a child to sleep. But there's nothing cute and comforting about this sea. There's a terrible undertow; if you swim you have to be careful."

"Get on with your story," he said.

"Yes. Well I never had any doubts about being accepted and wasn't surprised when it happened. Delighted, however, really delighted, and I couldn't wait to get going. After orientation, and after a couple of days in London and a night at an airforce base somewhere in Germany and after dropping people off along the way—it was like a big party, really, up until then—when we came to land in Accra a group of volunteers who were leaving that day held up a big hand-lettered sign against the fence: YOU'LL BE SORRY. It was a joke, of course, and we took it as such: veterans trying to scare rookies.

"Those were such different times, you know. We could take two years out of our lives, even three or four and be confident of jobs—good jobs—when we returned. I read somewhere that the Peace Corps is third after Harvard and Yale in providing members of Congress. And COW people are all over the place in Canada: Parliament, the CBC, universities, aid agencies. Not that I see any of them, but it comes out in interviews and articles and sometimes I just see a name I remember from way back then. It was a very good thing to put on your c.v.: 'served with COW in Africa'—or India, South America etcetera. Proved you had moral fibre or something. Proved you could *endure*. Very few of us actually had any marketable skills at the time; we were going out to teach (with no teacher training), to build schools and community centres, to dig latrines, to do whatever was needed. And for very little pay; we'd come home rich in experience, not rich in dollars or pounds. 'Sacrifice' is a wonderfully seductive word to the romantic young. Not that most of us did much sacrificing—some did, and a few even died, but mostly it was simply a grand adventure.

"The heat. I think the heat is a factor in all this as well. The heat is so intense and the humidity—and being so *other*, so white. It was interesting that the black Americans had problems as well. I don't remember any black Canadians or native COW people. Don't remember any Japanese or Chinese Canadians either. A lot of the American blacks were disappointed. They were seen as *American*, didn't matter how they dressed or how they wore their hair. Skin colour didn't really enter into it and that was a shock to most of them. Sometimes people laughed at their 'Afros' and they had as much trouble with the language as we did. I think young Afro-Americans were sentimental about Africa in somewhat the same way Irish-Americans are sentimental about Ireland or Canadian Scots are sentimental about Scotland, with the very important difference that they are descended from slaves. And so the politics are different. Hard to be seen as 'American' when what you want to be seen as is 'African.'"

William could hardly sit still. "What has all this to do with you?"

"I'm sorry. I've thought a lot about those years and I guess I'm trying to give you some background."

"Get to the point; if I want background there are books I can read." He was so angry his voice was shaking.

"I still have to go back, whether you like it or not, in order to go forward to what you call 'the point.'

"I was assigned to a school in Kumasi, along with a girl called Flossie French. Her real name was Margaret, but her hair had been almost white when she was a child, so she got the name Flossie—"

"Jesus Christ! What do I care how this girl got her nickname?"

Her reply came low, furious: "Sit down. This isn't *your* life, it's mine. If you want to walk away, then do it; I can't stop you. But I came all this way to tell you something and I have to do it in my own fashion. This isn't easy for me, you know."

"Poor you," he said, just loud enough for her to hear.

Even in the dark her aim was excellent. The slap came high up on his cheekbone, hard. She had never slapped him before and did not apologize. The cicadas stopped for an instant, even the noise of the sea seemed suspended, but then the water came rushing in and he heard the hissing sound as the tide pulled the water back across the sand. Somewhere near by a coconut fell with a thud.

(The silly grade three joke: What goes ha ha ha plop? A man laughing his head off.)

She continued. "Flossie and I were assigned to a big house off the ring road outside the city, a very large, very African city house with lots of rooms, polished cement floors, paint peeling on the outside, a general smell of mustiness, cockroaches in corners and drains and a big kitchen which we didn't have to worry about as we were also assigned a cook-steward, Nathaniel, who lived in a small concrete cube out back. His wife and family lived near Agogo and I think we just became two more of his children; he certainly spoiled us rotten.

"One Sunday Flossie and I were sitting under the fan, trying to decide whether we had the energy to hitchhike out to the university for a swim. 'What I'd really like,' she said, 'is an orange.'

"'But who would peel it?' I said. It was Nathaniel's day off.

"That remark really gave us pause for thought. Needless to say we never cooked on Nathaniel's day off. 'Cold chop on Sunday,' we said. He left us things or we went out and bought stuff from the stalls. We never lacked for things to eat and after a few months became quite blasé about buying off the roadside stands. Quite a change from the first day I went to Kumasi market and was afraid to try anything but a banana and a Coke.

"All in all Flossie and I got on very well, even though she was pretty ignorant about Canada and used a lot of annoying clichés: 'Up and at 'em,' 'Rise and shine,' 'Let's get the show on the road,' 'Hit the deck'—that sort of thing. But she was kind-hearted and I think we 'adjusted' a lot more quickly because we had each other. We heard stories about people who were all by themselves in remote places with no electricity, no running water. It sounded romantic but they couldn't stop talking when they came through on a visit. One guy had gone fifty miles on a moped, over a terrible road, just to smoke dope with another Canadian. Not even someone he was particularly close to, either.

"School was another matter. We taught at a large secondary school in town and the way the masters, particularly, treated the students was appalling. The girl students especially. They considered it their right to sleep with these girls and when we tried to talk to the girls about it they just gave little shrugs—this was the way it was. Since our general impression of Ghanaian women was that they knew very well how to stick up for themselves we couldn't understand it. Was this the price they had to pay for good marks? Did they even *care* about good marks? There were beatings too—both boys and girls. We went to the headmaster. He listened to us very seriously. I can still see him, leaning forward in his chair, rolling a yellow pencil between his finger and thumb.

"'Give me please,' he said, 'the names of the girls who have complained. We shall look into this, have no fear.'

"He knew he had us. The girls hadn't complained, not directly, and even if they did we would never give out their names. Who knew what reprisals would follow? We were talking, after all, to a man who took bribes to ensure the sons of local chiefs would pass the GCE. The whole school seemed to be corrupt, from top to bottom. We resolved to stick out the year but to ask for a transfer to another school, perhaps in another region, for our second year.

"Many of our visitors told us similar stories. The female teachers did the best they could, but often they were afraid to speak out in case they got the sack. And some of them believed in beatings too. It was pretty discouraging. A friend in Accra said boys at Legon University told her they didn't want an educated wife; she wouldn't know her place!

"But aside from what we were there to do—teach school—it was not an unhappy time. We loved the markets and dancing at the various hotels on the weekends, visiting and being visited, talking, talking, talking. The Cultural Centre had a pile of books from the British Council and there was the university swimming pool, care packages from Flossie's parents in Highland Park, Illinois.

"The male volunteers thought the African women were lovely—and they were—but were as shocked as we were at their attitude towards sex: very practical. They wanted presents—'ready made' dresses, not dresses from the market, radios, shoes, money. These nice American, Canadian and English boys were shocked and excited. This was pre-AIDS, of course. Not all the girls were like that, but the girls in and around Kumasi and Accra seemed to us both cynical and grasping. Not for them *The Feminine Mystique*.

"In February we heard that a third girl was going to join us, to replace someone who'd been invalided out with amoebic dysentery. Lillian. We had a telegram three days before she was due to arrive. I had to be in Mampong on arrival day and Flossie was going to be away as well—a field trip I think—but Nathaniel had promised to put flowers in her room and have her bed made up early in the day. We put copies of *Drum* magazine and some local books on the bedside table and left a pretty piece of indigo cloth for a bedspread. We wrote a note: 'Welcome to the Garden of Earthly Delights.'

"The lorry I was on broke down so I was late getting home. I was also hot and dusty and began dropping my clothes as soon as I walked in the door. I never even thought to shout 'hello' or anything and was stark naked by the time I reached the bathroom door. All I noticed was that the electricity had packed in again.

"By the light of a candle a man—very obviously a man—stood in the tub, pouring a bucket of water over his head. He had swim goggles over his eyes, duct tape over his mouth and earplugs as well, which is why I startled him as much as he startled me. I screamed and retreated. This was 'Lillian'—William—your father.

"He stayed with us because there was really nowhere else for him to stay; the local education authority didn't blink an eye. We were quite rude to him at first—he upset our balance—but after a while we got used to him. After a while we got to like him a lot. He fitted in very well, once he got over his initial squeamishness, and we had better Scrabble games, went out more on Saturday nights, stayed out later—we were with a man now, it was safer, although I can't remember ever feeling unsafe here, not really. There were some awkwardnesses of course; we didn't walk around naked any more and there were certain things we didn't discuss as fully as before, but in general our house was a happy one and Flossie and I stopped getting on each other's nerves. She still said 'Rise and shine' or 'Up and at 'em' in the mornings and still thought that America was the land of the free and the home of the brave, just like in the song. Her heart was in the right place, though, and she was very generous."

"So now Nathaniel could peel oranges for the three of you."

She laughed. "Yes. He and Sandy became great friends. The school term ran on the British system so we didn't finish until July. By that time Flossie and I both had our transfers—to the same school!—and a married COW couple was coming to take our place and live in the big house on the ring road. Sandy didn't like the school either but he felt he should stick it out because he'd come later, it was his first year and so on. I think, as a man, he was even more shocked by all the goings-on between the masters and the students, which is ironic, considering what…what happened later.

"You know, the real bonus, for me, was in the evenings; after we'd had our supper and the marking was done, we'd talk. And talk. And talk. He was thoughtful like Flossie, and although he was very nervous at first about disease, snakebite, all the usual things, he was determined to keep going. He didn't like the food and lost a lot of weight, which he could ill afford to lose but gradually he came round. He told me later that if there'd been, in those first few months, any honourable way he could have quit he would have done it.

"But he didn't leave, and we talked. Talked about all the great themes—love, marriage, war, death, talked about ourselves, about this country, how everything was so strange. We talked by kerosene lamp and candlelight. The electricity was always packing in and it was nice, anyway, talking in that soft light.

"Outside there was nothing but Africa.

"He talked about his mother, Seonaid, how she'd had a great deal of tragedy in her life, a still-born child and a child who died of meningitis at the age of six. He was the only one left and felt an enormous responsibility. I told them about my parents. He told us how he'd played the Gold Coast in a Commonwealth pageant in fourth grade: 'I am the Gold Coast. From my shores comes cocoa for your bedtime.' Dressed up in a grass skirt. Not a single black kid in his school.

"Friends visited from other places—Techiman, Tamale, Bolga, Ouagadougou—and we talked some more."

She looked up at the moon.

"Shine on, shine on Harvest Moon, up in the sky. Funny to think the same moon shines on everybody. One of the things we used to do, in those long evenings after the marking was done, was sing. All those old, corny songs we learned at camp and elementary school. 'My paddle keen and bright,' 'The Lonely Ash Grove,' 'Shine on Harvest Moon.' We'd sing in the dark; Flossie could do wonderful harmony."

"I can't remember ever hearing you sing."

"Well, I used to sing to *you* when you were inside me, lullabies, nonsense songs, wordless croons. Then, after all the trouble...it was as though my voice dried up. You don't have to have joy to sing—some of the most beautiful music sings of the most sorrowful things—but you have to have an impulse for joy. It all dried up, like the streams in the dry season. I had to get by on records and tapes and Saturday afternoon at the opera. They talk about soldiers in a war losing their nerve. Well, I lost my joy; I became witty, instead. Amusing. Not the same thing at all. I became cruel."

"To him."

"To him especially. To myself. To his lovely parents,

whom I couldn't bear to see again."

"*Why* didn't you ever see them again?"

"I was afraid, with my new cruelty, I'd tell on him, tell what he'd done. What *we'd* done. He was their only son. I owed him that much—silence."

"What *had* you done? What *did* you do?" William stood up, leaned on the sill of the verandah. "Why did that nun say you were murderers—or I was?"

"This is a story that takes a long time to tell."

"I haven't got a long time. You've spent most of the evening talking about the good times; let's get to the bad, shall we, before the moon goes down and the sun comes up. I really am not very interested in 'Shine on Harvest Moon.' I've been called a murderer by someone who is dying. It was like being cursed. Out here, you start to believe in things like curses."

"Yes. The Ashantis used to drive a knife through the cheeks of a man condemned to death so he wouldn't curse his executioners."

"Skip it. Right now I'm not interested in the customs of the Ashantis."

"I have to tell you how Sandy got up north."

"That was one of your dinner-party stories too, wasn't it? Flossie got sick and had to go home so Sandy—Father—came up as her replacement."

"Yes and no. Sandy and I fell in love—by letter, such an old-fashioned way to fall in love. Then Flossie got really sick—an ovarian cyst—and was invalided out. Sandy and I had some telephone conversations from the post office in Wa to the post office in Kumasi. I wanted him to take

Flossie's place—he'd be even better than she was, for chemistry was his specialty and they desperately needed a science teacher—but there was no way the nuns would ever let a single man and a single woman live together without marriage. We had decided to marry anyway, when Flossie and I had made the long trek down to Kumasi at Christmas; now we'd just hurry it up. I took some of my precious money and flew down to Kumasi from Bolga, then a whole crowd of us went off to Accra in a bush-taxi and Sandy and I were married by an American Methodist minister who was a friend of the High Commissioner When we arrived back in Jirapa we were man and wife and very very happy.

"I still am not sure how she managed it, but Flossie had sent a crate of champagne to the wedding and we saved one bottle for when we arrived at the school. After all that bumping and bouncing, of course it frothed and fizzed all over the place when we drew the cork. But there was still enough to drink a toast, pour a libation. 'To us,' we said, 'to the future.'"

"And the girl?"

"Grace Doulo.

"'The moon moves slowly but it crosses the town.' Have you come across that one yet? When I lived out here I used to collect the sayings; I've got a notebook full of them somewhere. 'Tell me, who is at fault; he who spread his mat across the path or he who stepped upon it.'"

"You tell me," William said. The moon made a long silver track on the sea out there in front of them.

"Grace was our pet," his mother said, "Flossie's and mine, then mine and your father's.

"The school was very strict and we didn't have a lot to do with the other teachers; all the rest were either nuns or Ghanaians. Because of this our life together was very intense and very different from our life in Kumasi. No Nathaniel, of course, but food itself was a big problem—the local diet was maize only. The nuns kept us stocked with corned beef and that was what we ate, along with yam chips and canned peaches and the occasional lovely parcel from home. Tomatoes for two weeks a year.

"There was a generator and we had electricity between 5 and 6 a.m. for mass and between 6 and 8 p.m. We used lamps and candles a lot. We read and read and read and went to bed early. There was no running water. A few times a week young girls would carry water in big pots on their heads and fill our bathtub. We would jump in and out of it several times a day to cool off in the hot season. We were very very happy. We even blotted out, after a while, the weeping of women walking back from the hospital with their dead babies in their arms. Our bungalow was very close to the road.

"There was a priest who came once a week; he was attached to the hospital at Jirapa and it was through him I became interested in speech therapy. He was a wonderful man, very jolly, who had an enormous liking for the northern tribes. He was officially an administrator but his real love was herbal medicine. He was also involved with the orphanage near the hospital. I had begun working with him before I was married and continued right up until... until we left. Grace was an orphan; the priests were paying for her education."

"How could there be orphans here? I thought these extended families took care of everybody; if your mother dies, your auntie takes you in."

"I don't know; I think those children were abandoned children. Grace had a shrivelled leg; she'd had polio when she was very young. That's all I know. She walked with a limp, a bad limp and so was left out of all those running and jumping games the girls were so fond of. But she was smart and feisty; she didn't go around feeling sorry for herself, not ever—or certainly not where anyone could see her."

"How old was she?"

"Fifteen at the time of... Fifteen. A lot of the girls were bright—they wouldn't have been there otherwise—but Grace was really bright. She turned out to have a real aptitude for chemistry and Flossie, bless her heart, back home in the U.S. and reunited with her boyfriend, sent all kinds of supplies in hollowed-out books, even once in the hollow handle of a tennis racket. The post office was very corrupt at the time and we had learned early on that you might never receive your parcel unless it looked like a book or something not too resellable. There had been a big scandal in Accra after the drains behind the post office backed up. *Hundreds* of soggy letters were discovered; the clerks had sold stamps, then offered to stick them on the letters, kept the money, put the stamps back in the drawer and sold the stamps again.

"I remember one evening when Sandy and Grace put on a 'magic' show with all their paraphernalia. It was a big hit with the girls, although the nuns weren't so sure. Magic—'ju-ju'—was already too much a part of the girls' backgrounds. But after the magic show girls flocked to his science classes so the nuns couldn't grumble too much.

"He had started wearing a hat, because he was already going bald. He wore it from morning to night and sometimes he forgot to take it off in class. Once he set it on fire, leaning over a homemade Bunsen burner. The girls loved it. Loved him. He was an inspired teacher and a really good chemist."

"And Grace was the sorcerer's apprentice."

"Yes. I guess you could say that. But she was good at most subjects: she loved poetry, for example. The set texts were all English, of course, but we gave them, as well, Langston Hughes, James Baldwin, Okot p'Bitek—*The Song of Laweno*. She gobbled it all up.

"We fantasized about her future; she was obviously destined for great things and we would help her. A scholarship to the U.S. or Great Britain or Canada; piles of books once our tour was over. Theoretically I would have to leave in another year and a half. Two tours was the maximum, give somebody else a chance; but Sandy was going to apply for a second tour and, as his wife, perhaps I'd be allowed to stay on. We'd be able to see Grace through her graduation from St. Clare's and launch her in whatever direction she wanted to go."

"Was Grace consulted in all this?"

"Oh yes. This wasn't a case of Eliza Doolittle. She knew she was smart and she wanted to go to university. She also wanted to get married and have children—she was quite open about this; and about the fact that, because her leg was weak, many men might not want her.

"'But I can sit down—in the fields I want to dig,' she'd say, with a big smile. 'I won't be messing about with yam mounds.'

"In the sixties everybody wanted to save the world, that was the dream. Give Peace a Chance. Give the poor a chance, women, blacks. And if you could do good in some exotic place so much the better. None of us seemed to be heading for the Indian reserves in our own country. I've thought a lot about that since. Missionaries go abroad, don't they? They don't go to James Bay or Lethbridge. Look at that moon. Soon it will be over the castle. Have you been there yet?"

"No."

"Perhaps we can go in the morning."

"I won't be here. Will you please get on with the story? *Please.*"

"In April of that year I got pregnant. We hadn't tried not to, hadn't given it much thought really, and discovered we were both delighted. I'd just been okayed for a second tour so we kept it quiet at first, not sure how COW would take it, but since we were legally married the nuns couldn't object, although we did have some trouble with one or two of the older ones. I guess it was hard enough preaching chastity to those girls without the growing evidence of *our* sexuality right there in the classroom. I felt terrific. Grannie and Granddad consulted doctors and sent boxes of expensive vitamins and even cod-liver oil, which Grannie swore by. The girls began knitting and crocheting little caps and jackets. My only real concession to being pregnant was that I gave up riding my moped. The roads weren't just too bumpy, they were dangerous—I see they still are. I went once a week to hospital in the Land-Rover and of course we went to Wa from time to time, but I stayed pretty close to the school compound. We decided to spend Christmas 'at home.'

"A married friend in the Peace Corps had a baby in Ibadan; she said it was wonderful and this bucked me up even more. The doctors and midwives at Jirapa already knew me and so I felt I was surrounded by one big solicitous family. What could possibly go wrong?"

William shivered. ("The child is not comin'.")

"Do you still have fever?"

"No, it's all right, go on."

"Well, some time in early December I began to get headaches and occasional blurry vision. I rested more, gave up even my one cup of Nescafé a day, tried not to go out in the afternoons at all. And then when I went for my check-up it appeared I'd had a terrific weight gain—I was such a blimp by that time I hadn't really noticed, although one of the girls in Form 4 had teased me about my 'elephant legs.' The doctor did some tests and said I had toxaemia—my blood pressure was way way up—and I'd have to be hospitalized.

"Grannie and Granddad said, 'Come home to have the baby. Don't take chances with your health, the baby's health.' At first I said no—I was out in Africa and I wanted my baby born out here. African women did it all the time and so could I. But I was frightened, I'll admit it. What if something went wrong during the birth? I wasn't so worried about myself but supposing I was jeopardizing my baby's life? The hospital at Jirapa was beautifully run but their emergency equipment for babies was minimal, to say the least. One of the things I'd never become used to was the sound of those women wailing, coming back from the hospital with dead children in their arms. And Sandy was beside himself. Apparently one of the nurses had told him 'toxaemia can mean dead babies or dead mothers.'

"So we drove to Tamale in the school Land-Rover—I think I cried the whole way—and I was put on an army plane to Accra, then a BOAC flight to Canada via London. They were giving me pills for water retention, pills for my blood pressure, pills to calm me down. All I remember of that long trip was little paper cups of water, pills and constant peeing. And a lot of tears."

"Why didn't Dad go with you? What if you'd gotten sick on the way?"

"Oh, there were doctors on the alert in Accra, at London Airport—everywhere. I was even travelling as far as London with a doctor going home on leave. He was an orthopaedic surgeon but he assured me he delivered babies when he had to."

"That still doesn't explain why Dad didn't go as well."

"I asked him not to. You see, term wasn't over and I felt I was letting the students down. I wanted him to take over my classes as well as his own and I also wanted to know he was *there*, watching over our little house, keeping it lived-in, keeping out the spiders and as many cockroaches as possible. He wanted to come; I was the one who said no.

"I was a mess by the time I got to Montreal, but Grannie put me right to bed with a hot-water bottle and an eiderdown and insisted I not be taken to hospital unless there was an emergency. She—both of them—were wonderful; they could have been my own parents, not my husband's. Remember, they'd never seen me in the flesh until I came down the steps of the airplane. And there was a lot of flesh by that stage. My borrowed coat wouldn't button, my eyes were all puffy from crying and I must have looked like something the cat dragged in. When we got to the house on Clarke Avenue Grannie had a doctor waiting, and after I had been examined gently she sat holding my hand and sort of crooning to me until I fell asleep. I was crying again and she just sat there in the dark, stroking my forehead and saying, It's all right lovey, it'll be all right." (Johnny's hand on his forehead.)

"I was treated like a queen and I felt like one. I spent most of every day in bed—doctor's orders—but I came down for supper in the evenings and sometimes Granddad would play the piano and we'd sing."

She turned and looked at him, sniffed.

"You were born just two days after your due date—Granddad called the hospital at Jirapa as soon as possible and they sent a boy on a bicycle to notify your father. I'd wanted it done that way so that he'd know first, before the nuns, and would have the fun of announcing it himself. And I was hardly downstairs before the phone rang and there he was—he'd run out to the main road and flagged down the first car—laughing and crying and me describing you, bragging, saying you had red hair like mine but you were an absolute MacKenzie. His voice seemed so far away! He *was* far away and the overseas operator kept coming on the line from London or Accra—can't remember—saying, 'Your three minutes are up, sir, do you wish to continue this call?' Later I thought about all those servicemen's wives, during wars, who had their babies alone and whose husbands were 'over there' getting shot at. I might be separated temporarily from my husband but that would soon be over and I knew where he was and that he was safe.

"I had a few minor complications and we had to wait until you could have your smallpox vaccination, so it was another two months, almost, before we could return. I was glad to be going; I was getting too used to all the pampering. If we didn't go soon I wouldn't want to go at all. Except I missed Sandy terribly. We wrote to each other every day, although the letters tended to arrive in bunches. He'd gone to Techiman for Christmas and had a good time—lots of beer and stories; there was quite a group of volunteers in Techiman and some had come up from Kumasi as well. Various gift packages had arrived and they'd managed a real Christmas dinner, soup to nuts—in that heat!—with chickens standing in for turkeys. He said he was loaded down with gifts for both you and me when he headed back up to Wa. He also said Grace had offered to help out with the baby in exchange for tutoring later on.

"Are you tired?" his mother said. "I do seem to ramble on without getting to the point. We could continue this tomorrow morning."

"No. I want you to go on. Please. Let's get to the end of the story."

"When I arrived back in triumph with you and after you'd been passed from hand to eager hand like some collective present, after the nuns had blessed you and we were actually in our own bungalow, the last of the well-wishers gone and you sound asleep in your mosquito-netted cradle—a present from the staff and made by the school carpenters—I asked Sandy where Grace was; I'd thought she was going to be a kind of nurse-girl in her time off and since I was anxious to take up my teaching again I wanted to talk to her about her schedule. She was in one of my classes and I didn't want her to think she had to miss lessons to look after you. It was very important that she pass her exams with flying colours.

"Sandy explained that she was at a nearby village—some funeral—but would be back on Monday. However, she'd decided she didn't want to be a nurse-girl, she was worried about her leg, her general strength, her marks, and so she'd opted out of that plan. He'd got another girl instead, Felicity. She was at her village but would be back soon. I made some joke about Felicity, in the end, being more useful in this life than Grace but he just looked at me. I thought maybe his nose was a bit out of joint because you'd cried when I put you in his arms.

"I said, 'I hope she understands we still want to tutor her, did you make that clear?'

"'Oh yes,' he said.

"That night he clung to me; he said, 'Promise you will never never leave me again.'

"'That's an easy promise,' I said, 'ask me something hard.'"

"Was she pretty?" William said.

"No, not particularly, not the way some Ghanaian girls

are. But she had such a lively, intelligent face and I don't think pretty entered into it."

"While you were away he seduced her, right?"

"It's not as simple as that."

"I'll bet." William stood up, angry. She was seducing him, wasn't she, with all this sweet talk about the past. But his father'd done more than seduce this girl—as if that wasn't enough!—he'd done something else.

"Why did that old nun call me a murderer? Can you get to the point? I can't stand much more of this. You go on and on and on. I can't stand it."

"Sit down. I'm nearly done.

"Grace wasn't the same towards me after I came back. It was almost as though she was afraid of me. I asked her if she wanted to hold the baby and she said no.

"'Go ahead,' I said, 'you won't drop him.' She shook her head and I accepted that. I didn't really think about it much at all—I was very busy teaching and playing with you, studying books on speech defects, writing letters to Grannie and Granddad and all our friends about what an absolute wonder you were, nothing bothered you, you slept when you were supposed to, stayed awake when you were supposed to blah blah blah. I was as boring as any new mother. And Felicity was a big, strong girl; she loved carrying you around, showing you off. The girls were constantly wrapping and unwrapping you."

"Was I ever dropped?"

"No. Why do you ask?"

"Just a strange half-memory. Banging my nose or something."

"I must have told you; you couldn't possibly remember that! You banged your nose on that big statue of St. Clare, but you weren't dropped. You'd been put down on a blanket—I can't remember why and we didn't know you'd choose that day to try to crawl. You must have moved about half a foot, put your head up like a little lizard, the way babies do, and then brought it down clunk. You had a bad nosebleed but no real damage. Of course I howled as much as you did—your first 'wound.'

"A few days later I saw Grace standing at the door of a classroom. She always stood favouring her stronger leg but when I got closer it seemed to me that there was something else about her. Whether I would have noticed if I hadn't just been pregnant myself I don't know.

"I thought, so that's why she's been acting strange, she's ashamed. At supper I mentioned it to Sandy; I thought maybe we'd invite her over and talk to her, see what could be done. Would the nuns make her drop out of school, for instance, when they found out? Did she want to marry the boy? Had she—God forbid—been *raped?* I kept on and on, tossing out ideas, should we do this, should we do that, had we any right to interfere? Then I heard a terrible sound. Sandy had his head in his hands and he was sobbing as though his heart was broken. Then he looked up and said, 'I'm such a shit, I'm such a shit, I'm such a shit.'

"I couldn't take it in. What was he talking about? That's what I actually said to him, 'Calm down and tell me what you're talking about,' and he said, 'I'm the father.' He hadn't known she was pregnant until I told him."

She took several deep breaths, as though she couldn't get enough air.

"I went berserk. Threw things, screamed at him, called him terrible names, said he had destroyed everything I held dear about him, that I wanted him to leave that very minute, just get out, I never wanted to see him again and I didn't want him as the father of my child."

"But he didn't go."

"No. You had begun to scream in sympathy and with all the noise the night watchman, thinking we were being murdered in our beds, came banging on the door, 'Madame! Madame!' So of course we had to open the door and let him see we were all right. 'No, no, perfectly all right. We thought we saw a big snake, but it wasn't so. Perfectly all right now, thanks.' And then, by the time I'd nursed you back to sleep it seemed to me that I needed to know what happened. Not so much to hear his side of the story—so far as I was concerned he didn't have one and I hadn't heard hers—but just so I'd have it on record, somewhere in my memory. I honestly felt that this was the last night we would ever spend under the same roof.

"Women always want to know *why*, William. It's not just vanity; it's that they feel so betrayed."

He wanted to say, don't you think it would be the same for a man, but he didn't want to get her off track. He felt so tired he could hardly keep his eyes open and he wanted to hear the end.

"He said that it was entirely his fault, but I expected him to say that. It didn't mean anything; it was like the opening phrase to something you'd learned long ago, like the Apostles' Creed: 'I believe in God the Father Almighty Maker of Heaven and Earth' and then you get down to the specifics. He said he'd been giving Grace extra tutoring in chemistry, with the nuns' approval. Even they had become excited by the possibilities—the possible future—for their star pupil. He went off for Christmas in Techiman feeling relieved about you and me safe in Montreal and pleased to feel that he might be making a real contribution to the future of the country as well as Grace's own.

"He said it never occurred to him to ask what she was doing for the Christmas break, but when he arrived back up north three days before the girls were due, there she was, with a couple of the other girls who came from Cape Coast and hadn't gone home for Christmas. She knocked on our door that evening—she was given a lot more freedom, in some ways, than the other girls. Whether the nuns felt she was so trustworthy she didn't need to be watched, or whether they felt, because of her limp, she wouldn't be out by the front gate flirting with taxi-drivers or whoever was passing (from time to time girls were caught doing this—the road was right there and the 'outside world' was represented by that road) or what else I don't know, but she'd asked permission to take some flowers to the bungalow and they'd given it. She knew the baby had been born and wanted to say how happy she was for us. She even had a tiny cap she'd made, all different colours, for the baby's head.

"Sandy had just finished his meal and was sitting at the table, wearing a cloth and cursing the heat. He'd been writing a letter to us and the sweat dripped down his arms and onto the paper. He was glad of Grace's interruption. I should add, I guess, that he'd been drinking a bottle of wine he'd been given as a Christmas present.

"Grace stood at the door with a flashlight, holding out the flowers and her gift, but shook her head no, she wouldn't come in. He insisted, said he'd love to have a chat with somebody besides the cockroaches and she finally agreed. She sat down at the table; he offered her wine, which she refused, and he admired the cap, said maybe she would make one for him to cover his bald spot and she laughed. But when he asked about her Christmas vacation she began to cry. It seems that her friend Veronica invited her to her village for a few days but Veronica's father and several of the men and boys treated them very badly, saying all this education-for-women business was a bad thing and he wasn't sure he was going to let his daughter go back to those ladies, those nuns. He and the others had been into the palm wine and were quite drunk. When Veronica's aunt (her mother was dead) told him to leave the girls alone he knocked her down. Veronica started screaming at him that he was a dirty, ignorant old man and then Veronica was knocked down. 'And I'd knock you down as well,' he said to Grace, 'if you were my child.'

"'Ho!' said one of the uncles, 'you would not want a child like that, that twig-leg, even to knock down.'

"They left in the middle of the night and Veronica vowed she would never go back to her village. She said she was going to stay with the nuns forever.

"Sandy said that as Grace wept he began to realize things—how these girls lived in two worlds, the world of

St. Clare's and the world of their village and although this might not be true for the wealthier girls from the big towns, parents in the villages might see education as an enemy, especially the education of girls. In one way, ironically, Grace had been spared that kind of conflict because she'd grown up in the orphanage and the nuns and priests had encouraged her from a very early age. She was shocked by the way this father had treated his daughter, her best friend. And by the way the other women, even the auntie/mother, who had encouraged Veronica to sit for the scholarship exam, bundled them off in the middle of the night, before there could be 'big trouble.'

"He said he probably fell in love with Grace that night. Men, especially men like Sandy—romantics—are a sucker for vulnerability. It beats big tits or dancer's legs every time."

"And she fell in love with her teacher?"

"I think she began to see him as her saviour. Me too, of course, but I wasn't back yet. She asked the nuns if it would be all right if she prepared an evening meal for Sandy in the school kitchen and took it over to him each day. Exactly when they first 'did it'—isn't that what kids say, when they are too young to actually come right out and say what 'it' is?—I don't know."

"Are you saying she seduced *him*?"

"Not consciously, I don't think so. Seduction is such a *Western* concept, somehow; it has such moral weight. She may have thought of it as making him happy; she may not have thought at all. She was *fifteen*, William, old enough to marry certainly but she'd lived in a sheltered environment all her life. She wasn't fifteen the way the girls outside were fifteen."

"Whatever it was, Dad could have stopped it."

"Exactly. He could have stopped it and he didn't. He fell in love with her, but after they had been together a few times her sense of sin and his sense of guilt got in the way. She said she couldn't 'visit' any more and he agreed. He assured her that it would make no difference in our hopes and plans for her and now they must both get on with their lives. We must all get on with our lives."

She stood up, sat down again.

"I've thought about all this for such a long time. He'd come back from the great Techiman Christmas party to his empty bungalow, not even school to distract him. Eating alone, worrying about us—when we would be back. Nobody much to talk to and the harmattan blowing so much dust around it was no fun going anywhere on the moped. Dust in your clothes, dust between your teeth, even. Maybe a lot of his original fears returned when he came back there alone."

"Get on with the story."

"He was a virgin when I met him. I suppose that sounds strange to you now—these days—but he was. And then, well, sex can become a kind of drug; if you are having sex regularly and you're young and healthy and it's suddenly taken away… But not with a student! It was worse than if he'd slept with one of the other volunteers. He said the first time he fell asleep and then woke up in the middle of the night, alone, he thought he'd been with me, in a dream, that none of this was real."

"Oh come on!" He turned on her. "I don't think I want to hear any more."

"Don't you want to know why we are murderers?"

"Forget it. You persuaded her to have an abortion and she did and she died. I think it's way past my bedtime."

"That's not exactly what happened. Please sit down, William, I've come all this way."

"I'm not a priest."

"I know that, but you're my son. I want you to know."

He sat down again. His chair made a harsh, raspy sound on the concrete of the verandah.

"The night after he told me all this he said he'd been in agony all day and had come to a decision. He felt he should help her, perhaps even marry her."

"'But you're married to me!' I said.

"'You're strong; you've got everything; she's got nothing.' He wanted to do the honourable thing."

"To make up for the dishonourable thing."

"Yes."

"And leave you, to go and live with Grace and her baby."

"I think that was the idea. Anyway, I went to find Grace that evening, after you were asleep. I told Sandy I needed to go for a walk, so I took the flashlight and waited for her outside the chapel. People knew we were special friends with Grace so no one thought it odd when I asked if I could 'borrow' Grace for a little while to help me with a project.

"I took her to one of the classrooms and asked her if she were pregnant. She said yes. I asked if Sandy was the father and she said yes. Her story was virtually the same as Sandy's except she said, 'I wanted to thank him.' So it wasn't 'seduction' on either side. Or so they said.

"And she said, 'Please, Missus MacKenzie, don't beat me.'

"I told her that it was Sandy who was to blame; he shouldn't have allowed it to happen; he violated a sacred trust. I told her she might not see it that way but I did. I asked if she wanted to have the baby; she hung her head and said no. It was ironic—thanks to all our encouragement she wanted to take her 'O' levels and 'A' levels and go to university. She didn't want a baby just then, but it was a sin to try and get rid of it."

His mother was crying. William wished for some clouds to cover the moon.

"Now here's a paradox, William. It was thanks to the nuns, to the Church, that Grace had her superior education and yet it was thanks to the Church she thought abortion was a sin. I knew for a fact that rural women had access to all kinds of herbs and roots if they wanted to get rid of a baby."

(William thought of Comfort. "There is a certain root they push up into themselves; you can buy it in the market.")

"I suggested to her that there might be a doctor in Accra—I was thinking of the Peace Corps doctor—who would give her a safe abortion and that I would pay for it. I would think up some excuse to take her there and I'd stay with her the whole time. I'd say you needed to have something that couldn't be done at Jirapa and would ask

Grace to go with me. She was terribly afraid; she kept saying, 'Please, it would be a sin.' I tried to jolly her up, said where was my cheeky scholar, my girl who wouldn't be intimidated, but it didn't work. Finally I told her to go along to bed and we'd talk again tomorrow."

"And she was gone the next day."

"No, she wasn't gone the next day. Perhaps in my heart I wished she would run away but she didn't. Both she and Sandy became very passive; they seemed to look to me to solve everything, but how could I? Maybe Sandy wanted me to leave, with you, so that he could 'do the honourable thing,' but I wasn't going to do that. I was damned if I was going to do that. I stopped speaking to him, except when absolutely necessary, and I tried to think of what to do. There didn't seem to be any way out except an abortion, which would save all of us here on earth but, in Grace's view, damn her soul to hell. Maybe your hair is so lush because it was watered with so many tears. I was angry and depressed and at the same time I loved you so much, was so delighted in you, that I felt guilty about even thinking of an abortion for Grace. I think I was a little mad by the end of the week, really ready to leave, when Grace stopped me outside my classroom and said she was willing to go to Accra. She looked terrible—I suppose I did as well, and Sandy, well I didn't look at him unless I had to. I told the nuns I needed to go to Accra, I wasn't well and asked if Grace could accompany me to help with the baby.

"'Why not Felicity?' they said, but I said I'd feel more comfortable with Grace and besides, it would be easier for her to make up a few days of missed classes. It was obvious to them that I was upset about something and I guess they thought it was something physical, something to do with having a baby, and they didn't want to pry.

"They weren't ignorant, those nuns; perhaps they even thought I would go all the way to Accra to be fitted for a diaphragm or an IUD. How could I go to the Catholic-run hospital for that?

"So we made the long journey to Accra, the three of us. Twice we had to stop the bus so Grace could be sick and women tsk'd the way they do. One asked her straight out if she'd been a 'bad girl.' I realized we should have flown but I didn't have the extra money."

"What did Dad say about the trip?"

"Nothing. I didn't speak to him at all about it, although he saw our preparations for leaving. When the taxi honked all he said was 'Are you coming back?' And I said 'Yes.'

"When we got to Accra we went to a women's hostel and then to see the Peace Corps doctor. He was very kind, but I don't think Grace had ever been subjected to an internal examination in her life. She thought he was going to do the abortion right there and then and we had a terrible time calming her down."

"Where was I while this was going on?"

"Playing with a volunteer who was there to get some shots. Did you think I would've taken you in with me!"

"I don't know what you would have done."

(Silence from his mother. The sound of cicadas; the sound of the wind in the palm trees; the sound of the sea.)

"We made an appointment for the following morning and took a cab back to the hostel. Grace hardly spoke. We lay down on our beds. You were hot and fractious so I nursed you and then we fell asleep. Later I asked Grace if she could go out and get some fruit and kenkey and bananas. When she came back I made a fruit salad but she said she wasn't hungry. I reminded her that she wouldn't be able to eat anything in the morning.

"She asked if she could go out again—to visit a chapel. It was getting dark by this time so I said no. She'd never been to Accra before and I didn't want her wandering alone at night in such a big city. She seemed so depressed that I asked her if she wanted to talk and she said no, lay down on her bed and turned her face to the wall. Soon you fell asleep as well so I turned off the one light and lay awake for a long time, listening to the night sounds outside and listening to the happy voices of women, coming in from wherever they'd been and getting ready for the night. Laughter and high spirits and here we were, on the other side of a door in a darkness more palpable than the usual African dark.

"'You don't have to do this,' I whispered. 'You really don't. Only if it's what you really want.'

"There was no answer. Soon I fell asleep again, very conscious of you asleep in the crook of my arm, my perfect child—and of Grace over there awake and terrified.

"In the middle of the night I woke up and I knew Grace wasn't there. Then you woke up and wanted to nurse. I turned the light on, worried, but I had to see to you first and I thought she'd probably gone down the hall to be sick.

"Then she came in and leaned against the door. Stood

there, in the doorway, her hand cupped around something, her hand and arm extended towards me.

"'Is this it?' she said. There was blood running onto the floor.

"'Is this it?'

"I was sitting propped up on the bed, holding you in my arms.

"'Don't!' I cried. 'Don't bring that in here! Get out! Go back!'

"I didn't want you to see—didn't want to see, myself, whatever it was she was holding in her hand. Not while I was holding you, not then.

"She turned and left the room. I never saw her—dead or alive—again."

William was on his feet, chair crashing to the floor.

"How can that be! She was lame, ill! How long did you sit there before you went after her? How could you let her go?"

His mother's voice was only a whisper.

"I don't know how long I sat there. Not long. I thought she'd gone back to the toilet, I thought... I don't know. It might have been only five minutes; it might have been half an hour. I woke up the matron; we got the police—but what did they care about a fifteen-year-old girl from the north? 'She's ill,' I said. 'She's had a miscarriage!' They promised they would find her. What else would they say to me?

"I went to all the hospitals. I called Flossie collect, told her the story I hadn't been able to write in a letter, asked her what to do. She said she would talk to the Peace Corps doctor herself, would see what pressure could be put on the police. She told me to go home, meaning home to Wa. I stayed three more days at the hostel, praying Grace would turn up, but she didn't. Flossie wired me the money to fly as far as Tamale. I don't remember much about the trip. I was a murderer; I knew in my heart she'd gone someplace to die."

"Oh, Mother. You weren't a murderer."

"I rejected her—in every way I rejected her. And now she's in Hell somewhere, doubly damned. It doesn't matter whether I believed; she did. She killed her baby and then, when I rejected her, she killed herself."

"You don't know that. You don't even know that she killed the baby. Maybe it was a miscarriage. All the tension, the exam—I don't know, but isn't it possible?"

She ignored him.

"And now I'll see her forever, stretching out her arm towards me, and me screaming at her, Go away! I brought her to that place and then I told her to go away. I didn't mean forever, not to go away forever. I just didn't want to see...whatever was in her hand." (Chantal's voice, suddenly, "There was no *father*, William, there was no *baby*.")

He had never held his mother before. She smelled of Lux soap.

"I told the principal," she said. "I had to. Told her Grace had been pregnant, had suffered a miscarriage and had run away. I didn't say we'd gone to Accra to get her an abortion, but I'm sure she figured that out.

"Sandy had a sort of nervous collapse; he'd be all right for a few days and then he'd have terrible bouts of weeping. Once he broke down right in the classroom. But because no one knew of the sexual side of their relationship, they didn't connect his behaviour to Grace's disappearance; they were two separate things.

"She brought him dinner every night. The nuns knew that; the girls must have known it as well. Probably everybody knew what was going on."

"Perhaps. Yes. Everybody must have known."

"I contacted our field officer, who came up to see us. We didn't tell him the truth, of course. I think I said I'd made a mistake, I didn't want my baby subjected to so much danger and disease, but he could see it was Sandy who was in some sort of hysterical state. He didn't want to go, but the doctor got some sedatives for us and we turned him into a kind of zombie to get him on the plane. He didn't speak to me at all on the way home and we flew directly from London to Vancouver, not to Montreal, as his parents had suggested. I remember looking down at the Sahara, all that desert, and wondering what on earth our life would be like from here on in.

"Well, you know what it's been like.

"We've never been back. He's never forgiven me for taking her to Accra; I've never forgiven him for sleeping with her in the first place. *He's* the one who committed a sin and she's the one who paid for it. There's a belief I read about—I can't remember which tribe now, but the image stuck with me and will haunt me forever. When a baby dies the child goes to hell and the mother follows it, squeezing milk from her breasts, trying to put the fire out with her milk. I see Grace wandering through hell, doing that, carrying her baby, who is on fire, trying to put the fire out, not only with her tears, but with the milk that was meant to nourish. I live with that image; I'm haunted by it."

"Oh Mother," William said, "what a mess."

Crying bitterly now. "And I loved it here, I loved it. I didn't really want to leave either. He ruined this place for me—and you—but that's not so terrible as what happened to Grace, that's not even important, except from a selfish point of view, except that I am still alive and suffering."

"Why didn't you leave him? Why don't you?"

"Because what happened is only partly his fault."

"Nonsense."

"No. Not nonsense."

"I think you should leave him. Start again."

"Too much baggage." She stood up. The moon was directly over the castle now. "Looks like a wedding cake from here but it's a Whited Sepulchre. If you want misery!" She put out her hand to him. "Could you stay another day? Could we just walk around and look at things?"

"All right."

He walked her to her door. "Perhaps she's alive somewhere? In another country?"

"I don't think so."

"She must have told that old nun most of the story. Or at least that you two were involved in some way."

"Or she guessed. Those nuns weren't as other-worldly as the girls thought."

"Good-night."

"Good-night."

There was only a wall between her chalet and his. He could hear her getting ready for bed, hear her blow her nose hard. Bedsprings. He tapped on the wall.

Tap Tap Tap.

Did it again.

Tap. Tap Tap Tap Tap. Tap Tap Tap.

And then her reply. Tap. Tap Tap Tap Tap. Tap Tap Tap. Tap Tap Tap.

"I love you too."

The next day was their last together, perhaps for a long time.

("Mother, will you come back?"

"To Canada do you mean? Or...home?"

"Home."

"I really don't know.")

There was an unspoken agreement that they would not talk about the night before. It was there and could never be not-there, but this day was for the two of them, mother and son. After that they would go, at least for now, their separate ways.

"William," she had said to him, at the end, "you are not responsible for your parents' youth. Nothing you can do can 'make up' for what we did—we have to live with it, not you. I just want you to know that although you may have felt you grew up in a loveless house, we both loved *you*. Never doubt that for a minute."

"I have never doubted your love," he said slowly, "but I guess I have always doubted your affection. Especially his, but yours too. Separately, you were very kind to me. Sometimes I used to wish I were twins, so you could each have one of me. But we weren't a family and I longed for a family. You were both so...closed."

"I will never be closed to you again, I promise."

"I want to go and see him—Dad."

"Let me see him first, let me tell him you know."

"I doubt I can forgive him, ever."

"I'm not sure your forgiveness would make much difference, one way or the other. Or mine. And I can't forgive. We're cursed, both of us. Cursed by regret, by endless 'what ifs' and 'might have beens.' At the same time we are blessed because we have you."

They ate breakfast late and decided to go to the castle.

After the glare outside, the large room just inside the castle doors was only a dark square for several seconds. William blinked; his mother took off her dark glasses. The man sitting behind a large table jumped up; he wore spectacles, but one of the lenses was cracked and mended with adhesive tape.

"Welcome!" he said, spreading his arms wide. "You have come to visit our castle?"

"Yes," said William, unzipping his moneybelt.

"Two hundred cedis," said the man. "Later on you may wish to visit the shop."

They bought the tickets and stood there, uncertain.

"I was here a long time ago," his mother said. "We went round with a guide. Is there a tour today?"

"Please. Wait over there. The guide is just returning."

"Over there" was a large couch covered in cracked orange Naugahyde. A black couple was sitting there, a very dressed-up, smart-looking couple, he in a stone-coloured suit, white shirt and tie, she in blue walking shorts, white blouse and a kente strip wound around her head. The man was looking at his watch.

"Do not worry," the ticket-taker said, "the guide will be here any moment, any moment."

"Is that a Gold Coast moment?" the woman said, but she smiled when she said it. She also smiled at William and his mother and nudged her husband to move over a bit.

They were Mr. and Mrs. Jordan, from Chicago. Mr. Jordan was in the hospitality business back home.

After another ten minutes the guide, an army officer, came into the room with a small group of tired, sweating visitors; two were white—they were discussing something loudly, in German—but the rest were black.

"Minerals in the cooler!" The man behind the desk indicated a red cooler in the corner. It said Coca-Cola. "He will be with you in one minute more," he said to the waiting quartet.

When they finally went down the wooden steps and into the vast courtyard the sun on all that whiteness was like a pain, a white pain. The guide stood in the centre and began to explain the history of the place, Portuguese, Dutch, before Columbus blah blah blah. William tried to concentrate, to imagine the courtyard filled with brown, sweating bodies chained together, the stink of fear, the shouts of the warders or whatever they were called in Portuguese, in Dutch.

"Costa da Mina, the Coast of the Goldmines...thousands and thousands...oiled their bodies...upside down...

The governor, he live up above."

They went in and out of dark places; it was like follow the leader: the male dungeon; the female dungeon, the dungeon for pirates. William's crayons came stacked vertically in their box the colour of a school bus ("non-toxic, *non-toxique*"); he couldn't get enough of their fresh, waxy smell. Here the "coloured people" as he'd heard a woman say on a radio phone-in show ("those coloured people" and the host of the show said excuse me ma'am, we don't say coloured people any more we say persons of colour), were stacked like his crayons, men and women separate, nowhere to pee and shit except on the floor. The guide showed them where a bit of the floor had been cut away; they were standing on six feet of hardened, eighteenth-century shit.

"You are standing on the excrement of all those sufferin' men and women, years and years of it, years and years." He poked Mr. Jordan, playfully but hard, right in the middle of his chest.

"Where you from?"

"Chicago."

"U.S.A.?"

"Yes."

The guide laughed loudly and poked Mr. Jordan again.

"Now aren't you glad your great-great-granddaddy's great-granddaddy's great-granddaddy was put on that boat. You a fine fine gentleman now."

Mr. Jordan wiped his forehead with a white handkerchief, but soon recovered when they went outside again.

The couple from Chicago became very playful with

their camera. Pictures were taken of a smiling Mrs. Jordan coming out of the women's dungeon, a smiling Mr. Jordan standing by the door of the tunnel that led out to the sea. The sea was closer then, the guide said; the ships were right outside. The tunnel was only one slave wide, so there would be no trouble.

After months inside those dark places, the sea air, sunlight, trees, and then back in the dark again. These were inland people, mostly. The sea was a fresh hell.

"One in eight," the guide was saying, "one in eight die before they reach the other side."

"How thick are these walls?" Mr. Jordan asked.

"Twenty, thirty feet, sir. Plenty thick."

Mr. Jordan had stopped smiling, his manicured hand resting still on the stone wall.

"I guess they expected slavery to last a thousand years."

His wife put her hand over his.

Bad ladies were brought out and chained to cannonballs in the open courtyard. Ladies were also brought out into the courtyard when the Dutch governor wanted a woman. He stood on his balcony and looked them over:

"There. That one. Bring her."

If the lady got pregnant by him she was set free.

In the gift shop each of the four bought a few postcards. There were kente strips in bright colours and fake ivory letter-openers shaped like big-breasted women. Everyone tipped the guide.

William didn't know what to write in the visitors' book so he simply wrote his name. Mrs. Jordan had written above him, "How can one fail to be moved by the terrible fate of these people." These people? Weren't they her people?

Outside the castle William said, "That place is *redolent* with misery; it's awful. I can't understand why they don't just blow it up."

"I suppose it serves as a reminder to the rest of the world, like the camps in Germany. If you get rid of the physical evidence sometimes you lose the horror. The guide said Cape Coast Castle is being used as a cultural centre as well."

"How can they?"

"William, the people who still live on this coast are descendants of the people who *didn't* go; it's not the same for them as it is for me and Mrs. Jordan."

"I could have slapped them."

"Don't be so superior. I don't know how I would react to such a place, to stand on my ancestors' shit, to sense, even for an instant, what it might have been like for them. I think they were embarrassed at first and then...then they changed."

The guide had told them one part of the castle was now a prison. As they walked away they could see police guards at a doorway to the right, stopping people, mostly women, with covered pans on their heads.

"I wonder how they treat the prisoners."

"It's ironic, isn't it? But I suppose it's an ideal building for a prison." She turned and took his hand. "You know what I'd like to do?" She had her dark glasses on again; he couldn't see her eyes.

"What's that?"

"I'd like to go to the fish market and buy some fish for

our farewell supper." They had arranged that she would drop him at the bus depot in Cape Coast the next morning. She was going to stay a few more days "just looking around." William knew that she would get up the courage to go to Wa. Maybe the courage to leave his father. They were bad for one another, *toxique* (he thought of his crayons); they might have a chance apart.

He was even more sure of this once they were in the market.

"Auntie!" "Madame!" She took a plastic bag and a string bag out of her purse and began to wander along the rows of seated women hawking their fish. She bargained and laughed. William stood to one side, watching.

"I must remember her like this," he thought. "Whatever she decides, whoever she might become, back home, I must remember her here."

A hand tugged at his belt. It was Kwame, leading a small girl of about three.

"Please," he said, "do you want fish?"

"My mother is buying fish—you should go talk to her."

Boys like Kwame were bringing in pails of fish from the dugout canoes drawn up in the lagoon. The castle might loom above them, over there on the promontory, but it couldn't hurt them any more and life must go on.

A woman went by with an enamel pan on her head. The fish it contained was so large it hung, head and tail, over the sides. She held her left hand up, to steady the pan. Caryatid.

His mother looked frail compared with the market women. She wasn't, really; she traipsed all over the world and was hardly ever sick. It was just that so many of these women were big. He no longer thought of them as fat, just big. They were tough, not flabby like the fat Americans he and Chantal had seen one weekend, eating banana splits and hot fudge sundaes at the Howard Johnson's near Times Square. Those people looked doughy, unhealthy—and their children were fat too. Had he ever seen a fat child in this country? A flabby child? Flesh looked good on these women and he liked the way they walked, their regal shuffle, but could like Chantal too, not a caryatid, more of a hummingbird, always on the move. She must have to will herself to stand still for the cameras. Did he love her, Chantal? What did it mean, what would the market women say to such a question?

"Ho, boy, all this palaver about this thing. Too much talk, *too* much. Not enough doing." Something like that. He loved her by his definition of love—(which was? which was?)—but he didn't think he wanted to marry, not just yet. He would have to tell her that, right away, in case she felt she was wasting her time. He didn't want to settle down; he wanted, instead, to be shaken up. Women were so strong; he wanted to be strong enough, sure enough, not to lean on a woman.

He'd always thought—been taught—it was the other way around, but that was wrong. It was the men who were frail, puny creatures, sitting under their metaphorical mango trees, playing Warri or the stock market, drinking palm wine or Molson's Light, telling lies. While the women were out there doing doing doing, keeping it all together. He thought once again of caryatids, the women here who seemed to hold up the entire life of the country. Rawlings could sit in his castle at Osu, his beret on a chair near the window in case any would-be assassins got ideas, or visit out-of-the-way places to press buttons—"let there be light"—but it was the women who carried on the real business of life. They had babies; they planted yam mounds, they bought and they sold, they carried loads he couldn't lift past his shoulder. They *endured.* Was it just possible that Grace had endured as well?

His mother came back with Kwame and his little sister and two long thin silver fish for dinner.

"What are they?" William said, as their little group went out of the market.

"Barracuda. I think we should probably go back straight away and put them in the fridge, but let's go by way of a cool drink stand; I'm thirsty."

William reached down to take Kwame's hand and then remembered.

"His sister's name is Margaret," William's mother said. "Also Ama; she was born on Saturday."

"Can you smile, Ama?" William asked the solemn child, but she just clung to her brother's hand.

"Does your brother put the flowers in your hair?" No answer.

The children left them at the edge of the town.

"Please, I will come tomorrow," Kwame said.

"Ah, I'm leaving tomorrow, Kwame. Very early."

"You are going home?"

"Yes."

"To Canada."

"Yes."

The children stood there, looking at him.

"Look," William said, tearing a page from his notebook, "I'm going to give you my address in Canada—well, my mother's address." She nodded. "And if you would like to write to me I promise I'll write back. I promise."

"Will you take me to Canada?"

"No. I can't do that. But I will write to you and send you a calendar, a map. Okay?"

He took their picture, standing by the side of the road, Kwame's good hand still holding the hand of his little sister. He couldn't really imagine their future any more than they could imagine his. He had asked one child, weeks ago, if he knew where Canada was. The boy nodded: "Far too much," he said.

Before sunset they went swimming, William way out, letting the breakers fling him back towards the shore, his mother, a poor swimmer, closer in. She was out of the water first.

"Lovely!" he shouted as he ran up the beach towards her. "Lovely lovely lovely!"

"William," his mother called, "look out!" He stopped, just missing a large coil of fresh human shit, already being picked at by crows.

William gave his mother Johnny's address—"in case you decide to go to Bolgatanga. And he'll welcome you with open arms if you take up some bottles of tonic."

"I just might do that. And I know for sure I'm going to Kumasi to see Mrs. Owusu-Banahene; we behaved very ungraciously to her. I'm sad that her husband is dead; he was a wonderful man. The story is that when he was in prison, under Nkrumah, they had to let him out because he was politicizing the other convicts. He told wonderful stories."

"If you go there say hello to the granddaughters, especially Alice."

She dropped him outside the depot and he went up the stairs and into the waiting area. It was Sunday morning and some sort of church festival was getting under way across the road. Singing and clapping, Amens and Praise Jesus. He tried to memorize the way the light was falling on an ochre-coloured wall. How unfortunate to have the painter's eye without the painter's hand. The sunlight like a huge bright triangle against that wall, the sleeping people they passed on their walk back to the motel yesterday—sleeping on top of walls, sleeping under trees; the three naked boys playing under a water tap who covered their genitals when William and his mother passed. "Who taught them that?" she said.

He couldn't stop thinking about his father and mother. How long had she really sat there before she went for help? How could a girl with a limp get so far away, in a strange city, that no one could find her. "Vanished without a trace." (But who would notice her, in the darkness? Limps, missing hands, all kinds of deformity and disease were not remarked upon here, even in daylight. Even her sobs would not seem unusual: she had been a bad girl; she had been beaten.) Was there any possibility that she sought sanctuary and shelter at a church? No, he didn't think so—not after what had happened.

Too young / too old / too many / too close: that's what Dr. Odonkoor had said about women and birth in Africa. And yet the children seemed, on the surface at least, happy and loved. If children are your only wealth how can you not rejoice in them?

Would Grace's baby have looked like his father? Would it have been a source of pride, in other circumstances, not shame? Would his father really have married her, and if so, then what? How many of Grace's dreams would have been fulfilled? It was no good. "No man knows the story of tomorrow's dawn." Johnny had told him that one. Better to look at the light moving across that ochre wall. Early that morning he had sat out on the verandah, waiting for his mother to wake, watching the dawn, watching the canoes set out from Elmina. Some of them, he'd seen yesterday, had eyes painted on them and the words *Onyame Naa*: God never sleeps. The wind rustled the palm fronds above his head; so hard did it blow, they sounded like canvas snapping. He made a simple sketch of the sun coming up out of the sea, then of the coconut palms near by. His long-ago Sunday School teacher was right, of course; in reality the branches were various shades of green. But he could, and did (as a tip of the hat to his six-year-old self), make them blue, magenta, canary yellow. "I love colour," he thought. "I will have to find something to do with colour. Or perhaps I will simply buy a house, someday, a blue house with yellow trim and all the walls inside will be, will be...."

The old colonial buildings, walls broken, some roofless, the taxis.

"Madame! Master! Where are you going?"

The long-legged palm trees, the silver fishes.

He knew one thing only; he didn't want to teach art history: a pointer pointing to an image of an image. "Notice the principle of composition here, the diagonal movement from bottom left to top right," careful not to linger too long on the curve of a buttock or pause with the rubber tip centred on a rosy nipple. He thought of Johnny's experience with lost wax and smiled. ("We are all lost.") Was it enough to know what you didn't want to do? For a while, maybe, but not forever.

He must try to love his father. First things first. That haunted man. Like Ham in the Bible, he had now looked upon his father naked—only Ham's punishment was to be burned black by the sun and become thus the founder of an inferior race. What he, William, would say to his grandfather was another thing—that, surely, must first be between father and son?

("Do you know the difference between guilt and shame?" his mother had asked.)

He could not go back through the door of not-knowing.

And what about this? Had Grace been intending to throw herself on the mercy of the Church or the mercy of his parents, both father and mother? Or had she not thought at all, too stupefied with fear to think of what to do?

A man could never know that particular terror—something growing inside, ocular proof whether you liked it or not. Pain whichever way you turned.

(His own mother had been, at first, an unwanted child, a "mistake." She did not talk about that but it was true. Had she talked about it with his father during those dark nights up in Wa?

The bus came hurtling round the corner; the driver honked three times. Come on! Let's go!

He had to spend one night in Abidjan, so of course he went back to the Grand Hotel. The desk clerk acted as though he'd never seen him before, but while William was lying on his bed, thinking about going out—his last night in Africa—there was a knock on the door and Bernard walked in.

"The desk clerk told me you were here."

"I thought he didn't even recognize me."

"Well, he's definitely still waters so perhaps he runs deep. Actually, what he said was 'your fren' is *en haut*.' I thought he meant on the telephone, 'on hold,' so I went to the phone box and no one was on the other end. When I came back he was asleep again but I shook him and managed to get an answer. He described you, called you 'the asparagus,' I think."

"Bernard, I'm really glad to see you! But what are you doing back here? Did you go to Bamako?"

"I did, I did. And other places too. Bought the rights to a couple of picture books, ate in some good Vietnamese restaurants. I couldn't figure out what the Vietnamese were doing there—I never was much good at political history. Thought, they can't be boat people—what boat crosses the desert? Then someone said 'French Indo-China' and the penny dropped.

"Bamako is so different from Abidjan, so *African.* I felt I had to scurry back here for some naughtiness before I went home. Besides, I'm taking my 'fren' with me."

"What friend? The tangerine man?"

"He wants to see New York."

"Oh, Bernard."

Bernard smiled. "I know you think I'm a dirty old man, William, but I'm not. Or not any more. I'm the clean boy of the Western world. Funny, all that stuff about 'seize the day,' *carpe diem*; we never saw the 'die' in that word, did we?

"But I'm lonely and he wants to see New York. We're going to be met with heavy overcoats and scarves; he'll be all right. After a while—unless he gets into the drug racket—he'll get fed up driving taxis and want to come back home."

"When are you going?"

"Tomorrow a.m. Tonight we are going to the late show at the Hotel Ivoire, *Dansant avec les loups*. Sounds like dancing with toilets. Very Dada. Want to come?"

"I don't think so."

"Have you *been* to the Hotel Ivoire? Oh of course you have, when Chantal and the black beauties were in town."

"That's what they call eggplant in Ghana—black beauties."

"Well those girls were certainly edible, but better-looking than an eggplant." He sat down on the edge of William's bed.

"Did I ever tell you about the time I made eggplant curry? No, I'm sure I didn't. Well, Blaise, my—the dear friend I used to live with—he loved curries and I learned to make a lot of different kinds from him. But one night, when we were due to have a *soirée*, I decided to branch out and try some new dishes. Curried eggplant sounded good so I rushed to a vegetable market, got three big plump eggplants and put them in the oven to bake as per instructions. I then went in the sitting-room to read while they were doing. About twenty minutes later I heard the most awful sound, like an elephant doing a shit—or three elephants doing three shits. I rushed to the oven and the eggplants had exploded all over the inside. It *looked* like three elephants had done a shit. I forgot to prick them. Needless to say I was still scraping away when Blaise came home."

He started to laugh heartily, remembering, and then suddenly stopped and turned away. "Do you know what they call it out here? 'Slims.'"

William put his hand on Bernard's shoulder. "I'm sorry, Bernard."

"Me too." He fished a handkerchief out of his pocket and blew his nose.

"Listen," William said, "I've seen that movie but is there time for us all to have a drink, my treat? There's something I want to do at the Hotel Ivoire."

"Of course there's time. But we'd better get some brochettes first; the drinks will be steep enough but dinner would be outrageous. I'll meet you downstairs in fifteen minutes. If you're down first look out for tangerine man; his name is Narcisse and no, I'm not making that up."

All three were quite drunk by eight o'clock. William waved to them as they went down the corridor to the cinema (it turned out they would all be on the same plane as far as Paris) and then went to find the manager.

Who said it was impossible, Monsieur.

Who said perhaps it could be arranged *demain matin* but in fact the facility was closed to get ready for a competition.

William's mother had given him a bit of emergency money after he told her about the oranges. This was an emergency—sort of. Anyway, it was something he wanted to do. Money changed hands. Perhaps it could be arranged after all. The manager snapped his fingers, once, twice.

Which is how, while Bernard and Narcisse danced with wolves up above, William sat lacing on some grey skates—700 CFA for rental fee—down at the *patinoire*. They had opened the doors and turned the lights on just for him.

He handed his jacket and his camera to the man who had brought him down and then he stood up and pushed away from the bench. "When I get going, when I'm ready, I'll yell 'Now' and you press this button, okay?" The man looked puzzled. What was button in French?

"*C'est automatique*," William said, "*pressez ici*." The man nodded but still looked dubious.

The rink was full size and he had it all to himself. He skated slowly to the far end and then turned and shut his eyes. Hockey Night in Africa!

Rinks were usually so cold that your face hurt when you skated but not here, not in the Montreal Forum. Here the air was so hot his throat burned and he broke into a sweat just thinking about taking a slapshot. Stanley Cup banners hung far above his head and the numbers of the immortals, No. 9, No. 4. Would they put his number up when he'd played his last game?

Like the banners, the fans seemed to hang down in sheets from the ceiling. Screaming and yelling, they crowded over the boards and glass watching his every move. He felt the weight of their constant scrutiny, but shrugged it off. Pushing all distractions aside, he began to skate.

Hearing his name echoing around the building he raised his stick to the crowd and then a few short powerful strides took him to centre. The national anthems dragged; minutes seemed like hours. He thought only of scoring goals, saw his shots as they hit the net, saw the red light blaze behind the glass. He shoots! He scores!

And later, with the game tied and under a minute left to play Scotty Bowman looks down the bench and thinks about who he should play for the most crucial shift in such an important game. He taps William on the shoulder.

"Here's your big chance. Show me what you've got."

Opposite William is the hulking frame of Gordie Howe. "Are you lost, rookie?" he says. "You don't belong out here with us real men. Do you even shave yet?"

William ignores him and concentrates only on the puck as it falls from the hand of the referee. It slides into his corner and he sprints after it, warding off Howe's slashing stick with an outstretched arm. With the puck nicely cradled on his stick he swings around from behind the net. A clear lane appears ahead and he races for open ice. Nothing can stop him; he fakes to the outside, cuts back to the middle, only the goalie left to beat. The fans go wild. Mac! Mac! Mac! Mac! He can hear Chantal screaming above the rest.

Pulling the puck around the flailing stick of the goalie he launches a backhand shot just underneath the crossbar and into the net.

Mac—Mac—Mac—Mac!

"Now!" he yells as he opens his eyes and gives a last burst of speed. The workman presses the button.

"Thank you," said William, laughing and sweating. "*Merci.*"

"Please," said the workman, "*d'où venez-vous?*"

"Canada."

"Ah. Canada. Guy Lafleur. *Un beau pays.*"

Suddenly there was a loud crashing and banging at the door and in came Bernard and Narcisse, still drunk.

"We didn't care for the movie," Bernard said, "so we had a little nip and have come to dance with you."

"I was just leaving." William pointed to the skate in his hand.

"Oh no no no no *no.* You must have a little twirl with us. I have been telling Narcisse about *le centre Rockefeller*; he has never been on skates so now is a good time to try."

"How did you know I was here?"

"Bernard knows everything."

The man who had accompanied William to the skating rink was shaking his head.

"*C'est fermé.*"

Bernard unzipped his moneybelt. "Ten minutes?"

The man looked at him doubtfully.

"Ten minutes and we'll be out. Cross my heart and hope to die, stick a needle in my eye. Just go get us some skates, will you? *Vite! Vite!*"

William looked at Bernard and then at Narcisse, who was shivering in his thin silk shirt.

"You're drunk Bernard. You might hurt yourself. Narcisse too."

"Oh hush, don't be such an old woman. Help the boy on with his skates. He'll warm up once we get going."

William stood there, undecided. Then he shrugged. If Bernard broke his head, too bad. *Carpe diem.* He began to see the humour in it and he bent over Narcisse, lacing his skates up tight, then holding him up as they stepped out onto the ice.

Bernard was there before them, took a couple of running steps on the points of his skates and then, much to William's surprise, began to skate in a most elegant manner, cutting and turning and gliding, doing perfect figure eights.

"Surprise, surprise," he called, as he whizzed past the astonished William. "I am the belle of Rockefeller Centre, the belle the belle the belle of Rocke fell er fell er fell. We'll have our friend out there strutting his stuff in no time at all."

Narcisse was clinging desperately to William, too terrified to move.

"Come," Bernard said, swooping down on them. "You take one arm, I'll take the other and we'll go slowly, slowly, yes, that's it, that's wonderful darling, we'll get you a nice warm outfit when we hit New York."

And so, as Bernard described the beauties of Rockefeller Centre at Christmas to the very wobbly Narcisse, the three of them skated in a (more or less) straight line to the end of the rink and back.

Bernard began to hum the Skater's Waltz: "Da da da dum, da da da dum. Oh!" he said, "I haven't been so happy in a month of Sundays."

At that moment Narcisse's feet shot out from under him and he sat down hard.

"You are the slippery boy!" Bernard said, as they hauled him to his feet.

"Out!" shouted the man with the keys. "*Fini. Allez-y!*" He flicked the light switch on and off impatiently.

"Okay, okay," William said. Then, "Wait a minute. *Un moment.*" He sped over to his camera. "*Encore une photographie*. Please."

He set the camera and then skated back to Bernard and Narcisse. Both were laughing madly.

"All right," William said, "let's go. When I shout 'Now!' please put on your best smiles."

"La la la la," sang Bernard at the top of his voice, "la la la la. Dum dum de Dum Dum de Dum Dum Dum." Then, very low, "I'm dying William; my last Rockefeller Centre Christmas tree."

"Oh Bernard."

"Just kidding," he said. "Anyway, it wouldn't matter, would it? Seize the day. Shout now, will you please."

"Now!" shouted William and the man pressed the button. Whirr. Click.

"Thank you," said Bernard. "Will you send me a print? Fairly soon?"

They unlaced their skates and the man turned out the lights behind them.

"A nightcap?" suggested Bernard.

"Why not?" said William.

"Shall we have it here at the very very grand or shall we repair to the barely grand?"

"The Grand, I think. I'm almost broke."

"Excellent choice."

They stumbled out of the Hotel Ivoire and into the hot night.

"Get us a taxi, my good man," said Bernard to the uniformed doorman. "A taxi to the Grand Hotel."

"Cheer up, William," he said, laying his hand on William's shoulder. "Everybody dies sometime and hasn't Africa been *fun*?"

"We must pray every morning and every evening," cried Brother Charles, "seeking the face of God."

"We must pray for our poverty, our sickness and our shame."

"A-men," replied the congregation.

"A-men A-men" and "Praise the Lord!"

"We must pray," shouted Brother Charles,

"That sickness will be healed!

"That the blind eyes will be opened!

"That the lame shall leap with joy!

"That all manner of beings will rejoice in the name of Jee-sus!"

"Amen. Amen. Amen. Oh Jee-sus."

"Blessèd be the Name of the Lord," cried Brother Charles, wiping his forehead with a white, white handkerchief. "Blessèd be the Name of the Lord!"

"Glory," they cried back at him. "Glory! Glory!"

"And we shall be *saved*."

(The drummers began to drum. The man with the trumpet raised the trumpet to his lips. The choir in their purple robes began to sing.)

"He was nice, wasn't he?" said Alice to her grannie over lunch.

"Yes," she said. "Yes he was. A thoroughly nice young man."

'Bronie / How are you?
I'm fine. Thank you.